While she's visiting Washington, DC, Princess Dominique's life is shattered when her beloved bodyguard is murdered during an attempt to kidnap her. She can't fathom what anyone would want with her, but whatever the reason, it is apparently worth killing for.

Ethan Moore, an ex-Green Beret, knows he can't refuse to accompany her back home when the request comes from the White House. Neither Ethan nor Dominique is happy with the arrangement, and though they just met, neither is exactly dazzled by the other. He thinks she's stubborn and spoiled, and she finds him rude and arrogant. To make matters worse, the raging attraction between them seems to add fuel to the fire.

Given Ethan's impressive military record and Dominique's escape from her would-be kidnappers, his superiors believe she is no longer in danger, but it isn't long before he and Dominique discover that she is not as safe as the White House believes her to be.

When her abductors track them down, Ethan and Dominique have to find a way to get along and deal with a past scandal in order to keep their wits about them and stay one step ahead of the kidnappers. Otherwise, she could be gone forever.

Royal Mission
Copyright © 2021 Josephine Valent
ISBN: 978-1-4874-3433-5
Cover art by Martine Jardin

Published by eXtasy Books Inc

Look for us online at:
www.eXtasybooks.com

Royal Mission
Royals Book 1

By

Josephine Valent

DEDICATION

To Gina, Debra, AJ, my publisher, and my editor. Thank you for helping me share the lives of my characters. Also, to my mother. Sorry, Mom, I had to keep the sex scenes.

CHAPTER ONE

"Wasn't that a splendid concert, Jean Pierre?" Princess Dominique brushed aside a tress of hair that had fallen loose from her French twist. "An absolutely divine conclusion to my visit here, wouldn't you agree?" As she glanced over, she noticed Jean Pierre, ever-vigilant, scanning the Grand Foyer of the Kennedy Center. She hoped he'd been able to enjoy the performance despite the distraction of his duties.

"*Oui*," he replied. She knew when he gave a quick, inconspicuous pull on the collar of his shirt that he was focused on something. He was always on high alert. She wished he could relax enough to enjoy the perks that his employment offered.

"Jean Pierre, how many times must I remind you?" she chided as she tugged his arm. "We are in the United States and at its capital no less. We should speak English while we are here."

"*Oui*—I mean yes. Of course." His eyes narrowed and he frowned. She followed his line of sight as he spied the hulking figure just outside on the River Terrace take a long, slow drag from a cigarette before dropping it to the ground and crushing it beneath his heel. She took note of the man's lack of grooming and wrinkled tux and assumed Jean Pierre's reaction was to his lack of polish. Jean Pierre was always impeccably dressed when he accompanied her to such events, and she knew him well enough to know it was just as much a desire to blend in as it was pride.

"It was a beautiful weekend here. It is too bad my schedule

1

did not permit a longer stay."

"*Oui* — yes."

"Are you all right?" she asked, a slight line forming between her brows.

"Let's just say that I'd feel a little bit more comfortable if there were two of me here right now," he answered. She noticed his focus shift as he glanced down the Hall of States and his attention settled on someone maneuvering through the crowd in their direction.

"Don't be ridiculous." She gave his arm a reassuring pat. "I'm sure the president's guards have had this entire forum secured for days."

"I'm sure the president's security was the first to leave the concert, along with the president and the first lady."

She felt his hand slide over her arm as he guided her back toward the Eisenhower Theater. "Jean Pierre, why are we going back to the theater?"

"Wait for my command, Princess." He had switched back to French, and she couldn't mistake the harsh yet controlled urgency to his voice. She didn't hesitate when he quickened their pace.

"You are to pass the entrance to the theater and go through the parking exit. Then find a way out," he instructed. "Do not go back to the hotel. Go to the police. I will come and get you there."

"What is it?" she whispered, returning to French. A numbing chill raced up her spine, but she knew enough not to react.

"No longer a coincidence," he muttered.

"What about you? Will you be safe?"

"Don't worry about me, Princess."

In the same split-second that the clammy fingers of a sweaty hand clamped down on her shoulder, she heard Jean Pierre's quick, tortured scream as his hand slid from her arm and he fell to the ground. A torrent of fear whipped through her, fast and fierce.

"Keep walking, lady," the throaty voice of her assailant ordered from behind her, his thick, vile breath heavy and disgusting on her neck. "And don't make a scene, or I might be forced to start shooting."

With no choice, she continued under his compulsion, concentrating through the haze of fear on Jean Pierre and the commotion behind her. "He's had a heart attack! Call an ambulance!" someone yelled, and for an instant, she felt her own heart freeze.

She allowed the anger to swell inside her, and from it, drew strength. "What did you do to Jean Pierre?" she demanded in a low, even voice, determined not to reveal even an ounce of fear to her assailant.

His rough, sweaty fingers answered, sliding to her neck and tightening their grip around her throat.

They passed through the exit and into the parking garage. She swept her gaze over the sea of automobiles while her mind raced to devise a plan of escape that would not endanger any other lives. She was going to have to do something before the garage emptied. And soon, she decided, as her assailant shoved her around a wall and out of view of the crowd filing through the exit.

She could feel the lethal mix of anger and fear explode inside her as Jean Pierre's cry echoed in her head. Propelled by the adrenaline whipping through her, she stomped the heel of her stiletto into her assailant's foot and drove it in with all her weight until she was sure there was bone crumbling beneath her foot.

Her assailant cut loose a muffled wail and thrust her forward off his foot, weakening his hold on her.

She jerked free from his clutch, spun around, and with the dead-on precision of a marksman, jabbed the pointed toe of her shoe into his groin, leaving him doubled-over and throttling for his next breaths.

She darted back around the wall and through a small crowd that had started to congregate in front of the exit. When a car horn provided a diversion, she ducked and wove a path through the parked vehicles. She didn't bother to look back until she was several rows down and several rows over. A second man had joined her assailant, and they were taking off in opposite directions, searching for her.

She stayed low and crawled between the cars as she listened to the chirping of car alarms being disengaged, the slamming of car doors, and the humming of car engines. She was running out of time. Soon the garage would be empty except for her and the two men chasing her.

As her hand brushed over the rear bumper of an enormous sport utility vehicle, the alarm deactivated and the locks popped. She peered through the vehicle from the darkened back window and watched the silhouette of a man and a woman strolling toward the vehicle. When they stopped and turned to a couple behind them, she opened one of the rear doors, slipped inside, and closed the door behind her. The windows were tinted dark and concealed the back compartment of the vehicle. She was certain no one would be able to see her from the outside as long as she kept low.

She lay down and nestled up against the back seat. She ran her fingers over the smooth stones dangling from her neck, relieved that the necklace hadn't been yanked off in the scuffle. She listened to the pounding of her heart and thought about Jean Pierre. She prayed that he was safe, and when a door opened, she prayed that she wouldn't be discovered. From the scent of heavy perfume, it was the woman who had stepped into the vehicle, and a moment later, after the driver's door closed, the woman spoke.

"My God, that woman has a neck like a football player.

And did you see the size of her hands? She has got to be a man underneath that dress."

"She is not a man. Senator Riley is married to a lovely woman," the man replied with what Dominique was sure was a hint of amusement in his voice.

"And what body part were you looking at?"

"I wasn't critiquing her looks. I was interested in the conversation."

"Yeah, right. Listen," the woman said, her voice softening to a seductive purr, "what's it going to be? Your place or mine?"

"Neither. And get back in your seat and put your seat belt on," the man ordered.

At the sound of the engine turning over, Dominique closed her eyes and released a long, quiet breath.

"We could always do it in here," the woman suggested. "I've never done it in an SUV."

"And you won't be. At least not in this one," the man replied. Dominique detected the mild annoyance that had replaced the amusement in his voice. "By the way, you know this isn't a date, right?"

"Maybe not a date . . . but fate, perhaps? You just happen to be going to the concert without a date. The general just happens to get sick and just happens to ask you to accompany his daughter to the concert. The concert just happens to be over, and the night just happens to still be young."

"And I just happen to be taking you back home to the general. And get back in your seat. I'm trying to drive."

"Oh, come on. Let's have some fun," the woman whined.

"You're too young for fun. And pull your dress back down over your knees."

"C'mon, Ethan." Her words were thick with disappointment. "I expect a little more from the most eligible million-dollar bachelor in Washington, DC."

Ethan. Dominique mulled his name over in her head, then shifted her thoughts to the men after her. She was sure they had mistaken her for someone else. She might be a princess, but she was by no means a celebrity. Outside of Monteaux, she was barely recognized by the paparazzi, who were only interested in her when she was in the company of much more popular personalities.

"What are you talking about?" There was surprise in his voice as he chuckled at the remark.

"I read the article about you."

"*Forbes* said no such thing. The article was about business."

"*Forbes*, pppff, who reads *Forbes*?"

"*Forbes* is the only publication I gave an interview to."

"The tabloids don't need an interview to publish something about someone."

"What are you talking about?"

"You didn't know?" She giggled. "Well, you weren't exactly front cover, but you were sure as hell in the pages. Picture and all."

"What? What picture?"

"Actually, you looked pretty hot. Kinda like you look tonight."

A relieved sigh escaped Dominique's lips as she felt the vehicle accelerate. She was safe for the moment and hoped, as she continued to listen to the conversation between Ethan and the woman, that wherever they were going, they'd be there soon.

"Shit." There was a slight hesitation before he spoke again. "Well, that explains it."

"Explains what?"

"The women coming to my office claiming to have appointments with me and lingering outside the building and in the parking garage. And the women slipping me their phone numbers in restaurants. And you. Look at you. I've known you since you were a little girl. What the hell are you doing tonight?"

"In case you haven't noticed, I'm no longer a little girl. I'm in college now. Don't you remember what it's like to be in college? Don't you remember those carefree, do-as-you-like days?"

"I went to *West Point*. We didn't have those days," he replied.

"Well, maybe I should show you what they're all about," she suggested.

"That's enough. One more time, and you're riding in the back seat," he warned. "Keep your hands in your lap."

The girl exploded with laughter.

He had his hands full. The woman, rather the girl, wasn't giving up on the object of her affection. Dominique was just grateful Ethan had scruples. The sooner he got the girl home, the sooner he'd get home. Then she could get to a phone and find out about Jean Pierre. She cursed herself for leaving her cell phone in her hotel room, but she really hadn't seen the need to bring it.

"You're lucky I'm not the general. If I were your father, I'd tie you up in a chastity belt and throw away the key."

"Geez. Chill out. You need like a drink or something. I know," she said, "let's go to Georgetown and hit a couple bars."

"I'm driving you home," he said.

"You are so uncool," she complained. "You're no fun at all. It's no wonder your wife dumped you. You probably bored her to death."

The girl must have struck a nerve, Dominique thought, as they rode in silence for what seemed like an eternity. Finally, she felt the vehicle slow as it made a series of turns and then came to a stop.

"I'm sorry," the girl apologized when she spoke again. "I

7

didn't mean that remark about your wife."

"Ex-wife. And I know. Don't worry about it. You're probably right anyway. C'mon, I'll walk you to the door."

Wherever they were, a brightly lit street lamp swept aside the night's darkness, spilling a beam of light over the vehicle. That made it impossible for Dominique to lift her head to look out of the window without the possibility of being noticed. It wouldn't matter anyway, she concluded. Even if she could see her surroundings, she was sure she wouldn't have the vaguest idea where she was. She wasn't familiar with any part of Washington, DC beyond the White House and the Kennedy Center. It was her first visit to the City, and it she hadn't been there long.

She stretched her legs but stayed hidden while she waited for Ethan to return. He hadn't lingered, and she was glad when he was back behind the wheel in a matter of minutes.

"Good luck with that one, General," he mumbled to himself as the engine fired up. "I certainly don't envy you."

After a few turns, by the vehicle's speed, Dominique assumed they were on some sort of a highway again when a phone rang.

"Ethan here."

"Ethan, General Bogart," another man's voice bellowed over a speaker. "Why the hell didn't you come inside for a drink?"

"I'm sorry, sir. I thought you were feeling pretty bad since you had to miss the concert. I didn't want to disturb you."

"Disturb me. Nonsense. I'm feeling fine. I told you, I just got the goddamn runs. Didn't want to crap my drawers in front of the president. It doesn't mean I can't drink. Hell, it'd probably do me good."

"Well, I'm glad to hear it's nothing more than a pain in the ass," he replied.

"Very funny," the general growled. "Anyway, what happened at the Kennedy Center tonight? I heard some fellow had a heart attack or something. They're still checking him out."

Dominique held her breath as she listened to the general. She was sure he was referring to Jean Pierre.

"I didn't see anything. When did it happen?"

"After the concert. The president had already left."

"How'd you find out?"

"The White House called me. They think it's a little fishy. Seems he was clutching a woman's scarf in his hand, but nobody seemed to be with him. The local police are involved, but the White House is keeping on top of it, since this was a White House affair. Right now, they're trying to figure out exactly who the fellow is."

"How is he? Can he talk?"

"In a coma."

Jean Pierre was in a coma. She bit hard on her lip to silence the scream that clawed at her throat. It was all her fault. He had wanted to bring another bodyguard, and she had dismissed the idea. It was a short visit, and she didn't want an entourage. He would be enough, she had insisted. She had told him there would be many people much more famous than she was attending the affair. Nobody would be paying attention to her. Had she listened to him, he would be fine right now.

"He's probably some old fart cheating on his wife," Ethan remarked. "The woman likely split to avoid a scandal."

"Probably," the general agreed with a chuckle. "I'll keep you posted. If it turns out to be anything more, the local police aren't going to be handling it. Are you on your way home?"

"Yeah. Let me know what they find out."

Dominique kept still, but her mind raced as she tried to figure out what to do. She needed to find out where they had taken Jean Pierre and get him the best medical care possible. She needed to go to him, but she'd have to disguise herself. The two men would likely assume she'd show up wherever he had been taken and would be waiting for her. She needed to call Lidia and make sure she was still at the hotel and safe. She needed to call her father. No, she didn't want to alarm him. Until they identified Jean Pierre, her father would know nothing. She'd keep it that way until she got things straightened out.

She'd call Lidia once they got to Ethan's home. She didn't want to startle him while he was driving and cause an accident. She'd stay quiet until they reached his home, she decided.

CHAPTER TWO

Bruno's gaze skipped over the graffiti defiling the brick wall along the side of the liquor store as he kicked the empty beer can by his foot. He watched the can sail at least fifteen feet before striking a scraggly figure hunched over a rusted shopping cart. The figure jerked around, ready to pounce, then backed down as Bruno's gaze met his. The figure scurried away, his cart clanging as it bounced over the cracked pavement.

Bruno's fingers fidgeted as he punched in the number. With his other hand, he swiped at a bead of sweat that trickled down the side of his face. It was still humid even though it was close to midnight, although he was aware it wasn't the humidity alone that was making him sweat.

"You better call," his accomplice grumbled from inside the rental car. Bruno glanced down at him and shook his head in disgust. The man's foot was propped up on the dashboard, and he scowled as he adjusted the bag of melting ice over his swollen foot.

Bruno cursed and then finished entering the last number. He listened as the line rang several times before it was answered.

"You failed," Helmuth Van Dousen said. His voice was caustic, a tone well-recognized by Bruno.

"But we've gotten rid of the bodyguard, Mr. Van Dousen," Bruno offered as consolation.

"Idiot! And how will that help you find the princess?"

"Uh . . . uh . . ." Bruno stammered as he shifted his weight from one foot to the other. He knew it was never a good thing to disappoint Van Dousen.

"You know what happens to the men who fail me," Van Dousen reminded him.

Bruno winced. "Yes, sir. I'm aware."

"Good. I will tell you where to find the princess, and you will not fail again, or else. Do you understand?"

"Completely, sir."

"According to the GPS, she has left Washington. You must get her before she seeks the protection of the authorities," he instructed. "You will need a boat."

"A boat, sir?" Bruno asked, clamping down on his tongue as the words slid out without his thinking.

"Is that a problem?" Van Dousen's voice boomed.

"No, sir," he replied.

"Good. You can reach the princess via the Patuxent River . . ."

Ethan cracked his window as he made the turn off the main road. Maybe I'll do some fishing this weekend, he thought. Definitely eat some crabs. They were in season now and plentiful this year. He inhaled, and the damp, fishy scent of the river filled his lungs. A smile crossed his lips. He was home.

He turned onto a gravel driveway flanked by thick woods, appreciating as he always did the privacy the trees provided. When he cleared the trees, he spotted the shimmer of the full moon dancing off the Patuxent River. He rolled to a stop in front of his farmhouse. Gazing over the front porch and noticing that the swing was motionless, he concluded that it was a still night in Saint George.

The house was dark and probably warm inside, he figured, from being closed up all week. Recalling that when he'd bought the house, he had envisioned filling it with half a dozen or so rambunctious kids, his heart sank a notch. That dream had been crushed. But even empty, he loved the house enough to keep it. Hell, he'd spent enough time and money restoring it to its original beauty, but it had been a labor of love.

He'd move his SUV in the morning to the old tobacco barn, he decided as he turned off the ignition. He wanted nothing more at that moment than to close his eyes and drift into unconsciousness until the morning sun woke him up.

"Excuse me, Ethan, I—"

"Holy shit!" He spun around, his eyes wide, his jaw hanging. "What the hell are you trying to do? Give me a heart attack? Jesus!" He shoved open his door and leaped out before she could answer, then stomped around to the back of the vehicle and flung open the rear door. "I can't believe this. Get out," he ordered, offering her a hand as she stumbled from the vehicle.

"I'm sorry," she apologized, accepting his hand and regaining her balance. "I didn't mean to frighten you."

"I am not frightened. I'm—I'm flabbergasted. I can't believe the lengths you women will go to in order to meet me." His voice was a fusion of disbelief and anger. He was sure that whatever had been published about him in the tabloids had been completely superficial and not the least bit newsworthy, and anyone attracted to someone displayed in that light likely lacked principles. And, obviously, dignity.

"Excuse me." Her voice remained even. "I'm not trying—"

"Listen, lady," he shot back. "You've gone too far. Breaking into my vehicle, stowing away, sneaking onto my—"

"If you'd just let me—"

"Look, I don't find this sort of thing flattering, so you can just—"

"I assure you, I am not some man-chasing floozy. My name is Dom—"

"I don't care what your name is, lady. Right now, I just want to get a good night's sleep."

"Fine. I would just like to use your telephone. I will call for a ride."

"No. I'm not up for any more company tonight. You can call someone in the morning to come pick you up. You can sleep on the sofa." He slammed the door, and turning on his heel, headed for the porch.

"No, thank you," she said. "I'm in a hurry. I have a sick friend waiting for me." He turned back just as she whirled around and headed in the opposite direction. "Rude, arrogant American," she mumbled in French under her breath.

"Where do you think you're going?" he called after her, the anger in his voice dissipating from fatigue. Sick friend. Right.

"None of your business," she shouted over her shoulder as she tried to navigate the stone driveway in her stilettos.

He made the last few strides to the porch and dropped down on the steps, too tired to care that he was in his tuxedo. A small grin crept across his lips as he watched her falter with each step. He'd give her three minutes. "You know, my driveway is at least a good mile."

"I don't care," she shouted over her shoulder again, then stopped. She lifted her foot, reached down, and slid off her shoe. Then she reached down and pulled off the other one.

"You should know, too, that I've seen wolves in those woods ahead of you," he called out. It wasn't exactly a lie. There were deer in them, and if she heard movement, she'd be back in a New York minute, he figured. He watched her gold gown shimmer under the light of the moon and couldn't help but notice how it draped over her curves in all the right places.

"I am not afraid of wolves," she declared.

"If you make it past the wolves, Route four is still about five miles down the road." She was one stubborn woman, he concluded, suspecting that the stones felt like glass under her bare feet.

"Maybe I'm not going to Route four," she shot back.

There was no way he would let any woman wander around Saint George in the middle of the night. It was pretty safe as far as crime went, but walking down the main road in the dead of night with cars buzzing by at fifty miles an hour wasn't a good idea. Before he could toss out any more discouraging remarks, his cell phone rang. "Ethan here," he answered, keeping his attention on her as she plodded down his driveway.

"Ethan, General Bogart."

"Hello, General, any news?" he asked, assuming that since he had called, he'd heard something more about the poor schmuck that went down at the concert.

"Yes, not good either. The heart attack victim. Turns out he's a royal bodyguard. The heart attack. Turns out it was induced by some shock-rendering device. The coroner found a round red burn on his back directly behind his heart."

"The coroner? I thought you said he was in a coma."

"He didn't make it. Died right after we spoke."

"Who was he guarding?"

"It gets worse." Ethan heard him take a slow draw on a cigar before he continued. "He was guarding a princess. Her Royal Highness Dominique Beauvais. Her father's the King of Monteaux."

"Where's the princess?" He frowned as he watched the woman still struggling down his driveway. Despite her undignified exit from the back of his vehicle and her bare feet, there was something incredibly graceful about the way she carried herself.

"Don't know, but the White House is anxious to find out. She was one of the president's guests. They're trying to keep the whole thing under wraps until they can get a handle on it.

15

The Secret Service is getting involved now."

"Any idea what this princess looks like?"

"Why do you ask? Do you think you may have seen something tonight?"

"No. Just curious."

"Late twenties, early thirties. Dark hair. Five-eight. Oh," he said, "one more thing. She was wearing a gold evening gown. That's all I've got. Sound like anyone you saw tonight?"

No, he told himself. It couldn't be. But he knew. It was her. The woman in his driveway was the missing princess. She had tried to tell him, but he had been too angry to listen. And too full of myself, he thought, as the sting of embarrassment slapped at his ego. "I'm looking at her right now."

"What? My God, Ethan." He heard the springs of a chair creak and knew the general was in his study. He'd listened to that damn chair screech a million times. "Oh, crap." He grinned as he heard the general fumble around. He had probably knocked over his glass of whiskey, he assumed. He knew there was one on his desk. Every time he'd seen the general light a cigar, he'd seen him pour a glass of whiskey. "What's she doing with you?" he asked after Ethan heard things settle down.

"I'm not sure. I assume she escaped whoever killed her bodyguard by hiding in my SUV."

"I'll be damned," the general said with a chuckle. "Don't let her out of your sight. I'll call you back."

It's just my dumb luck, he thought. Hopefully, the White House would dispatch someone to pick her up as soon as they hear from the general. At least he was counting on it. He didn't want to be stuck with a stubborn spoiled princess all night. He pushed himself up from the step and dragged himself down the driveway toward her.

"Okay, that's far enough," he said as he came up behind her.

She whipped around, and trying to keep her feet still on the sharp rocks, lost her balance. She fell backward, and just as she was about to land, he caught her.

It had been a long time since he'd held the soft, warm body of a woman in his arms. He'd forgotten how good it felt as visions of his ex-wife flashed through his head. Damn, it had taken him years to erase his ex-wife from his heart and from his mind. And once he had, he'd avoided women to keep the memory buried and prevent it from coming back and haunting him. Now, in a split second, this privileged little princess was stirring up urges better left dormant.

"How dare you touch me. Put me down," she demanded.

"Trust me, I don't like this any more than you do," he replied as he carried her up the driveway back toward the house. The feel of her long, luscious body and the thought of nothing but the paper-thin fabric of her dress draped over it threatened to push repressed desires to the surface. It surprised him more than anything else had that evening. He ignored her protests and tried to shake off the slight pangs of pleasure that assaulted his gut as she tried to wriggle free.

When he reached the porch, he lowered her to her feet and noticed the depth of her beauty for the first time. Her skin was flawless. Her lips were just the right amount of plump, and her eyes, well, a man could get lost in those eyes. He pulled his gaze from hers as he pushed the front door open, irritated with himself that he had even noticed. He reached inside and flipped a few light switches.

"Never touch me again," she warned as she swept past him into the expansive foyer.

"Don't give me a reason to." He followed her inside, averting his gaze from the silhouette of her body under the clinging gown. He didn't need a distraction like that, nor did he want one. He hadn't thought of being with a woman since his wife had left him, and he didn't want to start now. He should have never reached for her when she lost her balance. He should have let her fall on her spoiled, tiny ass and bruise her tender little feet hoofing it back up the driveway.

"I don't see a telephone. Do you have one, and may I use it?" There was an unmistakable expectation of compliance in her voice as she turned toward him.

"Yes, and no," he answered and continued past her, tossing his tuxedo jacket on a small table and heading into the kitchen. He didn't want whoever was after her tracing any calls to him and paying him a visit. Besides, she didn't need to call anyone. The wheels were in motion. Someone would be picking her up soon.

"Why not? I promise I will not call for a ride this evening," she offered. "I know you don't want any more company."

"Because I said so." He tugged his bow tie loose and flicked open the top button of his shirt.

"That's not an answer." She followed him into the kitchen, her annoyance with him evident.

"It'll have to do." He tossed open the refrigerator door and surveyed its contents. Aside from a carton of milk that he was sure was spoiled, there were a few bottles of beer and a couple bottles of water.

"You're infuriating," she remarked and dropped to a stool next to the counter.

"You can add that to the list. Beer or water?"

"Water, and what list?"

"You know. Rude, arrogant."

"Oh." A hint of pink reached her cheeks. "I didn't think you'd understand French."

He tossed open a few cupboard doors, most of them empty.

"It's all right. I can drink it from the bottle."

"I think you'll have to." The few glasses his wife had left behind when she had moved out were probably still in the dishwasher, he guessed. They generally stayed there for months, since he didn't cook much. He supposed he should get around to replacing what she had taken, which was, essentially, everything not nailed down, but the thought of going shopping for those sorts of things just didn't appeal to him. Besides, he didn't have guests often, invited or uninvited.

He sauntered over, straddled a stool across the counter from her, and slid a bottle of water in front of her. He twisted off the cap on his beer and swallowed a mouthful before he spoke again. "Do you know who's after you?"

"What?" A flash of surprise shot across her face, then just as quickly disappeared, replaced by an expression of controlled calm. "How do you know someone is after me?"

"I got a phone call while you were walking down the driveway." He set his beer down and continued. "You've had quite an evening."

"How much do you know?" Her voice was calm, but her hand trembled as she picked up the water bottle and tried to open it.

"Not much. I was hoping you would fill me in." He reached over and took the bottle from her, twisted off the cap, then slid it back across the counter. "Relax. You're safe here."

"Thank you." She released a long, slow breath. With a steadier hand, she lifted the bottle and took a sip. "Who are you?"

"Nobody." He took another swig of beer, aware she was studying him. "Just a regular Joe." He glanced down at his watch and frowned. It was almost one o'clock in the morning. If someone wasn't on their way to pick her up, it was going to be at least another hour before anyone came, he figured. He really wasn't up for chatting with her for the next hour, princess or no princess.

"If you're just a regular Joe, why is a general calling you?"

"We're friends. It's about time," he mumbled as he leaped

from the stool and tugged his ringing cell phone from his pocket. "General?"

"Yeah. Is the princess still there with you?"

"She's here. Is the White House sending someone for her?" He strolled out onto a deck that overlooked the river. He was used to conducting his telephone calls in private. He settled against the railing and watched as a faint breeze skimmed across the river, forming barely noticeable ripples across the top of the water.

"No. It seems they're satisfied with her safety where she is."

"What's that supposed to mean?"

"It means that she's in your custody."

"You're joking, right?" He pushed himself off the rail. He could feel the irritation that had nagged at him for the past half hour intensify.

"Sorry, son, I'm not. The princess made a clean escape. Only a few people know where she is, and she's in good hands with you. You can appreciate that the more people that get involved from this point, the greater the risk to her safety."

"What am I supposed to do with her?"

The general chuckled. "Well, that's up to you. Everyone agrees that she should stay the rest of the night with you. The White House has spoken with her father. He wants her home pronto. In the morning, you'll be accompanying her back home. I'll call you in a few hours with the details. Oh, and don't worry about her things. Her secretary was staying with her. She'll pack up her things and take them home with her. We're sending her home separately. It'll be less risky in case anyone's watching her, waiting for the princess to contact her."

"What if I don't want to do this?" He swallowed his anger, knowing he had too much respect for the general to mouth off to him. Even though he no longer served under him, he still considered him his superior and always would.

"You don't have a choice. The White House volunteered you."

"They can't do that. I don't work for the government anymore."

"They're aware of that, but they're also aware of your training and background. You know, you still have a damn good reputation in Washington, especially after the Embassy mission. You saved a lot of lives on that mission."

"And I'm retired now. Remember my leg?"

"Screw your leg. You and I both know it hasn't slowed you down. Besides, this is a relatively low-risk mission."

"Mission?" he growled. "This isn't a mission. It's a damn babysitting job." He knew he was going. He hadn't refused, and he knew he wouldn't. He owed the general, and for more than just closing the contract with the Army for his software, but he reserved the right to complain a little.

"Think of it as a vacation, then, if that makes a difference."

"It doesn't."

"Too bad. I'll call you in the morning with the rest of your orders, son."

He shoved his cell phone back in his pocket. *I'd better get CIA and Homeland Security contracts for this one,* he thought. When he looked up, the princess was standing in the doorway, fire burning in her eyes.

"I can assure you, I do not need a babysitter." Her voice was a controlled heat. "I am perfectly capable of taking care of myself. Now, if you'll permit me to use your vehicle, I'll be on my way. I'll pay you for my use and for any damage that I may cause during my use."

"It's not for rent," he said as he brushed past her, annoyed that she had listened in on his conversation.

"Then I'll buy it from you."

"It's not for sale."

"Then call me a taxi," she demanded.

"You're not going anywhere, and you're not calling anyone." He searched for his tuxedo jacket, trying to recall where he'd tossed it. "You're in my custody, and I call the shots."

"And exactly what are the shots?" she asked, following him.

"You're staying here, and I'm taking you home in the morning." He yanked his jacket off the table, pulled his keys from it, then flung it back over the table.

"I'm not going anywhere without my bodyguard and my secretary." Her voice was a combination of defiance and stubbornness.

"That's not going to happen."

"I cannot stand to be with you another minute. You are abhorrent. I demand that you take me to Jean Pierre. Now," she yelled before catching herself. "I'm sorry, but your ego is pushing me to my limits, and I think I should be on my own."

"Jean Pierre is dead," he yelled back. There was only so much a man was required to take, in his opinion, and he'd taken enough from her with her demands, insults, and her disrupting his life.

"That is not true. He is not dead. I heard the general tell you he was in a coma. He is not dead."

He stared down at her. The anger in her voice was unmistakable, but so was the desperation. He had a feeling that her bodyguard was more to her than just protection, and he wished he could take back his words. Regardless of what he thought of her, he didn't want her to find out like this, in the middle of an argument with a stranger, that her lover, if that was what he had been to her, had died.

His eyes told her he wasn't lying. She covered her mouth, gasping for her next breath. "That can't be." Her voice had softened to a whisper. "Jean Pierre has been with me for twenty-five years. When my mother died, he took over my protection. He's been by my side ever since. He can't be gone."

He watched as the anger in her eyes turned to shock and then to sorrow. Her face turned pale against her red lips. She reminded him of a painting of a beautiful woman that he had once seen in a small shop in Italy. The woman in the picture was exquisite, and everything about her had exuded a quiet, graceful strength. Her eyes, however, had held deep sadness in them.

"And Lidia?" she managed. "Do you know anything about Lidia?"

"She's fine. She'll be returning home separately." He assumed she was the princess's secretary or assistant, the woman the general had referred to.

She nodded, and her gaze fell from his as she turned away.

"I'm sorry." He had lost his patience and hadn't bothered to consider the consequences of his words. He was tired, not that it was an excuse. There was no excuse for hurting a woman like that, he told himself.

She didn't answer.

"I didn't mean to hurt you. Really, I didn't." He had just wanted to shut her up, he reasoned, and he'd gone too far. But he was paying for it. The guilt tore at his conscience and he deserved it. "I'm sorry."

"Please, I'd just like to be alone."

He nodded. He'd give her some space. It was the least he could do. He'd put his SUV away and take his time doing it. He decided he could putz around in the barn for a little while. Sleep was probably out of the question now anyway, he assumed.

He walked her into his living room and to the only piece of furniture in there, grateful that his ex-wife hadn't taken it. She lowered herself to the sofa. He watched her brush her fingers over a ruby-studded necklace, unclasp it and slide it into her purse. "I'll be in the garage if you need me," he offered and then strode from the room.

CHAPTER THREE

So far, so good, thought Bruno. The marina had been easy to find, and it was a decent size, making it easy for him and Edgar to prowl around without being seen. He glanced over the selection of boats moored to the far dock and spotted a nice little ski boat. By his estimate, it looked to be about a twenty-footer. It should work, he decided.

"Stay low," he said as they made their way to the boat and crawled in.

"Release the lines," he ordered as he yanked wires from under the dash and ripped them from the ignition. He trimmed their casings with his knife, exposing several bare wires. After a few failed attempts, he pressed two wires together, and the engine sputtered and then turned over.

He eased down on the throttle, and the boat skimmed over the water with hardly a wake. "Okay, let's go over the plan," he said when they were far enough away.

"We get the princess to the boat," Edgar began. "We come back up this way and you drop me off. I get the car and meet you at the dock by the bait shop on the Bay."

"Good." He nodded. "Then we proceed with the original plan."

"She was wearing the rubies tonight," Edgar said. "I should have ripped them off her when I had the chance."

"No, you were right not to. We will have the princess and all of the jewels very soon, and then Mr. Van Dousen will be pleased. It should make up for our failure earlier."

He continued down the river in silence, studying the structures along the shoreline. When he neared the location Van

Dousen had given, he cut the engine and allowed the boat to drift, staying close to the bank of the river. A few yards from direct view of the house where he had been told he would find the princess, he ran the boat aground.

"Give me the binoculars," he ordered.

Edgar tossed them to him, and he surveyed the house. It was well lit, and he smiled when he spotted an opened back door off the deck. He peered through the door and spotted two bottles on a kitchen counter, but there was no sign of anyone inside.

"Do you see the princess?"

"Not yet. But I think there are just two of them here." He scanned the grounds, then lifted the binoculars to the barn. The doors were partly open, obscuring most of the view of the inside. He climbed from the boat, and crouching down, crawled a few yards closer. A partial view of a man inside the barn came into view. His back was to the doors, and he was sitting on a stool.

He signaled, and a moment later, Edgar slithered up beside him on the sand.

"What do you see?" Edgar asked.

"There's a man in the barn," he replied and lifted the binoculars for another look.

"Do you want me to take him out?" Edgar asked.

He heard Edgar release the clip on his three-fifty-seven semi-automatic magnum, then snap it back in. "Shh!" he hissed, lowering the binoculars and flinging his arm across the bridge of Edgar's nose. "No, not until he is a threat. Follow me and do as I say. First, we check the house for the princess."

He crawled through the tall sparse reeds that grew along the shoreline up to the steps of the back deck, keeping an eye on Edgar behind him. They climbed the deck without a sound and slipped through the door that had been left open.

He listened to the sound of a woman weeping and watched

a sadistic grin form across Edgar's face. He allowed a menacing grin to cut across his own face in acknowledgment and nodded toward the living room. He gestured to Edgar to wait, then crept through the foyer and into the living room.

He sneaked up behind the sofa and, in one swift movement, slapped one hand over the princess's mouth and the other around her neck. He yanked her over the back of the sofa and before she could resist, dropped his hand from her neck, forced her arms behind her back, and clamped his fingers around her wrists.

"Let's go, sister," he snarled, jerking her forward. Her attempt to pull free was no match for him. "You can fight all you want, but it's not going to do you any good," he warned as he forced her through the kitchen and back to the deck.

"Get the hell moving," he ordered when he saw Edgar hesitate.

"Wait," he whispered, "the necklace."

"Go," he ordered again. "We'll get it later." He followed Edgar from the deck, then into the reeds while holding the princess in his grip. She was no challenge for a man of his size, and he was sure her feet were barely touching the ground as he propelled her toward the river. He knew he had underestimated her, however, when she stopped struggling and went limp. At the momentum he was moving, when she dropped her weight, she caught his next step. He tripped over her and they tumbled to the ground. The impact tore his hand from her mouth and she emptied a deafening scream into the night.

The scream cut through Ethan's concentration like a knife through butter. He jumped from the stool with such force he sent it crashing to the floor. He dashed toward the house and flung open the front door, nearly ripping it from its hinges. He ran into the living room, then heard another scream, this time muffled. He sprinted out the back door. Anger sliced into him as he witnessed a burly figure dragging the princess toward the water. They were almost at the water's edge. He leaped off the deck and raced after them.

"Hold her down," someone yelled as he watched the burly figure toss her onto a boat and then heave the boat backward off the sand and into the water.

"Hurry, someone's coming," someone warned.

He saw the burly figure jump into the boat and another figure draw a gun. He watched as the figure aimed and squeezed the trigger. The shot was muffled by a silencer, but the bullet struck its target. When it sliced through the surface of the water next to the boat, there was no doubt it had ripped clean through the hull of his boat tied to his dock. A second shot to his hull followed.

His heart slammed against his ribs when he watched the figure aim again, this time at him. In the same instant he saw the princess kick at the gun, he dove into the reeds. The gun fired, and the bullet sailed somewhere over him.

He was up in an instant. He knew time was not on his side. The boat's engine fired up, and the princess and one of the figures flew backward onto the floor of the boat when it took off.

He dove onto his boat. Water was gushing in through the hole left by the bullets. He ripped off his shirt, stuffed it into the hole, and prayed that it would hold. If he lost the princess now, he'd never be able to find her. There were too many avenues of escape. He knew if he didn't catch the other boat, she would be gone.

He turned the key and jammed his hand against the throttle, snapping a pile in half as the boat lurched forward and broke free of the dock. The boat tore through the water. The other boat was already almost a hundred feet ahead and was pulling away fast. He could feel the drag on his boat from the broken pile. He glanced down at his shirt stuffed into the bullet hole. It was soaked, and water was seeping in. His boat was sinking.

He saw the driver of the boat look back, then jerk the boat to the right and then left, leaving a series of choppy wakes in the water ahead of him.

He kicked open the tackle box on the floor by his feet, then knocked it over, spilling out its contents. The blade of the fileting knife gleamed under the light of the moon. He snatched it off the floor and released the steering wheel for a split-second as he reached back and sliced through the rope, cutting the pile free. Instantly, he could feel the boat gain speed. It sailed as it hit a wake and slammed back down hard on the surface of the water. He braced himself as his boat sped toward the second wake.

A flash of light sparked from the boat ahead and he knew he was under fire once more. He swerved his boat to the left, then right. The shots came in a steady stream. He lifted the throttle, keeping his eyes focused on the other boat.

He released a breath as he saw the princess's gown shimmer under the light of the moon. He watched as she clashed with the figure armed with the gun and then flew backward. It looked like the figure then leaned over her and was ready to strike when he fell to the side. He saw the shimmer of her gown come into view again and fixed his gaze on her. "What the —" was all he managed as she climbed onto the edge of the boat and pushed herself off into the dark water.

He steered his boat wide to the left to avoid the area where her body had plunged into the water, lifted the throttle to neutral, and dragged his gaze over the expanse of water to his right. He prayed that she would surface as the seconds ticked by. He allowed a grin when he spotted something break through the water and recognized her.

The whine of the other boat's engine winding down and

then winding up again drew his attention. The boat was circling around to the right. It was coming back for the princess, no doubt. They had taken her once on his watch. They weren't getting a second chance.

He snatched a gas can from its holding place, unscrewed the cap, and wedged it under the dash. Then he hit the throttle and his boat lurched over the water. He concentrated on the other boat, gauging its speed and the angle of its turn. He swung his boat to the right, aiming it at the other boat. He pressed his throttle down to full speed, the wind slapping at his face. He reached down and grabbed his fishing pole, sliding it between his fingers as he stared at the boat dead ahead. It was still on course.

"Three, two, one," he muttered under his breath, then jammed the fishing rod through the steering wheel, turned, and took a flying leap over the seat and onto the stern of the boat. He felt something tug at his leg as his shoe got caught on something. The other boat was right on target. He yanked himself free and dove deep into the river.

He was still under the water when he heard the explosion and felt the force of it. When he surfaced, what was left of the boats was a fiery blaze. Beyond the wreckage, he could see splashing in the water and assumed that at least one of the men on the boat had jumped overboard and survived. He was swimming toward the other side of the river. He and the princess were safe for now. As he turned to search the water where he had seen her, he spotted her swimming toward him.

"Are you all right?" she called out as she neared him.

"I'm okay." He swam the few strokes over to her. "You?"

"I'm fine."

"You owe me a boat," he said, swallowing his relief. He wasn't about to admit how glad he was to see her. As far as he was concerned, she was turning out to be nothing but trouble.

"Put it on my tab," she quipped.

"And a pair of shoes," he added, realizing that he'd lost one along with his prosthetic leg. "Can you make it to shore?"

"I think so."

"Good. Then let's go. We won't have much time. Swim diagonally toward the house." He was going to have to swim as far as he could. It was easier to swim than to walk without a leg. "I'll follow you."

"Wouldn't it be faster to swim straight to shore?"

"Just do as I say." He didn't need her questioning him, and he certainly wasn't about to waste time with explanations.

"Fine." She spun around and with a fierce kick, sent a torrent of water whacking into his face. "Royal pain in the ass," he grumbled, slicing through the water as he took off behind her.

"This is the second time you let her escape." Bruno was seething as he pushed himself up from the surf. He staggered to the water's edge, bent over, and spit up the murky water that had filled his lungs.

"It was not my fault," Edgar fired back, stumbling onto the beach next to him. "I had to stop the boat that was chasing us."

"And you did a fine job of that, too, didn't you?" He swung his arm with such force that when it smashed against Edgar's face, it sent him toppling backward into the surf.

He crawled from the water again and choked up a mouthful of water. "What do we do now? Call Mr. Van Dousen?"

"No." Bruno lifted himself upright. He squinted as he stared across the river. A slight smile touched his lips as he strained to see a quiet splashing a few hundred yards away on the other side. "We go back to the house."

Chapter Four

Dominique crawled from the river and collapsed onto the sand. Her chest ached as she swallowed gasps of air into her lungs. She was surprised her silk dress had survived as it clung to her body like a layer of skin, making her feel exposed. Grateful to be alive, she was annoyed by her modesty and dismissed the idea as she struggled for her next breath and watched Ethan climb onto what was left of his dock.

She allowed her gaze to drift over him. He was handsome, she had to admit, with his dark hair and crisp, blue eyes. He could probably melt a woman's insides with those eyes. Well built, too. His tuxedo had concealed a body of well-sculpted muscles. Each one perfectly defined, she thought, noticing the flex of those muscles with each breath he took. A *Forbes* interview. He must be wealthy. And likely intelligent, if he was friends with a general. It was no wonder women were throwing themselves at him. All things considered, she supposed his enormous ego wasn't surprising.

It was pointless to think about those sorts of things, she told herself. She didn't have flings with men, or any other kind of intimate relationships, for that matter. Her life was much too demanding for a man. Her royal duties consumed her life and left little time for anything else. Besides, men only complicated things, she reminded herself, recalling the actor she had mistakenly allowed in her life. That experience had pretty much sealed her fate of a life without men for the foreseeable future. Feeling she had let her gaze linger long enough, she dropped it and noticed his empty pant leg dangling from the dock. A wave of horror blew through her as she scrambled to her feet and, tearing the bottom of her dress to fashion a tourniquet, rushed toward him.

"Oh, my gosh! Your leg!" When she reached for his leg, his hand swooped down and his fingers clenched her wrist before she could touch him.

"No. I lost it before," he said with dead calm as he drew her hand away from his leg.

She thought she saw a hint of humility flash through his eyes when she looked into them.

He released her wrist and slid off the dock into the hip-deep water beside her. "We can't afford to waste time. We have to get back to the house." He slid an arm around her shoulders. "I'm going to need to lean on you. Are you ready?"

"Yes." She shifted into the crook of his arm and slid hers around his waist. "Let's go."

It took only a few steps to emerge from the water, and only a few more before they fell into rhythm with each other. Her dress was a worthless barrier between them, and every movement of his body against hers ignited tiny sparks of heat in her belly. It had been a long time since she had felt such sensations. That a man could do that to her with no effort at all surprised her.

A princess is always in control of her reactions, she reminded herself as she concentrated on what she would do when they reached Ethan's house.

"I don't want to involve you in this any further," she said. "I'll continue on my own from here."

"We've already had this discussion," he replied. "And it's a little late for that, don't you think?"

"No, I don't. You're still alive."

"Yeah, but I hardly think that if I'm here when your friends come back, they're just going to leave with a handshake if I tell them I'm not part of the deal anymore."

"Then I'll drop you off somewhere safe."

"Forget it, Princess."

"I'll have my father call your president and tell him to re-voke his orders to you, if that's what you're concerned about."

"I'm not concerned about that," he said. "Besides, nobody ordered me to do this. I was asked."

"But you agreed reluctantly. I heard you. You told the general you didn't want to be a babysitter."

"That was before things got interesting. And it's personal now. Those guys blew a hole in my boat, shot at me, ruined my tuxedo, and stole you on my watch. I can manage from here," he said, hoisting himself up onto the deck. He grabbed a nearby shovel, and using it as a crutch, hobbled across the deck and through the door.

"Please," she continued, following him inside. "I can't be responsible for another person's death, and you have nothing to do with this. I am not your responsibility."

"And you're not responsible for what happens to me. No one is responsible for me except me." He kept a brisk pace as she followed him through the house, back to the foyer. Be-tween the banister and the shovel, he maneuvered the stairs ahead of her easily.

They headed into a bedroom at the end of the hall. It was as empty as the living room, with only a bed occupying the space. He reached into a closet, grabbed some clothes, and tossed them to her.

"You can change in the bathroom," he said, nodding to-ward a door on the far wall. "And make it quick."

She did as he said. She slid the straps of her gown from her shoulders and let her dress fall to her feet. She stepped from the heap of fabric into the sweat pants, yanked the t-shirt over her head, and hurried back to the bedroom.

She saw that Ethan had already traded his trousers for a

pair of jeans and a t-shirt, had attached a prosthesis to his knee, and was stuffing a duffle bag. He looked up at her and frowned. "You need shoes," he said, yanking the zipper closed on the duffle bag.

"They're downstairs," she answered and remembered the jewelry. It was in her purse by the sofa, with her shoes.

"Grab them and meet me in the barn." He tossed the duffle bag over his shoulder and bolted from the room. "Let's move."

She was right behind him as they raced down the stairs. When they hit the foyer, he tossed open the door and took off toward the barn. She dashed into the living room, snatched up her shoes and her clutch, then ran out after him.

A couple of motorcycles in different stages of assembly or disassembly—she wasn't sure which—sat among an older model green sports car, an older model red sports car, and the SUV. She hurried to the passenger side of the green car when she caught Ethan stuffing the duffle bag behind the driver's seat.

"Oh, no." She spun around and started back for the house. "I forgot to close the front door."

"Forget it," Ethan said. "Leave it open. That way, they won't have to break it down."

She turned back and pulled the passenger door open. As she slipped down into the seat, he started the engine and the car purred.

"Where are we going?" she asked, locking her seatbelt in place. It had been one of Jean Pierre's rules. Seatbelts and door locks. Minimize your risk, maximize your safety, he had always said. The thought of his words tugged hard at her heart.

"Back to DC," he replied as the car shot out of the barn and flew down the driveway.

"To my hotel?"

"No. Whoever's after you most likely has someone watching the hotel. We're going to my offices. You can rest there," he offered. "And I'll see if I can get any information on these thugs that are after you."

"Then what?"

"Then we wait for the general's call."

"What about Jean Pierre? I can't leave without him."

"Don't worry about Jean Pierre. He'll get his own ride home."

"I need to accompany him home. I cannot leave him here." She let her head fall back against the headrest. Her eyes were starting to burn, and she was getting a headache from the adrenalin that had been blasting through her all evening. Just a little nap was all she needed. "And I need to find out who these men are. I must have justice for Jean Pierre."

"Got any ideas, Princess?" he asked.

"No. Ethan?"

"Yeah?"

"You can call me Dominique," she said as her eyes fluttered and then closed.

Bruno squinted as he looked down on the river from the bridge. Things were quiet on the water. Apparently, no one else had heard the explosion, or if so, they didn't care enough to check things out. There was no sign of the boats, either. He assumed they had already sunk.

"He's mine," he grumbled. "Wake up," he shouted when he saw that Edgar was fast asleep in the passenger seat. "You can sleep when our job is done." He threw a map at him. "Read this and tell me where to turn."

Edgar shifted in the seat and picked up the map.

Bruno stomped down hard on the gas pedal, and they darted across the rest of the bridge.

"Turn here," Edgar finally instructed. "Then down that gravel road."

"It's about time," Bruno growled. He made the last turn and guided the car through the trees. He drove over the gravel a few yards before he stopped and eased the car between two trees.

"Let's get out here," he said, and they continued down the gravel road on foot until he found an unobstructed view of the barn and the house. He saw that the front door was open, as were the barn doors, exposing a vacant spot where a vehicle obviously had been parked. They had wasted no time getting out of there. "God damned bitch," he snarled as he kicked a fallen pine cone, scattering it into a million pieces. "We're too late. She's gone."

"Maybe they left a clue where they're going in the house," Edgar suggested. "Let's check it before we call Van Dousen."

"They wouldn't be that stupid," Bruno fired back.

"Then let's at least get some dry clothes."

Bruno nodded. "But let's not waste time."

CHAPTER FIVE

Ethan pulled into the parking garage and scanned the ground level. There isn't another car or another person in sight, as to be expected at this hour. He parked in the space across from the warehouse and glanced over at Dominique. She was beginning to stir, and a soft moan escaped her lips. When he cut the engine, she awoke.

"Where are we?" she asked, looking around.

"Anacostia," he answered. "DC," he added when he saw no indication of recognition.

"Oh. Are we at your offices?" she asked.

"Yes." He snapped off his seat belt and reached behind the seat for his duffle bag. "Across the street. In the warehouse." He tugged the bag free and placed it in his lap. "Let's go," he said, reaching over and releasing her seat belt.

He led her across the street and unlocked the metal door to the warehouse. Through the door, they were greeted by a long, empty hallway, at the end of which was another metal door. He slid aside the cover to the reader and tapped his fingers across the pad. The metal door swung open, and he escorted her into a small lobby.

"ESM Defense Tech, Inc.," Dominique said, reading the words written atop the glass partition that separated the receptionist's desk and the lobby. "Is that the name of your company?"

"Yes," he answered as he entered the code and another door slid open. He guided her through the door into the suite. He scanned the cluster of cubicles and surrounding offices.

He knew there was nothing fancy about the suite. He hadn't decorated it for aesthetic purposes — if you could say it was decorated at all. He had designed it for function. And functional it is, he thought, as he listened to the clicking, beeping, humming, ticking, and buzzing that reverberated throughout the space from the computers and equipment scattered among the work spaces. "This way," he said and guided her down the hall to the last office at the end.

"What exactly does your company do?" Dominique asked as she strolled around the office.

"Basically, it compiles and disseminates data," he explained as he set down his duffle bag, lowered himself to a chair, and began punching a series of codes and passwords into a keyboard.

"What kind of data?" From the direction of her voice, he knew she was behind him, and from her scent, he knew she had closed the distance and was leaning over him. He thanked God she was no longer wearing that dress. He'd barely survived the assault on his gut when he'd had to hold onto her to get from the dock to the house. It had taken every ounce of willpower to keep from ripping that skimpy little dress off her.

"All kinds," he answered, concentrating on the series of large monitors built into the office wall.

"From what sources?"

"That's classified information," he said with a grin. "That's one of the things that makes ESM unique. Our computer program can intercept and download data in any form from virtually any source capable of receiving or transmitting data. The other thing that makes ESM unique and its program invaluable," he continued as his fingers danced over the keyboard, "is the program's ability to cross-reference the data, analyze it, and organize it."

"Sound's impressive," she remarked. "Who has access to

your program? It sounds like it could be dangerous if used by the wrong kind of people."

"It could be, but we have the ability to shut the program down anywhere in the world from a private, secure location. And we sell to friendly governments and private enterprises that have established reputations and that we know they will use the information for valid purposes." Talking about ESM is a good distraction, he thought.

"What are you doing now?" she asked. He sensed she had taken a step back and knew she was watching the monitors across the wall. Numbers and images were flickering and flashing across the screens.

"Nothing yet. I'm just booting up the access system." He struck one more key, turned his chair to avoid tilting back on her, and then leaned back.

"Are you going to try to find out who killed Jean Pierre?" She slid a nearby chair next to his, sat down, and dropped her clutch in her lap.

He swiveled to face her. "I'd like to try, but I can't get any information from the system until I give it something to work with." He saw the stress of the evening in her face, yet she was still more beautiful than most women he knew. There was a natural exquisiteness about her despite the mangled river-washed hair and the dowdy clothes. It must have something to do with coming from generations of royalty, he figured. "Do you know anything at all about these men?"

"No. I've never seen them before tonight." She shifted in the chair.

"Did you get a good enough look at them to be able to describe them, or did you notice anything in particular about either one? A birth mark, a scar, a tattoo, missing tooth?"

She was quiet for a moment and then shook her head. "I'm sorry. I couldn't even see one of the men. He held me from behind, and I can't recall anything distinctive about the other one." The corners of her lips turned down, and she lowered her gaze. "I should have made it a point to notice. For Jean Pierre."

"It's okay." Instinctively, he placed his hand on her arm and then drew it back. It was foolish to touch her. No, he corrected himself. It was dangerous to touch her. She had already nearly sent him into convulsions once, and just the thought of those luscious legs simmering in the back of his mind was enough to make his gut stir. He was convinced the dowdy clothes he'd given her weren't going to do much to quell the rumbles in his gut now that he knew what was underneath them. "Do you have any idea why they're after you?"

"No. I don't think — " When she crossed her legs, her purse slid from her lap and fell to the floor. She reached down to pick it up and her face lit up. "Wait. One of the men mentioned the necklace."

"Necklace?"

"The one I was wearing tonight." She unsnapped her purse and pulled out the necklace she had worn that evening. She turned it over in her hands, studying it.

"You think they're after the necklace?" he asked, watching the huge rubies glisten under the fluorescent lights. He estimated the smallest one to be easily the size of an almond.

"I think so," she replied, handing it to him.

"Was this purchased or inherited?" He threaded the necklace through his fingers, then turned it over and examined the setting into which the stones were mounted. He could see a tiny, almost illegible inscription of some sort on the back of the setting in which one of the rubies was secured.

"Inherited, but not by me. It belongs to my secretary, Lidia. Her grandfather made it. He was a jeweler. She asked me if I would wear it. She said she would never have occasion to wear it and that it was a shame for it to be stored away and never worn."

"She's right about that. It would be a shame to keep this hidden away," he said, trying to make out the inscription. He had no doubt there were millions of dollars of jewelry worn inside the Kennedy Center that evening and wondered why the necklace was so special to the person who was after it.

"Have you worn this necklace before?"

"No, not this one. But I've worn others made by Lidia's grandfather. I was wearing one about a month ago. It was made with sapphires."

He pushed himself up from the chair, grabbed the duffle bag, and headed out of the office with the necklace. "Come with me."

"Where?" she asked, catching up to him in the hallway.

"Upstairs." He pushed open a door and held it while she passed through. She took the flight of stairs ahead of him and stepped aside when she reached the top.

He placed his index finger against the small pad on the wall and held it there. In a matter of seconds, the heavy, vault-like door swung open on its own. They stepped into a large room.

"I'd like to see if I can pull anything up with this necklace," he said, placing the duffle bag on a table and then leading her to a machine a few yards away. He lifted the lid and positioned the necklace on a glass plate. "There's some sort of mark on it." He lowered the lid and then pressed a series of switches located on the front of the machine. Several images of the necklace from varying perspectives appeared on a small monitor. He pressed another button, and an enlarged image of the inscription emerged.

"It looks like some sort of symbol," she said, leaning closer to the monitor and him.

"Or initials. One on top of the other." He could almost taste her. She was so close. It would take minimal effort to cover those lips with mine, he thought before reminding himself that it was not an option.

"Possibly. Yes, I can see that," she said, studying the monitor.

"Do you know the name of Lidia's grandfather?" He took a few steps back, annoyed that she was triggering reactions he had for years managed to keep suppressed. The last thing he wanted was to be at the mercy of a woman. The sooner he got her home, the better.

"No. All I know about him is that he made the necklaces for her grandmother."

He moved to a keyboard and tapped his fingers over the keys. A series of lights began to flash inside the lid covering the necklace. When he finished, he lifted the lid, removed the necklace, and handed it to her. "Let's give the necklace some time to work its way through the network."

He watched as she tucked the necklace back into her clutch, then led her back to the office.

"I don't want to leave Washington until I find out who killed Jean Pierre," she said as they entered the office.

"That's not an option." His tone made it clear that there was no room for discussion. He had instructions coming with the plan to take her home. Pronto. That was the word the general had used. He slid the chair she had sat in before a safe distance away and dropped into his chair. He struck a key on the keyboard to rouse the computer, and the monitors lit up.

"If I go home now, my father will never let me out of his sight." She eased herself down to a chair on the opposite side of the desk. "And I'll never find out who killed Jean Pierre. I'll never get justice for him."

"I'll e-mail you if anything comes up on the necklace," he said as he slid his fingers over the keyboard.

"I need to know more than just about the necklace. We have an opportunity now while the men are still here. Maybe we could set a trap for them."

"You're going home. You don't have a choice." His voice was firm. Despite as intriguing as things were getting, she was going home. That was the plan, and he wasn't going to subject himself to her any longer than he had to. He didn't need the constant drain on his willpower.

"Once I leave Washington, no one will investigate Jean Pierre's murder. Your police will have no interest in the matter, since Jean Pierre is not a citizen here, and I am no longer under threat here."

"Don't you have detectives in Monteaux?"

"Of course, but while I am here, the men will be here, and there will be evidence here. There is none in Monteaux. We need to strike here while the iron is hot."

"Sorry, but that's not in the cards. Once I get instructions from the general, you're going home."

"Stop it," she snapped, pushing herself up from the chair. She slapped the palms of her hands on the desk, and he felt her heat as she glared down at him. "Just when I was beginning to like you, despite your incessant arrogance, just when I was beginning to think you had some measure of decency, you had to start up with your smug, condescending attitude."

He lowered his gaze to the keyboard and began typing. "I'm going to ignore this little outburst. It appears you are not used to not getting your way and are having difficulty accepting that." He wasn't going to lose his temper this time only to regret it again, he told himself as he tried to remain calm. Arrogant, he thought, and despite his best effort, felt the prick of her words.

"Stop treating me like a child. Who do you think you are? You can't order me what to do as if I am some subordinate."

"I think you might be wrong about that," he muttered between clenched teeth as he continued typing.

"Look at me when you speak to me," she demanded.

"I'm busy working here," he said, shifting his gaze past her to the monitors.

She marched around the desk, grabbed his chair, and jerked it around until he had no choice but to face her. Then she dropped her hands to the arms of the chair and leaned down to within inches of his nose.

He could taste her passion. He was drawn to it like a magnet to steel, and that pissed him off even more than her huffy little tantrum.

"I've got news for you," she seethed. "I'm not going with you. This is where we part company."

He knew full well as he clamped his hands over her wrists that it was a mistake to touch her. The fact that he couldn't stop himself told him that he was losing control. He could feel her heat, and that it was fueled by anger didn't matter. It was infectious, and it stoked the fire already simmering in his gut.

She tried to jerk her arms free, but he ensured that any attempt to liberate herself from his grip was useless. His hands were like vises around her wrists.

He debated whether he could trust himself. His self-control had been chipped away at all night by her constant minor assaults. He wanted nothing more than to pull her into him so close that not even a molecule of air would separate them. He just hoped that there was an ounce of willpower somewhere within him as he forced her to back up a step so he could get to his feet.

"I've got news for you," he said, standing over her. There was only a whisper of air between them, but she didn't retreat. He stared down at her, knowing his control was slipping away. Impulse was taking over. His voice disappeared as he covered her mouth with his, his tongue diving deep to quench the long-endured drought. When she kissed him back, what little control he had left shattered. He felt her needs unleash. They were as desperate as his. He was already hard when he yanked her into him. He tugged at the sweatshirt, knowing what awaited him. She tore at his t-shirt. Clothing was ripped off and thrown aside.

They stumbled to the conference table in a tangled embrace, their hands groping, exploring, and taking. He lifted her onto the table and climbed on top of her. Famished, he wanted all of her all at once. The hunger consumed him. He pawed at her silky flesh. He mauled her breasts. And when the moan of pleasure escaped her lips, he almost went mad.

He dragged his tongue down her neck. When he reached her breast, he could have swallowed it whole. She spread her legs, and when he slid his fingers inside her, he felt her breath catch. Her hands clawed at him. He sensed their impatience. When her fingers circled his penis, he lost all rational thought.

Overwhelmed by needs too long ignored, he plunged inside her and felt her shudder. She arched under him and drove him to the edge. He knew he was at her mercy. Each of her movements demanded more. Each delivered more. He responded with wild fervor, pounding harder, deeper. Their bodies collided in a fit of frenzy. He teetered on the brink. When she whispered his name, his insides exploded. He felt her spasm around him as he took her over the edge with him.

His sanity flooded back, and with it, a mountain of regret. All those years of stringent control had been swept aside so easily. Before he could utter a word, a beam of red light flashed around the perimeter of the ceiling, signaling a break-in along the rear of the warehouse. He slid off the table in one swift move, taking her with him and lowering her to the floor. He lifted his finger to her lips. When she nodded, he gathered their clothes and tossed hers to her. He slid into his, then leaned over her. "Stay here," he whispered and then headed for the door.

Without a sound, he slipped out of the office. He hugged the wall as he made his way down the corridor and past the other offices. He'd been sloppy forgetting his duffle bag up-stairs. He knew better. Now, he was going to have to rely on the element of surprise.

At the end of the hallway, he stayed low as he maneuvered his way through the cubicles toward the back. He ducked be-hind a partition when he heard a sound. He saw a figure emerge from one of the offices along the wall. He had been right. At least one of the men had escaped the boat collision. And he'd been right about him returning to his house. The son of a bitch was wearing a pair of his khaki pants and one of his shirts.

He waited behind the partition while he watched the figure check the other offices along the back wall. Then he crept along the cubicles as the figure started to snake his way through the suite. Be patient, he told himself as he studied the path the figure was taking and his pace. Every four or five strides, the figure stopped to glance around and listen, and he was poised to shoot. He stayed in rhythm with him, moving when he moved and waiting when he paused as he closed the distance between them. He had to be careful. The pistol the figure was carrying was a forty-five caliber.

He watched as the figure changed direction and headed to-ward the corridor. Damn. He knew he had to make a move before the son of a bitch reached the hallway. He cut across a few rows of cubicles and then quickened his pace to three to every one of his. When he snuck ahead of the figure, he made his way back toward him. He ducked into a cubicle one over from the figure's path and waited.

He listened as the figure got closer. He could hear the son of a bitch breathing. It was rapid. The asshole was nervous. He should be, he thought, as he planned his attack.

He heard him pass the row of cubicles. He crawled from his as he counted the figure's strides. He waited as he paused, and after the first stride, he drew a breath and curled his fingers into a fist. He was pretty sure one blow to the back of his head would have him out cold. He stood up and took two steps toward the asshole. Before he could strike, the son of a bitch whipped around, lifted his hand, and aimed his pistol at his chest. He swung his fist hard against the gun, causing it to discharge as it tore loose from the figure's hand.

He wasted no time following up with a punch to his jaw, sending the son of a bitch backward and slamming hard against the wall. The asshole returned with a kick, catching him in the gut and sending him through a cubicle panel. He saw the asshole scramble toward the gun. He grabbed a chair and hurled it at him, knocking him off balance and giving him enough time to force him down.

They rolled into another cubicle panel, and he felt it tumble down on top of them as he saw the asshole grab a pair of scissors. He moved out of the way just as the scissors plunged against the floor, barely missing him. He landed a punch to the asshole's left kidney, but the man recovered and scrambled to his feet. He blocked a punch but took a kick to the leg. He stumbled backward into an office door, regaining his balance just in time to see the son of a bitch charging toward him, wielding the scissors above his head.

He twisted the doorknob and forced his weight against the door. It flew open and the asshole sailed past him. He leaped onto his back and propelled him into a metal file cabinet. The son of a bitch's head slammed into the cabinet with such force, the blow snapped his neck, and he collapsed to the ground.

Winded from the struggle, he dropped to his knees beside the asshole's motionless body. He lifted a limp arm and checked for a pulse, then tossed the limb aside. He was dead. He checked his pockets next. They were empty.

He got up and searched for the pistol. When he found it, he hurried back to the office where he'd left Dominique. As he opened the door, a bronze statue came whirling toward him. He ducked just in time to avoid being struck.

"It's okay. It's me, Ethan," he called out. When he flipped on the light, he saw Dominique standing in front of the desk clutching a letter opener. Her cheeks were a pale shade of gray.

"Thank God," she said, clutching her heart. She set the letter opener down on the edge of the desk. "I heard a gun go off. I thought they killed you."

"I'm fine." He walked over to her. "I'm not that easy to kill."

"Are they gone?"

"There was only one. We don't have to worry about him anymore, but the other one might be coming."

She nodded.

"Take a slow breath," he instructed, placing his hands on her arms to steady her.

"I'm okay," she replied but did as he said.

"Good." He urged her forward. "We have to get moving."

She took a step, then turned back and grabbed her clutch off the desk.

They hurried up to the second level, and Ethan opened the vault door. He grabbed his duffle bag, tugged the zipper back, and retrieved his *Sig Sauer*, a souvenir from his service days. Then he slid the zipper closed, swung the bag over his shoulder, and they hurried down the stairs without a sound. He checked the hallway, then pulled Dominique through the door behind him. He shielded her as they made their way through the suite to a side exit.

He pushed the door open a crack and scanned the alley between the warehouse and the other building. Satisfied it was safe, he led her into the alley. He kept a tight grip on her arm while they hastened toward the front corner of the building. He considered a strategy for crossing the street to get to the parking garage. He knew they would be most exposed in the street.

When they reached the corner, he shoved her behind him. He peered around the corner and canvassed the area. "Son of a bitch," he said under his breath. His sweet little red Italian sports car was parked about thirty yards down the street near the front entrance to the warehouse. He dug out his binoculars from his duffle bag and focused them on the car. It appeared empty. Either the other dirtbag hadn't survived the boat explosion, or he was looking for his buddy inside the warehouse. He figured they had only one option for getting to the parking garage, and they couldn't waste time taking it. He kept an eye on the front of the warehouse and his car as he stuffed the binoculars into his duffle bag and gave orders to Dominique. "We're going to haul ass across this street as fast as we can, and while we're doing that, you're going to use me as your shield. Once we get to the side of the parking garage, we're going to climb over the wall, then haul ass to the car. Any questions?"

"No."

He pulled his gaze from the front of the warehouse and planted it on hers. Other than the fear her eyes divulged, they told him she was ready. "Let's go, now," was his last order. They bolted across the street quicker than he expected, given that she was wearing stilettos, and she tackled the wall just as impressively. In less than twenty seconds, they were exiting the parking garage.

He glanced in the rear-view mirror as he turned down Pennsylvania Avenue and spotted his little red car about half a mile behind them. It was running with its headlights off, and if it weren't for the light cast by the city's street lamps, he might not have seen it until it was right upon them. He took a sharp right onto the Anacostia Freeway and looked over his shoulder.

"Damn it," he muttered, stomping down on the clutch and shoving the gear shifter into fourth gear. From the corner of his eye, he saw Dominique look behind them.

He kept an eye on his mirror. He knew it was going to be a close race between German engineering and Italian engineering. With the speeds and maneuverability of both cars, it was going to come down to skill, and that, he had. He slid the shifter into fifth gear and punched down on the accelerator. "Put your seatbelt on," he ordered. He glanced at the speedometer. They were now cruising at over a hundred miles per hour, and the asshole behind them was closing the distance. The street lights above them were a blur of white ribbon.

"It's on."

A pair of red taillights came into view ahead of them, and in an instant, they passed a minivan as if it were standing still.

They were approaching the end of the Anacostia Freeway. He had to decide whether to take the Beltway toward Baltimore or over the bridge into Virginia. As he considered both routes, the blast of a ship's horn in the near distance cut through the morning calm. He glanced at his little red car in his rear-view mirror and grinned. It's worth a shot, he thought, as he slowed toward the exit ramp just before the bridge. The car was so close he could almost feel the heat of its engine on his neck. He rounded the ramp and shot onto the bridge. The traffic lights on the bridge flashed a bright, foreboding red as a ship proceeded in the dark water below toward the bridge.

"Ethan?"

"Uh-huh?" He stomped down on the accelerator. His little Italian car swerved out from behind and pulled alongside them, its engine roaring. He watched the mid-section of the bridge separate and begin to lift ahead of them.

"Ethan?"

"Yeah?"

He raced alongside the car, barreling toward the rising roadway.

"Ethan!" Dominique's voice pitched, and he heard her hands smack against the dashboard.

"Hold on," he warned, his voice calm, as they approached what was now almost a thirty-degree angle of pavement. He slammed the clutch to the floor and jammed the gear shifter into third gear. When the clutch sprang back, the engine howled and the car jerked as it slowed.

He watched his little Italian sportster blast past them. He hit the brakes and the wheels locked. The tires screeched and smoked as his little German baby skidded across the bridge. The smell of burning rubber filled the air.

His little Italian car skyrocketed up the elevated portion of the bridge and catapulted out of sight.

His German sportster slowed but continued skidding toward the raised roadway. He yanked the steering wheel to the left, and the car spun around two full turns before it came to a rest at the foot of a wall of road.

He pressed in the clutch, slid the shifter into first gear, and started back over the bridge in the opposite direction. He glanced over at Dominique. She was as white as a sheet and was still clinging to the dashboard.

"I take it you're not a fan of roller coasters?" There was a hint of amusement in his voice, and he allowed the grin to sweep across his face. He had lost the son of a bitch. The asshole and his Italian sweetheart were either in the Potomac or on the other side of the bridge. Either way, he was sure his car had suffered some major damage. But Dominique was safe.

"Excuse me?" The words alone told him she was displeased.

He swerved to the left as the eighteen-wheeler headed toward them, its angry horn blaring. "Relax," he said, still grinning. "I've got everything under control." Once they were off the bridge, he steered onto the median and toward Balti-more's northbound lanes.

"You call that under control?" she asked, her voice simmer-ing. "You almost got us killed."

"You're kidding. I saved your life. You're still alive, aren't you?" he shot back.

"Only by the grace of God, I'm sure." She slumped back into her seat. "If you think I'm going to be grateful for that Kamikaze ride, you have another thing coming."

"We wouldn't even be here if—" he began, then stopped. He veered off the next exit and pulled to a stop on a side street. He reached over and dragged his hands through her hair, sifting it through his fingers.

"What are you doing?" She didn't bother to conceal her an-noyance as she slapped his hands away.

"We weren't followed from Saint George to my office. I'm certain of that." He looked down at her feet. "Give me your shoes."

"What? Why?"

"Just give them to me."

She reached down, slid off her shoes, and handed them to him.

"And I'm pretty sure we weren't followed from the Ken-nedy Center." He snapped the heel off one of the shoes and inspected it. Finding nothing, he handed it back to her.

"What do you think you're doing? What am I supposed to wear now?"

"I'm sure I would have noticed," he continued, ignoring her remark and snapping off the heel of the other shoe. "Well, what have we here?" He turned over a tiny disc in the palm of his hand and studied it.

"What is it?"

"This," he said, holding it up between his fingers, "is a GPS dot. A global positioning system transmitter. It's been transmitting your location to a receiver somewhere."

"Where?"

"Could be anywhere. The receiver could be halfway around the world and be able to pick up your signal."

"Is it transmitting now?"

"I'm sure it is." He dropped the dot on the floor and smashed it with the heel of his shoe. He leaned down, picked up the smashed piece of metal, and slid it into his pocket. Then he pressed in the clutch, nudged the shifter in gear, and pulled away from the curb. "Who could have put that in your shoe?"

"I don't know. Those shoes were just one pair of ten that were given to me."

"Why would someone give you ten pairs of shoes?"

"Designers occasionally give me products so that when I wear them, they get free advertisement. I received these shoes in ten different colors."

"That certainly increased the chances of you wearing a pair and whoever sent them being able to track you."

"I think I shouldn't accept any more promotional products."

CHAPTER SIX

"Imbecile!" Helmuth Van Dousen's voice thundered over the line, and Bruno was sure he heard glass breaking in the background. "Dispose of the body immediately," he ordered. "Then get out of the country before you get caught. You've screwed up enough!"

"Yes, sir," Bruno replied, swiping at the bead of sweat that had rolled down and caught in his brow. He knew he couldn't blame the humidity this time. "There is no way anyone can trace Edgar to you," he assured Van Dousen. "We used false identification to get into the country, everything has been paid for with cash, and we are using disposable phones. We did everything as you instructed." He heard the desperation in his own voice. It was the desperation of a condemned man, a man who knew that his failure meant certain death.

"Just do as I say," Van Dousen ordered.

"I can finish the job alone," he offered.

"No. It's too risky now. Just dump the body where it will not be found and leave," Van Dousen ordered again before the line disconnected and went dead.

"Didn't take you long to get here. C'mon in," the general said, pushing the door aside to allow Ethan and Dominique inside and taking a quick glance down one side of the street and up the other. "Margaret's got coffee on. She'll serve us in the study."

He looked groggy-eyed even though he was dressed in

khaki slacks and a starched shirt, Ethan observed as the general ushered them across the foyer and into his study. He looked over the general's impressive military paraphernalia, as he always did when he entered the study. "I'm sorry, sir, to get you out of bed at this hour."

"Hell, I'd be up in a couple hours anyway." He turned with a smile to Dominique. "General Bogart," he said, extending his hand to her. "I understand you've had quite an interesting evening, Your Royal Highness. Please, sit." He gestured toward an overstuffed leather chair. "I'm sorry about your guard."

"Thank you, General. He was a dear friend, as well."

Ethan heard the earlier sadness as she lowered herself to the chair.

"And I'd like to express my apologies, as well, for intruding on you."

"No need. As soon as Margaret brings our coffee, she'll show you upstairs. You can get a little rest."

"That's very kind of you, General. Thank you, but please, I don't want to put you and your wife to any trouble," she said. Ethan noticed the touch of pink that had reached her cheeks and watched her brush aside her hair and smooth down the sweatshirt. He was pretty sure she was mortified by the remnants left from the river and the clothes he'd given her. And she was probably dying for a shower.

"It's no trouble, and Margaret's our housekeeper. She's happy to get you whatever you need." He turned to Ethan and gestured toward an empty chair. "Seems escorting the princess home has been a little more exciting than you anticipated, huh?"

"It's been a little more complicated," he admitted, appreciating the gist of the remark as well as the raised eyebrows and smirk that accompanied it. He supposed he deserved it for the complaining he'd done.

He glanced at Dominique to see if she had caught the im-
port of the remark, but it was clear that either she hadn't or
didn't care. Her somber expression brought sharp barbs of
guilt stabbing at his conscience. Amid all his complaining and
grumbling, he'd forgotten that she had lost a friend, a dear
friend by her own account, and was probably blaming herself
for his death.

"Good morning, all." Ethan turned to see Margaret burst
into the study, balancing a tray in her hands. It was obvious
from the rollers under her scarf that she had been unexpect-
edly awakened by the general. "There's some nice warm muffins here to have with your coffee." She set the tray on the
edge of the desk and poured the first cup of coffee.

"Good morning, Margaret," Ethan said with a warm smile,
returning the greeting. "The muffins smell wonderful."

"I've got your favorite here," she said with a wink.

"Margaret," the general interrupted as he sat down at his
desk, "Ethan and I will serve ourselves. Would you take the
princess here up to one of the guest rooms? She'll have her
coffee upstairs. And could you make sure she gets whatever
she needs," he added.

"Certainly." She cleared the tray except for a cup of coffee
and a plate with a couple of muffins, then gestured to
Dominique. "Come, dear. Let's get you comfortable."

"Thank you, General, for your hospitality." Dominique
pushed herself up from the chair and followed Margaret.
"Oh," she began as she turned back, "please understand that
I will not leave for Monteaux without Jean Pierre."

The general nodded, and she followed Margaret from the
room.

"Good Lord, son," the general bellowed as soon as
Dominique was out of earshot. "I didn't want to insult the
young lady, especially given the fact that she's a princess, but
you two look like you were sucked into the rotting belly of

some freakish beast and then shit out. And good God, what the hell was she wearing on her feet? I want a full briefing."

"You've always had a way with words, sir." Ethan took a long sip of his coffee, then told the general everything about their evening.

"I'll be damned. It didn't occur to me that she might have a transmitter on her." He leaned back in his chair, his brow furrowed. "Are you sure she's clean now?"

"Positive. I checked her myself," he was quick to answer. "Head to toe."

"Hmm." The general nodded with a grin. "And don't tell me you didn't enjoy that." He pushed forward and lifted the telephone receiver. "Let's see what we can find out about your trip to Monteaux. I'll have someone pick up that stiff in your office and see if there's any sign of your sports car, as well."

As the general made the calls, Ethan helped himself to one of Margaret's muffins and allowed his thoughts to drift. He had to admit, Dominique had held up well through the evening, all things considered. There was amazing strength and determination under that exquisite exterior. And he had enjoyed every remarkable inch of that exterior, but it was going to make things much more difficult for him now. Damn princess. He had lost control with her. She wasn't easy to resist.

"Okay, that's in the works," the general reported as he hung up and took a bite of his half-eaten muffin.

"What's the plan for today, General?" he stifled a yawn and took another sip of coffee.

"A plane is being prepared for your trip. It'll be flown into Andrews. You and the princess can board it there. The Royal Family has its own airstrip in Monteaux, but the problem is that it's part of a commercial airport, which makes things more complicated. It'll be safer and give us more control to fly you into the nearest US military base, then have a helicopter transport you directly onto the palace grounds. No one would expect that. We're working on that end, too. We want to make sure we deliver the princess to her father safe and sound."

"Sounds easy enough. Who's being filled in?"

"No one." Ethan recognized the band from the *La Perla Habana* cigar the general lifted from his humidor and watched him clip the cap. He knew *La Perla* was one of the general's favorites. "Not even the pilot will know the princess is his passenger unless he recognizes her. But security will be beefed up at both ends."

Ethan nodded and took another swallow of coffee.

"What do you want in terms of firearms?" He watched him hold the lighter steady, then roll the cigar just above the flame and take a draw, careful not to let the flame touch the cigar. He'd watched him light a lot of cigars. It was a science to the general.

"I've got my *Sig*. I wouldn't mind having some more ammo with me."

The general nodded and took a few slow, steady draws, then waited for the burn to establish. "I'll have it waiting for you on the plane. Any idea who's after the princess?"

"No." He shook his head and lowered his cup to the table. "There's a chance her secretary might have something to do with it."

"Oh?" The general arched his brows. "What makes you think that?"

"Well, for starters, I'm not convinced that it's the necklace someone's after and not the princess. The necklace could be a smokescreen. And the necklace belongs to her secretary, who asked her to wear it. And, I have to question how the GPS dot was placed in her shoe."

"So you think her secretary wants her kidnaped?"

"I don't know. It's just pure conjecture at this point."

"Well—" The shrill of the telephone interrupted him.

"Let's hope they've got some information for us," he said as he snatched up the receiver. "General Bogart."

For a man who has just turned seventy, he has the energy and agility of a man half his age, Ethan mused as he smiled to himself. He was as loyal to the men who served under him as he was to the country he served. He had no doubt that the general had mentored other young men who felt just as loyal to him in return as he did. Theirs was more than a relationship of mutual loyalty, though. It was a relationship of trust, respect, and in his case, love. The general was more like a father to him and the closest to one he'd ever had.

He thought about how lucky he was that the general was a part of his life. He couldn't imagine what would have happened to him had his mother kept him. By the time his useless addict of a mother had realized she was pregnant, she had no idea which of the endless stream of losers she had slept with had gotten her pregnant. Not that it mattered. Like her, none of them had a pot to piss in and wanted nothing more than to have a pint of whiskey in one hand and a syringe in the other. His aunt, Charlotte, threatened to have his mother arrested if she didn't enroll him in school. Afraid that a teacher might call the cops if they saw the scars on his back, his mother gave him to his aunt in exchange for a couple hundred bucks to, as she put it, compensate her for the loss of her property.

Aunt Charlotte was determined to give him some self-respect and honor. She was the one who had made him apply to *West Point*. After graduating at the top of his class, he was assigned under a hierarchy of officers under the general's command. It hadn't taken long for his heroics to get him noticed by the general.

"What do you mean there's no goddamn body?" the general barked into the phone. He lowered the receiver and looked across at Ethan. "The body's not in the vault, is it?" he asked.

"No, it's in one of the offices on the lower level. The third one down on the left side of the suite."

"Recheck the offices and make sure you look in the third one down on the left side of the suite."

Ethan pushed himself up from the chair, his mind churning. He was sure, now, that his little Italian sweetheart hadn't been driven into the Potomac. It had made it to the other side. The driver must have gone back to his office to pick up his accomplice, and finding him dead, took the body to get rid of it.

"All right, all right. Anything on the car?" the general continued. "Okay. Call me if you find it." He tossed the receiver into the cradle as his gaze followed Ethan. "Are you sure you killed the goddamn bastard?"

"Yeah. I'm sure."

"Well, there's no sign of the body at the warehouse. Listen," he said, getting up from his desk, "there's nothing more for you to do right now. Why don't you grab a few hours of sleep? Get refreshed. I'll have Margaret wash your clothes for you."

"I don't—"

"And don't argue with me. That's an order." He dropped a hand on Ethan's shoulder as he guided him from the study. "You can grab one of the guest rooms upstairs."

"I suppose I could use a couple hours," he conceded. "Thanks, General."

"Hell, I'm partially responsible for getting you into this. It's the least I can do."

"Remind me to thank you for that later."

"Yeah, yeah."

Just as Dominique stepped from one of the bathrooms, she saw a young woman stumble from a bedroom half asleep and stagger down the hallway toward her.

"What's going on?" the woman asked, wiping her eyes and pushing a tangled mop of hair from her face.

"I'm so sorry if I've awakened you," Dominique answered in a hushed voice. She recognized the dazed woman from the prior evening as the one with Ethan in the garage at the Kennedy Center. She looks much younger without make-up, she thought, but still adorable. She had the general's round face and slightly protruding chin, although not as pronounced.

"Who are—" she managed before her jaw unhinged. "I know who you are. You're Princess, Princess—"

"Dominique Beauvais," she finished for her, doing her best to suppress a yawn.

"That's right. I'm Bailey, by the way. I didn't know you were going to be staying with us. My dad didn't say anything about any guests."

"It's nice to meet you, Bailey. We weren't expected and won't be staying very long. I'm sorry to have disturbed you," she apologized again as she inched her way toward the guest bedroom. Now that she was showered, she couldn't wait to crawl between a set of sheets and be able to sleep, even if for only an hour or two.

"We? Who else—"

"Good morning, Bailey," Ethan interrupted as he cleared the stairs and strolled up the hallway toward them. "You're certainly looking chipper this morning."

Bailey's gaze danced from her to Ethan and then back to her before settling on Ethan, and Dominique could see her mind spinning. The corners of Bailey's mouth formed an impish grin. "Well, well," she said. "I see now why you were in such a hurry to dump my ass off last night."

"And you're looking refreshed," he said to Dominique, ignoring Bailey's remark. "Don't let her talk your ear off," he warned before slipping into another room.

Dominique watched Bailey tuck her arms across her chest and, with the grin still painted on her lips, lift a brow to her as she waited for an explanation.

"Oh, please," she muttered as she turned to enter her room. "The man is insufferable."

"Insufferable?" Bailey repeated. "That doesn't sound like Ethan."

"And how long have you known the man?" She sat down on the edge of the bed, then remembered the remark Ethan had made when they were in the SUV.

"Most of my life," Bailey replied as she plopped across the bed.

"Well, that explains it," Dominique said. "You've gotten so immune to his behavior that you don't notice it anymore." Not to mention the fact that you've obviously got an enormous crush on the man, she thought.

"I'm not the oblivious type," Bailey returned and propped herself up on an elbow. "And exactly how long have you known Ethan?"

"You needn't worry." Dominique folded the top sheet back and squeezed between the sheets. "Only four or five hours. And I have absolutely no interest in the man, personal or otherwise. The sooner we part company, in fact, the better. Could you please . . ." She tugged on the comforter.

"What's that supposed to mean?" Bailey continued, rolling off the comforter.

Dominique drew a hesitant breath, then decided she was just too tired to choose her words any more carefully than as they came to her. "I was at the Kennedy Center this evening at the concert, and a man tried to kidnap me. I escaped by hiding in the back of Ethan's vehicle. I heard your conversation with him as he drove you home."

"Did that have something to do with the man that died tonight?" She pushed herself up. "My dad asked me if I had seen anything."

"Yes, it did." She lowered her gaze and blinked back the tears. "The man was my bodyguard."

"Holy shit!" Bailey leaped off the bed, then sat back down on the edge of the bed beside her. "I'm so sorry. Had he been your bodyguard long?"

"Yes." She nodded. "Most of my life."

"I'm sorry," Bailey repeated, then reached for the tissue box from the nightstand and offered it to her.

"Thank you." She forced a weak smile. "Anyway," she continued, changing the subject, "as I was saying, I overheard your conversation with Ethan as he drove you home. Obviously, you have romantic feelings for him, and I'm sorry to have intruded on such a personal exchange."

"Oh, my God." Bailey flopped backward on the bed, her sides trembling with laughter. "That's hysterical."

"What is?"

"That you heard all that. And that you think I have a thing for Ethan. Not that he's not hot. You can see just how hot he is, but he's not my type. That was all an act."

"Oh." She'd accept that. It wasn't her intent to embarrass Bailey. She just wanted to let her know that she wasn't in competition with her for Ethan's affection. If Bailey wished to deny that she had feelings for him, she had no problem going along with it. Being rebuffed was one thing, but having it overheard was another.

"I'm glad to know I was so convincing. Maybe it'll work."

"Maybe what will work?"

"My plan to convince Ethan that he doesn't repulse women, to remind him of what he's been missing out on, and to bring him back among the living." She rolled over and sat up, crossed her legs in her lap, and started explaining. "You see, Ethan lost his leg about four years ago. Well, not his whole leg, only half of it."

"And he's so vain that he's embarrassed by it?" She'd add that to the list, vanity.

"No. That's not it at all. Boy, you sure are a bad judge of character, at least when it comes to Ethan. Anyway, Ethan was married when he lost his leg. Granted, he had other injuries, too, and it took him a while to recover, but the leg was a permanent injury. His wife couldn't deal with it. And she wasn't nice about it, either. She told him that she didn't marry half a man and didn't want to stay married to one. She called his leg a stub and told him it repulsed her. She left him within a week of his being discharged from the hospital."

"That's horrible." A little touch of guilt nipped at Dominique's conscience for judging him so harshly.

"Yeah, it is. Ethan was so in love with her, and she crushed him like a bug. What happened to him physically was nothing compared to what she did to him emotionally. And he's never recovered. He hasn't been with a woman since. It's been about three years now."

"How do you know that? Maybe he's just discreet." She lifted a hand to cover a yawn and prayed that her eyes wouldn't betray her.

"Not discreet," Bailey corrected her. "Celibate. So I decided to do something about it."

"By advertising him in the tabloids and causing all the women he complained about to harass him?"

"Yes." The pride was evident in her voice. "That was my brilliant idea. I called the tabloids to spark an interest in him, exploiting the serious interview he did for *Forbes*."

"But Ethan doesn't seem to appreciate the women that maneuver has attracted to him," she pointed out.

"That's because he's forgotten what it's like to have sex. That's where I came in last night. I just wanted to jump start his testosterone so he'd start looking at these women as possible candidates."

"I don't know if you're a genius," Dominique said with a giggle, "or just a little off balance."

"I prefer genius." She uncrossed her legs and rolled off the bed, then stretched. "I'll let you get some sleep. I'm still kinda tired myself."

"Thank you."

"I'll see you in a few hours," she tossed over her shoulder as she closed the door behind her.

Dominique rolled over and thought about Ethan. His wife's cruelness pricked at her heart as she remembered the look of embarrassment in his eyes when she had reached for his leg on the dock. As for Bailey's claim that he was celibate, it was possible, she supposed. After all, until a few hours ago, it had been years since she had been intimate with someone. She was going to have to cling to the memory of what had happened in Ethan's office, because she was certain it wasn't going to happen again. It couldn't happen again.

CHAPTER SEVEN

"Thank you for washing these clothes, Margaret, and thank you for breakfast. It looks lovely," Dominique said as she and Bailey sat down in the dining room.

"You're welcome. Fortunately, you can shed those clothes when Ethan gets back with the general," she replied, setting a pitcher of juice on the table. "They have very nice clothes at the exchange on the military base here. I'm sure he'll pick you out something that fits much better than what you're wearing now. Honestly, I don't know how you've managed to hold those baggy pants up. They look ten sizes too big. Now let me know if I can get you, ladies anything else."

"Thanks, Margaret," Bailey called after her as she went back into what Dominique assumed was the kitchen. "So, are you looking forward to going back to Monteaux?" Bailey asked.

"Of course," she replied. "I'm sure things will be a little different for a while, but that's to be expected."

"If someone tried to kidnap me," Bailey said, popping a strawberry into her mouth, "this place would be like Fort Knox and my father wouldn't let me out of the house for the rest of my life."

"I'm sure there will be restrictions on my freedom once I get home," she replied, setting down her cup of coffee, "and security will be heightened until this matter is resolved."

"How is that going to affect your dating life?"

"It won't. I haven't dated for over two years," she replied as she sliced into a piece of bacon.

"What? You've got to be kidding?"

She released a small sigh as she recalled the turmoil the last man had caused in her life. "My life is much less complicated without that to worry about."

"What — oh," Bailey said, and when Dominique looked over, she saw her catch herself before swallowing a forkful of eggs. She knew Bailey must have read about the scandal and remembered it. "Nobody believed any of that garbage."

"None of it was true." She frowned and avoided Bailey's stare.

"Of course not. That guy was so transparent. It was obvious he was using you to jumpstart his acting career, for which he had no talent at all, by the way." From the corner of her eye, Dominique saw Bailey reach for a muffin. She hated looking people in the eye when that topic was brought up. She still felt the sting of humiliation from the ordeal. "And no video ever surfaced. He had no proof to back up his lies."

"It was irrelevant that he didn't have any proof." She took a sip of coffee and looked down at the eggs on her plate. "People believe what they want to believe, and the more sensational the material, the more they want to believe it. The image that he created with his lies was damage enough."

"It must have been horrible for you having all that personal sort of stuff reported in the tabloids."

"It was," she acknowledged. "The public shamed me. They expected better of me, but the worst of it was the look on my father's face every time something was printed about it. I had betrayed him. It was naïve and dreadfully irresponsible of me to have ever dated that scoundrel."

"So, are you letting this one self-serving asshole ruin your life?"

"What do you mean? My life isn't ruined."

"No date in two years. That's not ruining your life?"

"No, it isn't," Dominique replied with a wave of her fork.

"I rarely dated anyway, and I'm much too busy now."

"Dating is sort of a precursor to marriage, you know. Don't you have to get married and produce an heir?"

"My brother has taken care of that, and quite frankly, I don't trust myself not to make the same mistake again." She finished her last bite, dabbed her lips with a napkin, and continued. "I would have never thought that Luis would concoct such vulgar and vicious lies about me just to promote his own interests. I'm a horrible judge of character when it comes to men. You said so yourself earlier."

"That's why you should let someone who is a good judge of character find a guy for you."

Dominique watched Bailey as she tapped her fingers against the table and knew the wheels were spinning in her devious little mind.

"Let's see. You need a guy who is already a success and doesn't need you to boost his career. And one who doesn't particularly like the attention of the news media."

Dominique raised a brow and smiled in amusement. It didn't take a genius to figure out who Bailey was talking about.

"Excuse me, girls," Margaret interrupted, poking her head through the door. "The general and Ethan are back. When you're finished, you can join them in the general's office."

"Thank you," Dominique replied. "May I help you clear the dishes first?"

"Of course not," Margaret shot back. "You are a guest here."

"That's my job," Bailey announced as she stood up and began collecting the silverware. "You should go see how Ethan did at the exchange."

Ethan greeted her as she strolled into the general's office. "Good morning. These are for you," he said, handing her a shopping bag. "The general has arranged for a helicopter to pick us up at the base here and take us to Andrews. We need to get moving, so you should get changed."

"What about Jean Pierre?" she asked. She hadn't been able to shake from her mind the image of him lying on top of a cold steel table in some strange morgue so far from home, his chest sliced open and a paper tag tied to his toe. It was such an indignity, and the thought pained her almost as much as his death. She was not going to leave him like that or risk any red tape delaying his return home.

"A full autopsy report will be sent to your father for him to forward to whomever takes over the investigation in Monteaux," he reported, his voice gentle. "His body has been properly prepared for burial, and my tailor made sure he is dressed in the finest suit he has available. I selected the casket for his transportation myself. I believe it is befitting a man who was a dear friend to a princess. He will arrive at Andrews in about an hour and will be with us the entire trip to Monteaux."

She stared at him in silence for a quick moment, relieved and surprised that he had made an effort to assure that Jean Pierre was treated so respectfully. With that one kind gesture, he had washed some of the sorrow from her heart. "Thank you," she managed, then turned to the general. "Good morning, General," she said with a nod and left to change.

She was quick, and she returned to the general's office in a matter of just a few minutes wearing the outfit Ethan had purchased. She noticed the jeans and blouse complimented the jeans and shirt he had apparently purchased for himself. The sneakers fit just as perfectly as the clothes and were much more comfortable than the shoes she had worn the evening before, which she had thrown in the trash. "I'm ready," she announced as she strode into the office.

Ethan grabbed his duffle bag and stood.

"I'll walk you out," the general said, then led them to the foyer. Margaret and Bailey joined them from the kitchen.

"Dominique, the clothes Ethan bought look very nice on you," Margaret said with an approving nod. "It was nice to meet you, and I hope you have a safe trip back."

"Thank you for everything, Margaret. It was nice to meet you, as well," Dominique returned.

Margaret said her goodbyes to Ethan and then returned to the kitchen.

Bailey threw her arms around Dominique and whispered into her ear. "You and Ethan are perfect for each other." She drew back and added, "It was so exciting to meet you. You're welcome to come back for a longer visit anytime."

"Thank you, Bailey. It was wonderful meeting you. Perhaps you could visit me in Monteaux."

"Yes!" she replied and then turned to Ethan. "I'll see you when you get back."

"Okay, squirt," he replied.

The general extended a hand to Dominique. "Young lady, I hope to see you again under better circumstances."

"Thank you, General," she replied, taking his hand. "And thank you for your hospitality."

"Anytime," he said, then extended his hand to Ethan. "Son, I know you'll be careful. Hopefully, you won't have any trouble from here forward. If you need anything else, I'll be here, and call me when you get back."

Ethan took his hand. "Yes, sir. Thank you, sir, and I will."

"They're a lovely family," Dominique remarked once they were in the car on their way to the military base.

"Yeah, they're good people," he agreed.

"How did you meet the general?"

"I served under him," he answered without elaborating.

"In what branch did you serve?"

"The Special Forces."

"Is that how you got hurt?" she asked.

"Yeah, in a helicopter crash. The tail rotor fell on my leg. And in that one split second, my career was over. And so was my marriage." She heard the bitterness in his voice. "Look, I don't like talking about my military career. It always comes back to the accident, and that's one chapter of my life I prefer to forget."

"I'm sorry. That must have been horrible for you on so many levels."

"It was, and that's why I don't like to talk about it."

"Of course. I'm sorry." She shifted uncomfortably, annoyed that she had brought up the subject. She wished he wasn't so sensitive about the loss of his leg. To her, it wasn't a flaw. It was a symbol of bravery and heroism that made her pulse beat just a little faster. "How long will it take to get to the base?" she asked, changing the subject.

"About ten more minutes. It's not far."

They rode the rest of the way in silence. Once they boarded the helicopter, Ethan sat in front of her, next to the pilot. The trip to Andrews hadn't taken long, and she stared out the window taking in DC as they flew over it.

CHAPTER EIGHT

Ethan took a quick sweep of the air strip as the helicopter began its descent. Two armed soldiers were waiting below near where he assumed they were going to put down, and two were standing guard near the jet. He spotted a fifth one positioned on the roof of a hangar. He brushed his hand over the *Sig Sauer* resting on his hip and glanced backed at Dominique. She was staring out the window.

"All clear, sir," the pilot advised when they touched down and the rotors slowed to a rest. He stepped into the back, slid the door open, and then tossed his bag to one of the soldiers. He hopped out and then helped Dominique to the ground. He took his bag, threw it over his shoulder, and helped her into a waiting jeep. Along with the two soldiers, they headed the short distance to the jet. No trouble so far, he thought. It's a good sign.

He boarded the jet behind Dominique. A young woman in a dark plain suit and crisp white blouse greeted them. It wasn't a military uniform, and he wondered if she was a civilian. "Welcome aboard, sir," she said with a nod toward him, "and miss," she added with a nod toward Dominique. She seemed oblivious to their identities, and he figured she didn't recognize Dominique. "Your third passenger arrived shortly before you and is comfortable below. Please follow me, and I'll give you a tour of the jet."

When she led them past the cockpit, he glanced in. The pilots looked busy, and he hoped they were checking whatever they checked to make sure the plane was ready for the flight.

He didn't want to waste time on the airstrip. "We can take it from here," he said when they returned to the lounge.

"Of course. Let me know if you need anything during the flight," she replied and then disappeared through a door.

He unbuckled his holster, placed his *Sig Sauer* inside his duffle bag, and set the bag on one of the swanky chairs. Pretty fancy, he thought. "This will do," he said.

"I suppose you're pleased to know that your tour of duty will finally be over soon," Dominique remarked, setting her clutch down on the chair next to the one with his duffle bag.

Relieved is more like it, he thought. It hadn't been easy keeping his hands off of her since he'd made that first fatal mistake in the driveway, and he'd failed at it majorly. He couldn't say he regretted it, though. Quite the contrary. He just hoped that once she was out of his sight, she'd be out of his mind, and at the moment, he needed to stop thinking about that, or he was going to be in trouble. "It hasn't been as bad as I expected," he admitted. "A little excitement," he said with a shrug, "and decent enough company."

"Decent enough company?" She lifted a brow and smiled. "I can't say that I've ever been referred to as such, but I'll accept that as a compliment."

He allowed the grin when he saw her smile.

"And I suppose that I might have done worse had I chosen someone else's vehicle in which to escape," she countered.

"Thank you for the compliment, as well."

The jet vibrated under his feet as the engines powered up, and the pilot's voice announced their take off from a speaker above him. He lowered himself to one of the two remaining seats, fastened the buckle, and watched Dominique do the same in the seat next to his. It didn't take long to reach the Atlantic, he thought, glancing out the window.

He snapped off his seat belt and strode across the lounge to a magazine rack when the plane leveled. He selected a sports publication hoping it would keep him distracted for a while. Beyond that, he wasn't sure how he was going to keep his mind off the fact that he was trapped in nothing but a tin can with Dominique. As it was, her scent had permeated the small space and was making it impossible to ignore her. With every breath of her, he had to resist the impulse to touch her. Despite that his leg was a deterrent, the urge was still there. If he didn't keep his mind off of her, his gut was going to be one big tangled mess by the time they landed.

He glanced over at her. He supposed he was going to have to apologize for his behavior in his office. He'd been rough. He'd pounced on her like a rabid dog. But at least it had been so fast and frantic that he was certain she hadn't seen his prosthesis or what was left of his leg. He'd know if she'd had. She would have been horrified like his ex-wife had been.

He flipped open the magazine and heard her release a quiet sigh, then watched from the corner of his eye as she pushed herself up and strolled over to a shelf lined with DVDs. She selected a movie, then wandered back.

"How about lunch?" he suggested. Maybe a full stomach and a shot of whiskey would do the trick, he hoped. He'd only gotten about two hours of sleep over the past thirty. If he could knock himself out, he'd probably sleep for at least a solid six hours, he figured.

"Yes," she agreed. "I'll make us something."

"I didn't mean for you to make it. Isn't that what the flight attendant is for?"

"I can guarantee you that I'm a better cook than she is." She slid up from the chair. "You won't be disappointed," she added as she disappeared from the lounge.

Curious, he got up and found the kitchen. "Are you here to help?" she asked as he strolled in.

"I'd say I'm more like a spectator," he replied with a grin.

"I see." He watched her rummage through the cabinets and

refrigerator. "I'm surprised," she said. "And impressed," she added. "This kitchen is well-stocked. I was thinking croquet monsieur," she said, then pulled a cut of what looked like filet mignon from the refrigerator. "But there's enough ingredients here to make beef bourguignon." She turned to him. "I can modify the recipe to cut down on time. How hungry are you?" she asked.

He shrugged. "Beef bourguignon sounds perfect."

"Good," she said with a smile. "Now, go. I'll come get you when it's done."

"I won't go far, then," he replied with a wink and headed back to the lounge. That'll keep her busy for a while, he thought, relieved knowing she wouldn't be as much temptation with a bit of distance between them.

A while later, just as the selection of decent magazines was running low and the aroma of the dish started to whet his appetite, she walked into the lounge. "Lunch is being served in the dining room," she announced.

"Let's see how you did," he teased and followed her from the lounge.

"I'm impressed," he commented as he scanned the table and observed the several little votive candles scattered over the crisp white linens amid the china and silver flatware. There was a glass decanter with red wine set on the table along with the stew, two small salads, and a basket of bread. "Allow me," he said as he dragged her chair out for her and then poured the wine.

"Thank you. *Bon appétit.*" A smile touched her lips in return as he smiled down at her.

He took the chair across from her and dished a plateful of the meat and vegetables into his bowl, realizing he was hungrier than he thought. "Mm. This is outstanding," he said. "And here I thought all you did all day was sit on your throne issuing orders and being served," he joked.

"Very funny," she replied. "I'll have you know," she continued as she smoothed a pat of butter across a slice of bread, "even the primmest of princesses like to get their hands dirty on occasion."

"I'll keep that in mind," he replied with a smirk.

When they were finished, they returned to the lounge, and she turned on the movie she had selected. In a matter of minutes, she was asleep. He found a bottle of whiskey, downed a shot, and reclined his chair. A few seconds later, he felt himself drift off.

He awoke after a few hours and grinned when he looked over and saw her still asleep beside him. Still groggy, he got up, checked the time, and went to splash some water on his face. When he returned, she was awake. "What time is it?" she asked.

"DC time, seven o'clock. We should be landing soon."

"I can't believe I slept so long." She stood up and stretched, then strolled from the lounge.

He took a few strides, then sat down and picked up the magazine he'd been looking through earlier. The long nap had done him good. He was feeling reenergized. He'd be alert for the final leg of their trip. Then I'll be home free, he thought. He'd return to Maryland, get Dominique out of his system, and get on with his life. "You missed your movie," he commented when she came back.

"I know," she answered, lowering herself to the chair. "I was more tired than I thought." After a minute, she got up and strolled over to the magazine rack.

He tossed his magazine aside and released a slow breath. He watched her searching through the publications and decided that a newspaper might be a better distraction. He pushed himself up and sauntered over.

"Find anything interesting?" he asked and knew that narrowing the distance between them had been a mistake.

"Not yet, but I'm sure there's something here that interests me."

A sudden strike of turbulence caused the plane to jolt. He braced himself against the wall and grabbed Dominique as she lost her balance and the plane shuddered. He pulled her into him and, with his arms around her, held her against his chest while he fought to keep them from being tossed around. Instinctively, she clasped her fingers around his arms and clung to him.

When the plane settled, he eased his grip. She was so close, he felt the impact of every inch of her. "I think we're through it," he said. "Are you all right?"

She stared up at him and nodded. "I'm fine."

"Good," he replied, unable to release her. The temptation was too great, the desire too powerful.

"You?" He felt her relax, but other than that, she didn't move. He was aware that she didn't try to release herself from his embrace.

"I'm fine," he replied. It was a mistake to hold on to her, he reminded himself. But it was a mistake he was willing to take at that moment, he decided. Though it mattered that he had just a stub for a leg, her effect on him rendered him defenseless. He slid his hands up her back.

Her grasp loosened as she slid her arms around his neck. He leaned down, and she drew him to her. He brushed his lips over hers and felt his gut tense. When he kissed her, any inhibitions about his leg that lingered were pulverized by the passion that plowed through his veins.

He lifted her, and she circled her legs around his waist. With lips locked, he carried her to the bedroom and lowered her to the bed. He was already throbbing. Patience, he told himself. Savor her this time. Methodical, he released each button of her blouse, one by one, then slid it off of her. He cupped her breasts, and her fingers slid under his shirt and down his back. He slid his hands down to her jeans and lowered his mouth to her breast. He unsnapped her jeans and pulled the zipper down. Then he tugged on her jeans and slipped his fingers inside her. Her back arched in response, and he let his fingers explore.

He took a slow breath as her fingers glided into his jeans. When they skimmed down his penis, the knot in his gut tightened. Be patient, he reminded himself. Her fingers tightened around him, and with each stroke, the knot twisted.

He rolled off of her and dragged his gaze over her as he unbuttoned his jeans, then pulled them off. He knew he was hanging by a thread as she wriggled out of her jeans. He straddled her and then lowered himself onto her. When she parted her legs, he guided himself inside her. He felt her contract around him, and he nearly exploded. Hang on, he told himself and eased back. Slowly, he pushed back in deep, then retreated. With each penetration, her muscles relaxed around him, and with each withdrawal, he felt them clench. She was driving him insane, and he knew he was doing the same. He thrust himself in and lingered. She held him there, and when he felt her pulsate around him, he almost lost his mind. He pulled back, then drove in one last time before his gut erupted.

He rolled off her, aware it was going to cost him. The lingering feelings were something he hadn't expected.

"Prepare for landing," a voice said over the speaker. "We'll be on the ground in twenty minutes."

"We're not finished," Ethan whispered before collapsing beside her.

Chapter Nine

Ethan peered out the window of the helicopter as they approached Monteaux. The sky was an explosion of a thousand different hues of crimson as the sun dipped over the horizon and dusk began to settle on Monteaux. There was still enough light to allow him to study the grounds while the pilot navigated the helicopter down. In his opinion, he could not overestimate the beauty of LaBuerge Palace. The palace itself was majestically colossal compared to the other structures surrounding it, and the grounds, with their impeccably manicured lawns and brilliantly vivid gardens, were magnificent. He imagined living there was like living in a fairy land.

He noticed the army of guards patrolling the perimeter of the grounds and a scattering of sharpshooters positioned on the rooftops of the palace and nearby buildings. Roads providing ingress to the palace were cordoned off, preventing passage. Flashbulbs popped like lightning during a summer heat wave from a group of news crews congregating outside the palace walls. A shower of light illuminated the helicopter pad like a football stadium on a dark night.

As they approached the landing, he saw a squad of armed guards proceed in formation around the helipad. He felt the helicopter tilt before righting and then settle on the pad, and he heard the whirl of the blades begin to slow. In the distance, he saw four figures just inside the entrance to the palace.

"Welcome home, Princess," he said, and the door next to him slid open with a thud.

"Thank you," she replied. He expected her to be relieved,

even happy, to be home, but he noticed a hesitancy in her smile. Maybe the reality of Jean Pierre's death is settling in, he thought.

He climbed out of the helicopter, and the half a dozen or so soldiers on both sides of him stood at attention. He offered his hand to Dominique, and she stepped down just as the blades came to a halt above them. The soldiers closed in around them and whisked them down the walkway to the palace entrance. They crossed an expansive veranda and entered into an enormous vestibule. He couldn't help but notice the crystal chandeliers dripping from the ceiling like chunks of icicles suspended by chains of gold and the spectacular paintings and sculptures adorning the room. Opulence came to mind, but it didn't surprise him. After all, he was in a royal palace.

He watched while an older, white-haired gentleman with a mustache embraced Dominique, assuming it was her father, the king. He wasn't tall, just under six feet, he figured, and slightly stout. "Dominique, thank God you're safe, my child," he said as three others huddled around them.

He observed them while they welcomed her home. The other gentleman was younger, not much older than Dominique, he figured. He had dark hair like her and was a few inches taller than the king. He was slim but obviously fit. There was little similarity between the women, who appeared to be separated by maybe fifteen or twenty years, he guessed. Although both were slender and tastefully dressed, the younger one clearly strove for high-fashion, the other for understated conservatism. The long blonde tresses of the younger woman hung loosely over her shoulders, while the chocolate strands of the other were swept up into a neat bun.

When the king finished with Dominique, he turned to him. "You must be Major Moore."

"Yes, Your Majesty," Ethan replied with a deep nod. "Retired Major, actually. It's an honor to meet you."

"Thank you for returning my daughter to me safely. I will be forever grateful to you."

"You're welcome, sir. It is my pleasure to do so."

"This is my son, Prince Andre," he said as the younger gentleman stepped forward.

"So nice to meet you, Major," he said, extending his hand.

"It's an honor to meet you, Your Royal Highness," Ethan returned, accepting his hand.

"Welcome to Monteaux. And it's Andre to you. This," he continued as the blonde woman stepped beside him, "is my lovely wife, Princess Francine."

"Pleased to meet you, Your Royal Highness."

"You as well, and please feel free to call me Francine."

"This, Major Moore," the king said, glancing at the other woman, "is Lidia, a long-standing member of our staff."

"It's a pleasure," Ethan said to Lidia, recalling that she was Dominique's secretary and that she owned the necklace.

"Thank you," she replied. He noted she had a demure presence but was very polished, and he wondered if he had been wrong to suspect that she would have anything to do with Dominique's kidnapping.

He strolled between the king and Andre as the king led the way from the vestibule. "I hope you will accept my invitation to stay with us for a couple of days," the king said.

"Thank you for the invitation, sir. I wasn't planning on staying, but I suppose I can see if I can arrange it." His mind was warning against it, but his emotions were telling him to stay. He had started something with Dominique, although he wasn't sure what it was or what could become of it, if anything.

"Good." The king lifted his hand, and a servant scurried over to them. "Fetch whatever bags Major Moore and Her Royal Highness have from the helicopter."

"Yes, Your Majesty," the servant replied with a nod and

then disappeared.

"It's late, but I trust your journey hasn't so exhausted you that a quick nightcap is out of the question?"

"No, sir. I would be delighted."

They turned down a vast hall before entering a spacious parlor. It was a contrast to the vestibule, Ethan noted as he looked around. The room radiated warmth and intimacy with its cozy seating area arranged in front of an enormous fireplace. He glanced at the handful of servants standing nearby.

"Please make yourselves comfortable," the king said, sinking into a generous-sized chair with plump cushioning upholstered within an ornately carved frame. When Andre and Francine made themselves comfortable in a plush settee, he took one of the matching chairs across from them next to the chair Dominique had chosen. Lidia excused herself and then lowered herself to a second settee facing the king when he insisted she stay.

He caught himself staring over at Dominique. He had noticed the perfect posture, the graceful, fluid movements, and the flawless manners before, but they seemed more pronounced in the grandeur of their surroundings, and he wondered if there was going to be anything else different about her now that she was back in Monteaux.

"Major Moore, what is your drink of choice?" the king asked.

"I prefer whiskey, sir, and please call me Ethan," he replied.

"You're in luck," Andre said. "I'm a whiskey man, myself. I like a single malt. I'm particularly fond of *Highland Park.*"

"I like that, as well."

Right on cue, he assumed, the servants delivered drinks and offered an array of canapes.

"If you wouldn't mind, Ethan," the king stated, "I'd appreciate it if you could meet with Dominique and me tomorrow.

I've scheduled a meeting with our head of security and Monteaux's police inspector about the incident in Washington, DC."

"Of course, sir. Anytime you wish. And I think it might be helpful if Lidia met with us, as well." There was no need to get into the necklace at this point, he decided. He'd likely have more information tomorrow. It would be two days since he scanned the necklace into the system. Something would have come up on it. He'd also had people lift the prints off the gun he'd retrieved from the asshole that had broken into his office, as well as run a search on the weapon itself. If he was lucky, they'd come up with something on the dot, too.

"I don't know what I can contribute but, I absolutely will attend the meeting," Lidia assured them.

"One more thing, Ethan."

"Yes, sir?"

"We have a small soiree planned for tomorrow evening, and since Dominique is home safely, we didn't see the need to cancel it. Some of our Italian acquaintances will be joining us, as well as Leonardo Parducci, the Italian opera singer. Perhaps you know of him?"

"I have heard of him, yes."

"I'd like it if you would join us. The dress is formal. I'm sure you didn't pack a tuxedo, but you will have a butler at your disposal who can help you with that. He will also provide you with anything else you may need while you are staying here."

"Thank you for the invitation, sir. I'd be honored to join you and your guests."

"Well, since Ethan's calendar seems to be filling so quickly, I'd like to ask if you shoot, Ethan. Since you were in the military, I assume you do." Andre's grin didn't escape him. He was expecting the challenge to follow.

"Yes, I've done a little shooting," he replied.

"He's going to invite you to a skeet shooting contest," Dominique warned him.

"I'm running out of decent competitors," Andre replied. "Dominique won't shoot with me anymore."

"You've gotten too obnoxious for my tastes," she teased.

"You must be a pretty good shot if no one wants to shoot with you, Andre," Ethan remarked.

"Well, I wouldn't want to brag, of course, but I am pretty accurate. And you?"

"Actually, I've got a pretty good eye, although I have to admit, I've never shot skeet before," he replied.

"Would you be interested in trying your hand at it tomorrow? That is if you're up to it. I promise I won't embarrass you. I'll even miss a few shots on purpose, so I don't beat you too badly," Andre added with a smirk.

"You're on, but don't do me any favors."

"Excellent. You all might want to watch this match," Andre offered. "It sounds like it just might turn out to be a little competitive."

"I think I'll pass, dear," Francine replied. "I can think of at least ten things I have to do tomorrow."

"It sounds like something I might not want to miss," Dominique replied.

"Father? Care to join us?" Andre asked.

"I'd like to, but I've got things to tend to. And, Dominique, I'd like you to stay close to the palace until we have a chance to meet with your security team."

"Yes, Father. Of course. I understand."

"Very good," he said with a nod. "Now, if you'll excuse me, I must turn in. I'm afraid I require a bit more sleep than you younger people."

"I'm going to retire, as well," Lidia said, getting up from the settee. "Good night, all."

"Good night, Father," Dominique said when he leaned

down to kiss her. "Good night, Lidia."

"Good night," Ethan said to both and stood.

"No need to get up. Sit down," the king insisted.

"Good night, Father, Lidia," Andre called after them before turning to Ethan. "You be sure to get your rest, too, Ethan." He stretched an arm across the back of the settee. "You're going to need it for our match. I wouldn't want jet lag to slow your trigger finger."

"Don't worry, Andre, my trigger finger will be fine," he returned.

"Excuse me," Francine said as Ethan watched her unsuccessfully fail to restrain a yawn. He could see the fatigue in her eyes. In Andre's, too. He assumed they hadn't gotten much sleep since they were told of the incident. "Please don't be offended, but I suppose with everything on deck for tomorrow, I should turn in myself."

"Not at all." Andre rose and pulled Francine to her feet. "All kidding aside, Ethan, I am eternally indebted to you for protecting my dear sister and bringing her home to us safely. Thank you again."

"You're welcome," he replied. He watched them leave, then turned to Dominique. She took a step toward him and rested her hand on his arm. "Thank you for agreeing to stay." She shifted her gaze past him, then drew her hand from his arm.

"For tomorrow," she continued as she slid her gaze back to him, "remember to hold your aim under the top of the trip house so you can see the bird when it leaves the house. And throw your pattern a little higher at the bird so it will run into it."

"I'll keep that in mind," he replied and allowed his gaze to linger on hers.

Dominique slid her hand along the molding and pressed

her fingers against the smooth wood. She waited until a portion of the molding snapped open and revealed a numbered keypad, then she tapped in a sequence of numbers. She watched the vault panel of the wall in her dressing room slide aside and expose the hidden, silk-lined drawers.

She knelt down and unlocked the long, narrow drawer near the bottom. Five necklaces, each as stunning as the ruby necklace she held in her hand, sparkled up at her under the lights. She admired them as she placed the ruby necklace into the empty space.

"I know how much these necklaces mean to you, Lidia." She was going to have to tell her before she found out the next day that someone might be trying to steal them.

Lidia bent down beside her and lifted a necklace from the drawer. Dominique noticed her smile as she held it in her hands and let the light dance over it. The emeralds were as big as dates and as green as the first rich blade of grass in the spring.

"I don't think I could ever choose a favorite, Lidia," she said. "Each one is as spectacular as the others."

"My mother told me that my grandfather used to say that these stones were as flawless as nature would permit, just like my grandmother. She told me that the necklaces he made for my grandmother were the most magnificent ones he'd made, much more intricate and unique than the ones he made for his clients. It's true. I've seen pictures of some of the necklaces he made for others. When I was little, my mother showed me a picture that had been published in the newspaper. It was of a queen, and she was wearing a necklace my grandfather had made for her. I can't remember which queen it was, though I remember the necklace was not as beautiful as any of these."

"They're breathtaking, Lidia. Look at how deep blue these sapphires are." She ran her fingers over the sapphire necklace. "I remember when I wore this necklace."

"They're more than just jewels. They hold a piece of my grandfather's heart. They hold his love for my grandmother." She paused before she continued. "I never told you this story. When Hitler started to invade Poland, my grandfather and his brother sent my grandmother, my mother, and my aunt out of the country. My grandfather made my grandmother take the necklaces with her. Each necklace has a matching pair of earrings, a ring, and a bracelet. My grandfather always made his pieces in sets. He wanted my grandmother to take the rest of the sets with her, but she refused. She said he was to bring them with him when he escaped, in case he needed to use them for bribes. He and my great-uncle were going to stay behind for just a few days to get enough medical supplies for my great-grandmother. They were going to bring her with them. They never made it, however. They were killed by Hitler's men."

"I'm so sorry." She stared at the necklaces and wondered how she was going to tell Lidia that someone wanted to steal them.

"I know." She lowered the necklace back into the drawer. "My grandmother was heartbroken. When she ran out of money, she refused to sell the necklaces. My aunt tried to convince her that my grandfather would want her to sell them, and that was why he had insisted she take them with her when they escaped, but she still refused to sell them. When she died, she gave the necklaces to my mother because she knew she wouldn't sell them. She made my mother promise to keep them all together and pass them down to only one member of each generation to be sure they wouldn't be separated. I think it was her way of preserving my grandfather's love."

"How can you allow me to wear them if they mean so much to you?"

"Dominique," she said, and a smile graced her lips. "I want

to celebrate my grandfather's love, not keep it hidden. And you're the closest thing I have to a daughter. I think my grandmother would approve."

"But it's a risk that shouldn't be taken."

"A risk?"

Dominique placed her fingers around Lidia's hand. "Oh, Lidia, I love you so much. I don't know how to tell you this."

"Tell me what?"

"I think the men who are trying to kidnap me are after the necklace or maybe all of them."

"My necklaces? I wasn't aware anyone knew about the necklaces. What makes you think they are after the necklaces?"

"Well." She released Lidia's hand, closed the drawer, and then checked it to ensure the lock was set. "One of the men said something about the necklace I had worn to the concert. He wanted to know where it was."

"Oh, my God," Lidia gasped. "Am I to blame for all of this?"

Dominique watched the tears spill from Lidia's eyes.

"I am to blame for Jean Pierre's death. I am to blame for your . . . your . . . they tried to take you."

"Shh, don't cry, Lidia. No. Of course, you are not to blame for any of this," she insisted.

"I *am* to blame if someone has done these horrible things because they want the necklaces."

"Lidia, you are not responsible for someone else's greed."

"We must put an end to this. I cannot put your life in danger. I cannot risk anyone else dying. Lives are far more valuable than necklaces. We must give the necklaces to whomever it is that is willing to kill for them."

"No." Dominique pressed a button, and the vault panel slid closed. "Absolutely not."

CHAPTER TEN

"How did you do?" Ethan heard Dominique ask. He turned to see her behind him as he was headed toward the drawing room to meet with the police inspector and the palace's head of security. He stopped and waited for her to catch up to him. He took a survey of her as she approached, and his heart gave a little kick. A strand of pearls was draped around her long, delicate neck, coming to a rest just above the hint of cleavage. The short red skirt hugged her waist and hips enough to showcase the curves of her body. It's enough to have any man drooling, he thought. He swallowed and tried to ignore the long, sexy legs.

"I held my own," he answered. "Ninety-eight out of a hundred."

"That's unheard of for the first time."

"Your advice was invaluable." He smiled down at her and slowed his pace as they continued toward the drawing room.

"Mm-hmm," she muttered. "And how did my brother score?"

"The same."

When she smiled up at him, he saw suspicion in her eyes. "And did he miss first?"

"I can't recall."

"Really."

"What are you suggesting? That I missed on purpose?"

"No one except a very skilled marksman shoots that well their first time at skeet, and a marksman that skilled wouldn't miss any birds. It was very generous of you."

"I don't know what you're talking about," he said as they entered the study. He saw the king seated at the head of a long, narrow table. Lidia was seated to his right. A burly gentlemen that looked to be in his late forties or early fifties and a much younger man were sitting a few seats down from her. He wondered who the younger man was and what he was doing there. He certainly can't be the head of security or the police inspector, he thought.

"Of course not," she replied. "But I'm sure you saved yourself a miserable morning. My brother is not a very good loser."

"Good afternoon, Ethan," the king said before turning to Dominique. "My dear," he added and then looked back to Ethan. He followed the king's gesture toward the older man seated at the table. "This is Frederique Crane, our head of security. Frederique, this is Major Ethan Moore."

"Major Moore, it's nice to meet you." He leaned across the table and took Frederique's extended hand, aware the man was taking measure of him. "I appreciate your taking the time to assist us with whatever information you may have."

"Thank you. I'm happy to do anything I can to help your investigation." He wondered if the meeting was going to be a waste of time. The man's security practices had already allowed someone to plant a tracking dot on Dominique, murder her guard, and nearly kidnap her. He hoped for her sake that he was more capable than he seemed.

"Ethan, the young gentleman here is Lidia's cousin's son, Brian Pontellier," the king said. "He is also in our employ. He's Lidia's assistant."

He certainly seems eager, Ethan thought as Brian sprung to his feet and shoved his hand across the table toward him. "I'm pleased to meet you, Major Moore. I'll do whatever I can to help, although I don't have much information about the necklaces."

Ethan nodded, shook his hand, then glanced at Dominique. She was the only one he was aware of, other than himself and the general, who suspected the kidnappers might be after the necklace. "I told Lidia that it's possible that whoever attacked me wants her necklaces," she said as she sat down.

"I see." That explained how Brian knew the necklace might be involved, but it didn't answer why he was at the meeting. He wondered if Lidia and Brian might both have something to do with what had happened. Brian does seem a little too eager, he thought, but then again, it can be attributed to his youth. He set aside the thought and lowered himself to the chair next to Dominique.

"Good afternoon, all." Ethan looked up as Andre strutted into the room. "Forgive my tardiness. I apologize. Father, Frederique," he said with a nod to each. When Andre's eyes met his, his lips lifted to a grin. "How's that trigger finger doing, Ethan?"

"A little stiff, but I'll survive." He returned the grin. Yeah, he thought, I could have kicked your ass at skeet, but I know better than to beat my host at what appeared to be one of his favorite sports.

"Glad to hear that," he replied as he strutted the length of the table and then took the seat at the end opposite the king.

"Inspector Laroche from the Police Internationale, Your Majesty." He turned to the door when he heard the servant announce the arrival of the short, balding man and studied him as he swept past everyone and took a seat near Andre.

"It is an honor to see you again, Your Royal Majesty, and an honor to be of service." His voice was deep, almost a growl, and his words rolled off his tongue with confidence.

Ethan observed everyone as introductions were made around the table. The meeting commenced with Dominique recounting the course of events in Washington. Despite the gloss of grief in her eyes, he thought she relayed the incidents with admirable poise and composure. After her, he followed up with the details of the attack at his house and in his office and the discovery of the GPS transmitter.

"Sounds like quite an evening you had, Your Royal Highness," Laroche remarked. "Sir," he said to the king, "I'd like to have our coroner take a look at the corpse. It hasn't been buried yet, has it?"

Ethan felt Dominique stiffen next to him.

"Inspector, can you have him review the autopsy report instead?" she asked.

"I did forward the report to him," he assured her. "I will check with him again to see if an inspection of the body is vital."

"We will be attending Monsieur Pierre's funeral service tomorrow." The finality in the king's voice was clear. "Whatever you need to do, get it done today."

"Very well." He leaned back in his chair when Laroche turned toward him. "Major Moore, I will need from you the GPS dot, the shoe, the gun, and copies of any fingerprints your people may have been able to lift from the weapon."

"I'll have them sent to you as soon as possible," he responded without hesitation.

"Good. Do you know if your car has been recovered?"

"I haven't heard that it has been." He watched Laroche scribble some notes in a small pad before he resumed his questions.

"Did your software program come up with anything on the necklace?"

"The information that came up pertained to the inscription on the necklace, which I'm sure Lidia can tell you more about." His program had found considerable information, and he wanted to compare it to what she disclosed. Whatever she missed, he'd tell the inspector later, and he figured Laroche could decide whether keeping an eye on Lidia was necessary.

Laroche shifted his gaze to Lidia and lifted his pen. "Mademoiselle?"

"The inscription consists of my grandfather's initials." Her hands twitched when she spoke. "It is the letter K superimposed over the letter S. The initials stand for Stanislaw Kaminski. He was a well-respected and well-known jeweler before World War II."

"Do you have any idea why anyone might want to steal your grandfather's necklace?"

"Other than for the monetary value of the stones, no. It is possible that my search for the matching pieces may have sparked an interest in the necklace." There was a rise in her voice as she offered her thoughts. "If someone has done all of this. If someone killed Jean Pierre and tried to kidnap Dominique for the necklace, I want it known that the necklace is available. No questions asked."

"No, it is not." Dominique insisted. "The necklace will never be available at any price."

"Matching pieces?" Laroche asked. Good question, Ethan thought, wondering why Dominique had never mentioned them.

"There are five necklaces, actually. Each necklace is part of a set with earrings, a ring, and a bracelet," Lidia explained.

"What happened to those pieces?"

"I don't know. They were in my grandfather's possession before he was killed."

"Killed?" There was surprise in Laroche's eyes.

"My grandfather was Polish. He didn't make it out of Poland before Hitler invaded it. He was killed by the Germans."

"I see. When did you begin your search for the matching pieces?"

"About four months ago. Brian can fill you in on that. I asked him to try to find the pieces."

"Brian?"

Brian jerked forward in his chair when Laroche turned his focus to him, and when he placed his folded hands on the table, there was a slight tremble in them.

Nerves, Ethan thought.

"Yes, sir," he replied.

"How did you conduct your search for the missing jewelry?"

"I designed a website and had my great, great uncle's name linked to search engines so that anyone doing a search with his name would come across my website."

"Did you provide a means by which you could be contacted?"

"Yes, sir. By telephone, address, or e-mail. You can visit the site. It's still running. But no one has ever contacted me."

Ethan wondered if that was true or if Brian had been contacted and tried to sell the necklaces instead of finding the missing pieces.

Laroche continued his interrogation until, Ethan assumed, he was satisfied that he had obtained enough information. He snapped his pad shut and tucked it into his pocket. Standing up, he addressed the king. "Sir, we will continue our investigation of this matter, which, as you know, is in its infancy. I believe we have more to go on now, and we will wait for the evidence Major Moore will be providing. I will contact you as our investigation progresses."

"Yes. Please do that. I want this matter put to rest."

"I understand, sir."

"I'll show you out, Inspector," Frederique volunteered.

Dominique was the first to speak after they left the room. "I found him offensive." She scowled. "I hope his investigative skills are better than his tact."

"Yes, he did lack a certain amount of sensitivity," Andre agreed.

"That doesn't matter as long as he does his job," the king said with a dismissive wave. Ethan saw his gaze travel around the table and hesitate on Lidia before returning to Dominique, and he wondered what was going through his mind when he looked at Lidia. "The important thing is that this matter gets resolved and that you will be safe. Now, if you all will excuse me, I've got some business to tend to before this evening."

Brian asked if he could leave, and Ethan looked at Lidia. She appeared upset, but he had to admit that he didn't know her enough to speculate why.

"Yes," she replied before turning to Dominique and pushing away from the table. "Dominique, is there anything I can do for you? Do you need anything for this evening?"

"No. I believe you've taken care of everything already. Thank you."

"All right. Then, all of you, have a wonderful evening," she said and strode from the room.

He looked at Andre. He had swiveled his chair in his direction, and it appeared that he wasn't going anywhere. He leaned back and clasped his hands across his lap. "Ethan, what did you think of Laroche?"

"He was a little rough around the edges but seemed thorough." He shrugged. "He took a lot of notes." He paused a second before continuing, unsure how his question would be received. "How long has Brian worked here?"

"Brian?" He saw the surprise in Dominique's eyes.

"Not long," Andre answered. "About a year. Lidia asked us if we would employ him. Seems he wasn't getting along with his mother, had no interest in going to a university or doing much else with his life."

"Lidia thought a change of environment might do him good." Dominique pushed back from the table and stretched her legs. "He's a rather innocuous presence around here. He's very polite. He's respectful. I haven't heard any complaints about him."

"Does he have any interest in the necklaces as an heir or otherwise?"

"Not that I'm aware of. Lidia told me the necklaces are passed down to one member of each generation to ensure that they will remain together and in the family. Brian's grandmother, Lidia's aunt, tried to persuade Lidia's grandmother to sell them, so they were all left to Lidia's mother, who then passed them down to Lidia."

"I doubt he's got anything to do with any of this," Andre said with a shake of his head. "Quite frankly, he's not exactly a rocket scientist, nor is he terribly motivated."

"Where'd he live before he came here?" Ethan asked, shifting in his chair.

"Somewhere outside of Paris, I believe," Dominique answered.

"Well, I'd better see if Francine needs me." Andre stood and slid his chair aside. "She likes my opinion when we dress for a formal occasion," he continued as he strutted past them. "Of course, I think she looks best with not a stitch on."

Ethan heard his chuckle as he left the room. He was sure that was how he preferred Dominique, as well, but kept the thought to himself as he let his gaze drift over her.

"Do you think Brian has something to do with this?" she asked.

"I have no reason to. I was just exploring the possibility."

"Major Moore." He lifted his gaze from her and spotted his butler at the doorway when he heard his name. "I'm sorry to interrupt, but the tailor would like you to try on the tuxedo for any final adjustments if now is convenient for you."

"I'll be right there," he answered and ran his fingers through his hair as he took one last look at those long, luscious legs. He leaned into Dominique as he stood up. "I look for-ward to seeing you tonight."

Dominique allowed her gaze to travel around the table. It was an intimate affair. There were just twelve of them in all. She rested her gaze over Leonardo Parducci and his date, a beau-tiful woman. She looked no older than his daughter. Marco was seated next to Leonardo's date. She knew she would have to fend Marco off all evening, and the more he drank, the more obnoxious he became. She wasn't looking forward to it.

Her gaze landed next on Ethan. He was placed between Marco's sister and Leonardo's daughter, both young, single, and already vying for his attention. It wasn't a surprise. He looked dashing, and he exuded nothing but charm. It's funny how my opinion of him has changed so quickly and so dras-tically, she thought, as a little current of heat drifted through her. She pushed the feeling aside and looked at Andre and Francine. They made a beautiful couple, and it was obvious to her that they were both deeply in love. She was happy for her brother, and she loved her sister-in-law. Though Francine appreciated the finer things in life and had been called pre-tentious by the press, she knew that there was an abundance of kindness and compassion under that flashy exterior. Marco's parents look lovely, she thought, turning her gaze to them. They had been friends with her father forever, it seemed, and had even known her mother.

She wished her father could find someone to love and who would love him back, someone with whom he could find hap-piness and share his life. It had been a long time since her mother had died, and he had been alone since. She slid her hand over his, gave it a little squeeze, then drew it back. He glanced over at her, then reached over and gave her hand a soft pat. Sometimes she thought she saw a hint of something between her father and Lidia, but it was always so subtle and fleeting. It was wishful thinking on her part, she assumed.

"Come on, Leo," Leonardo's date pleaded. "Let's dance. The king hired this lovely ensemble to play for us. Let's not allow it to go to waste."

"She's right, Leonardo," her father added. "Enjoy yourselves. Dance."

"All right, Victor," Leonardo relented, "but don't let us be the only ones having fun. Andre, take your wife's hand."

Andre didn't need any more persuading than that. He whisked Francine from her seat and twirled her in his arms. Before Dominique could prepare herself for Marco, he was sweeping her up from her chair. From the corner of her eye, she saw Ethan watching Marco, then saw Gianna whisper something in his ear before Marco spun her away.

She felt Marco slip his hand under the fabric of her gown, where it draped open down her back. "Marco, please take your hand out of my gown," she said.

"My, how did that happen?" he asked. "Do forgive me."

"Am I going to have to fight you off all night? When will you learn?"

"Dominique, my sweet Dominique," he said with a sigh. "When will you realize that you cannot live without me?" He slid his hand from inside her dress and then circled it around her waist.

Dominique heard Ethan's voice as Marco led her across the floor. "Why don't you allow me to lead, Gianna?"

"You can lead me wherever you want," Gianna replied.

She detected a slight slur to her voice, and when she glanced over, she saw Gianna clumsily toss her hair in what she guessed was an effort to be flirtatious.

Ethan pulled her into him and tightened his grip around her when she almost fell over.

"Mm. Your arm feels good around me," she cooed as she

settled into his arms. "You are so strong," were the last words she heard before Marco led her in another direction.

"You fit perfectly in my arms, Dominique. It's like you were made for me." Marco tilted his head and dragged his lips over her shoulder.

"You forget, Marco, that I've known you for my entire life. I know what a playboy you are, and those are nothing more than the shallow words of a philanderer."

"*Au contraire.* Let me prove it to you. Let me show you, tonight, that we are a perfect fit." He looked down at her and cocked a brow. "In more ways than one."

"I'm afraid that's not going to happen," she answered.

"We shall see."

Ignoring Marco's constant innuendos, Dominique looked for Ethan and Gianna. She found them not far away. Ethan must have said something funny, because Gianna erupted in a fit of giggles. It looked like they were having fun. This is interesting, she thought, as she spotted Antonia approaching them.

Antonia said something and then took Ethan's hand and placed it around her waist, elbowing Gianna out of the way. That was seamless, Dominique observed, and Gianna wasn't too happy, she concluded, as she watched her stand there for a moment with her mouth agape before she marched away.

He must be in heaven, she thought, averting her gaze, with two beautiful women slobbering all over him. He certainly appeared to be enjoying them. If what Bailey had told her about Ethan being celibate was true, their encounters had likely unlocked a door that was now snapping off its hinges, waiting for any young lady to waltz through it.

The third song was ending when she looked up and saw Francine smile at her, then toss her a wink. She broke from Andre's embrace, gave him a little push in her direction, and then headed toward Ethan.

Dominique kept Francine in her sights. By the time she reached Ethan, both Gianna and Antonia had him surrounded. She swooped down on the two girls and placed herself between them. She locked an arm around Gianna's waist, looped one through Antonia's arm, and then led them away.

"Marco, my friend." She heard Andre behind her and, when she turned around, saw him slapping an arm around his shoulders. "We've hardly spoken this evening," he continued as he led Marco away.

"You look ravishing tonight," Ethan said from beside her as he took her arm. "You take my breath away." She looked up, and his gaze locked on to hers. His hand slid down her arm, took her hand, and then lifted it to his lips. He brushed his lips over her hand and let them linger.

"I could say the same about you." The touch of his lips was enough to kindle the warmth, and the intensity of his gaze was enough to make it simmer.

"Really." He cocked an eyebrow.

"Indeed." She allowed the corners of her lips to curve up.

"May I have this dance?" he asked when the next song started.

"Of course."

She stepped into his arms, and he swept her across the floor. She moved under his lead like a feather floating on the wind. "I've been waiting for this," she whispered and felt him draw her closer.

They glided across the floor without another word. She was oblivious to the others, relishing the opportunity for the moment together.

"I want to see you, alone," he said, finally breaking the silence.

"I'll come to you tonight after everyone has retired for the evening," she promised.

"I'll be waiting."

They managed to indulge in another song before deciding to rejoin the party, which had moved to the terrace.

In minutes, Marco resumed his pursuit of her and insisted she join him for another dance. She couldn't insult a guest, and knowing he was harmless, she obliged. When she left the terrace, she glanced back and saw Andre approach Ethan.

"Three, young, beautiful women," Andre said with a sigh. "What a dilemma for an unattached man."

"How so?" Ethan asked. He rested his weight against the railing and settled his gaze on Dominique.

"Who to choose, my friend." Andre fell back against the railing beside him.

"That would assume the man finds them all equally intriguing."

"Hmm. I suppose it would," he agreed. "And how do you find them?"

"A diamond among rhinestones," he quickly answered.

Andre traced the path of Ethan's gaze. "Ah."

"It's a beautiful evening, isn't it, gentlemen?" Francine asked, strolling toward them with Gianna and Antonia.

"Yes, I imagine just as lovely as Paris in the fall," Andre remarked with a grin.

"I'm sure it is," Francine answered with a soft laugh.

"How are you finding the evening, Ethan?" Gianna asked.

"It's been enjoyable."

"I agree, but the night isn't over yet."

"I'm afraid it is," Antonia said. "It looks like our parents have called it a night. They've all turned in."

"It is getting late," Ethan agreed, pushing himself up from the railing. "And I'm still adjusting to the time change."

"Yes, it does look like the party's over," Marco added as he strolled in with Dominique. "I'll escort you to your room," he offered.

"There's no need, Marco," she replied. "I can find my way."

"You can't blame me for trying. Ladies, shall we?" He tucked Gianna's and Antonia's hands under his arms and led them from the terrace. "I believe we are all going in the same direction."

"Good night, all," Andre said as he slid his arm around Francine and headed to a staircase off the terrace. "I suppose Francine and I will see you all for breakfast in the morning. Sleep well."

"I'm surprised Marco gave up so easily," Ethan remarked as he stared down at Dominique.

"He knows it's an exercise in futility. He behaves like this every time he and his family come for a visit. I don't think he can help himself. He likes to do the dance."

"I can't say I blame him," he replied. "Shall we?" He offered an arm to Dominique, and she led him inside.

After they passed through the ballroom, she stepped to within an inch of him, brushed her cheek along his, and whispered in his ear. "I'll see you shortly."

It wasn't long before Ethan heard the knock on his door. He tossed his bow tie onto a chair and strode across the suite. When he reached the door, he wrapped his hand around the knob and pulled the door open.

The dim light illuminated the outline of her body through a transparent negligee.

"Gianna?"

"I was hoping you'd still be awake," she purred.

CHAPTER ELEVEN

"Gianna? Ethan?" Dominique made sure their names rolled off her lips with mild shock as she strolled down the hall toward them.

"Dominique, what are you doing still up?" Gianna asked. Dominique noticed the guise of innocence in her words.

"I went down to the kitchen for a snack."

"Then to the guest wing?" Suspicion intruded on the innocence in Gianna's voice.

"Not to. Through. It's a shortcut to my suite." She turned her gaze on Ethan and shot him a scornful frown. "What would your wife think of this?"

"It's not what it appears, I assure you." Good job, Dominique thought. He made sure to inject a sufficient amount of regret in his voice without a trace of amusement.

"And I suppose your wife would believe that? And what about your children? You would risk your family for an affair?"

"You have a wife? Children? You didn't mention any of this when you invited me to your room," Gianna said and spun on the heel of her feather-adorned, strapless slippers, then charged up the hall.

"Goodnight, Ethan." Dominique delivered the words with a wink and marched down the hall. When she was sure Gianna was gone, she tiptoed back and slipped into Ethan's room.

"Wife? Children?" He chuckled as he slipped his arms around her. "Did you have to make me into such a cad?"

"I was hoping it might kill the intrigue for Gianna," she replied with a grin as she slid her arms up his chest and around his neck. She tilted her head, and her hair fell to one side. His lips traveling down her neck felt like little wisps of air brushing over her.

"And just how many children do I have?" he whispered.

"How many would you like?" She let her head fall back, and a soft, little sigh escaped her lips.

"I think six might be enough." She felt his hand slide through the opening in the back of her dress. His fingers skimmed over her flesh, then grazed the side of her bare breast. It triggered the warm pulls.

"That's a good number."

She concentrated on his lips as they floated from her neck over her chin, leaving a trail of soft little kisses. When they reached her mouth and she parted her lips, she stepped in closer to him and pressed her lips into his. It was enough to set the simmer of heat.

She slid her arms from his neck and unbuttoned his shirt. He pushed the straps of her dress from her shoulders, and she felt her own breath quicken.

He slid off his shirt and tossed it aside.

When her dress slid to the ground, she thought she was going to melt into a pool of lust. She dragged her hands over his flesh and felt every chiseled muscle tense under her touch. Her hands trembled with anticipation as she unhooked his trousers and lowered the zipper. When they fell to the floor, his penis spilled into her hand, and she closed her fingers around it. She slid her hand down the shaft, then back up.

He pulled her into him, and flesh against flesh, they tumbled onto the bed. He rolled on top of her, threaded her fingers through his, and stretched her arms above her head. He planted his hard penis between her legs. It ignited a firestorm inside her. When he lingered outside of her, she knew he was teasing her. When he glided against her, she knew he was testing her. Her body writhed beneath him, begging for more. When he refused to give more, she pulled her hands loose and pushed him off. She rolled on top and, straddling him, slid down his erection, taking it all. It was her turn now. She oscillated her hips, and when she felt his hands cup her bottom, she pulled away.

In one swift movement, she was beneath him again. She spread her legs, and he drove inside her. With every retreat, he plunged back in. She met each assault with equal furor. He danced her to the brink and held her there. If a perfect state of bliss existed, she was sure she was in it.

His body jerked above her, and as he propelled himself inside her one last time, she took him with her. The fire in her belly turned to liquid. Her muscles melted, and a series of glorious little convulsions swept through her.

It was minutes before dawn when Dominique left Ethan's suite and made her way up to her own. If she was lucky enough to be able to fall asleep, she hoped she might just be able to squeeze in a couple of hours before she had to get ready for Jean Pierre's funeral. It was the one exception her father had made to her confinement to the palace grounds.

She closed the door to her suite behind her. When she passed the salon, she was startled by the sound of Gianna's voice. "That was some shortcut," she remarked. When she peered inside the room, she saw Gianna stretch her legs before tossing them over the side of her silk-upholstered chaise. She wondered how long she had been waiting for her.

"Gianna, what are you doing here?"

"I thought we might have a little chat." She watched as she rose from the chaise and wandered across the room, picked up a porcelain figurine, and turned it over absently in her hands. "You know, girl talk."

"About what?" she asked, knowing it was Ethan that was going to be the topic of their discussion.

She set the figurine down, and Dominique met her gaze. "You almost had me fooled. That was quite an act you and Ethan put on."

"We didn't want to embarrass you, Gianna," she offered, slipping out of her shoes.

"So you opted for taking me for a fool? I'm going to make this very simple for you, Dominique." Leaning against a table, she crossed her arms over her chest. "I'm a very spoiled little girl. I've been given everything I've ever wanted all my life. I want Ethan, and that means that you can't have him."

"That's ridiculous, Gianna. You can't make someone want to be with you," she said, hoping she could reason with her.

"I beg to differ. Now, to make things clear, I intend to spend today with Ethan, which means that you will not."

"He's my guest, Gianna. I have to see him, and he has plans to attend Jean Pierre's funeral."

"Let me put it this way, Dominique." She dropped her arms and sauntered toward her. "If you spend time with Ethan today, I'll call the tabloids and tell them about the self-righteous little act you staged to get me out of the way so you could spend the night with Ethan. I even have a photo on my cell phone. See?" She lifted her phone, and Dominque stared down at the picture of her entering Ethan's room. "I'm sure they'll have no problem filling in the rest, especially when I tell them that you left his room just before daybreak looking tired and disheveled," she continued, snapping a photo of Dominique. "That funeral you're going to today will be a circus, and it will be two years ago all over again."

"Are you blackmailing me?" she asked, but the look in Gianna's eyes left little doubt in her mind.

"Call it what you like." Gianna turned and sashayed toward the door. "I prefer to think of it as evening the score."

Stunned, Dominique dropped to the chaise when the door closed. She knew if Gianna called the tabloids, they would hound her. She couldn't have Jean Pierre's funeral shrouded by chaos with dozens of reporters and photographers tripping over themselves trying to get to her. Even worse, she couldn't disgrace her family again. She had no doubt the press would take the opportunity to dredge up Luis again. They had all but crucified her for letting him into her life. She couldn't bear to go through that or to put her family through it again.

The sting of regret cut through her. She should have never let her guard down with Ethan. There was no room in her life for him, she reminded herself. Her royal duties left room for little else. She had been born into a life of wealth and privilege. With that came sacrifice.

She pushed herself up, knowing there was no way she was going to be able to sleep. She was going to have to try to figure out how to avoid Ethan and keep him from attending Jean Pierre's funeral.

"Ah, Major Moore, good morning," Frederique said as Ethan watched him stride into the vestibule, a radio transmitter wired in his ear and a pistol in his belt. "I'm afraid your services will not be required at the funeral proceedings."

"My services?" Ethan asked, assuming that Frederique didn't get the memo. "I think you have misunderstood my purpose in attending the funeral. My presence at the funeral is not service-related. His Majesty invited me to stay here as a guest, and I will accompany Dominique as a friend, not as a bodyguard." The fact that he would be keeping an eye on Dominique was secondary.

"Be that as it may, we have not considered you in any of

our strategies. With all due respect, your presence could jeopardize the safety of the Royal family."

"With all due respect, it sounds like your strategies are a bit inflexible if they don't provide for contingencies. In any event," he continued, managing to conceal his annoyance, "I can assure you that I will not be in the way of your security team."

"What's this?" Ethan turned when he heard Victor's voice and watched him stroll into the vestibule. "Is there some sort of a problem here?"

"Good morning, sir," he said, greeting him with a smile and remembering the slight nod. "It seems that Frederique is uncomfortable with my attending the funeral. I was just trying to explain to him that my being there would not be a detriment to the safety of the Royal family."

"Frederique, why do you think Major Moore would be a threat if he accompanied us?"

"If I may, Your Majesty." Frederique leaned into Victor and lowered his voice to a whisper.

"That's nonsense," Victor responded with a dismissive wave of his hand and loud enough for him to hear. "What is with that child this morning? Missing breakfast with our guests and now this." He turned to him and continued. "You are welcome to come with us. And you will ride with us, as well."

"Thank you, sir."

"Good morning, Father." Dominique greeted her father, then turned to him. "Good morning, Ethan. I didn't expect to see you here." She was as cool as a cucumber. There was not a hint that anything had occurred between them. There was not the subtlest indication that they were anything more than just acquaintances.

"Why is that?" he asked, trying to read her. He knew she was aware he would be accompanying her to the funeral. He could appreciate that she might not want anyone to suspect that she had spent the night in his bed, but he didn't see how that had anything to do with his attending the funeral. There had to be another reason. "I would be honored to attend Jean Pierre's funeral."

"Please don't feel obligated to attend," she insisted. "You are here for just a few more hours."

He searched her eyes. It was like staring into a stranger's. They were as blank as the face of a poker player. Whatever was going on, it was tucked deep away. "You should spend it enjoying Monteaux. I'm sure Gianna would be happy to show you around."

Gianna, he mused. Why would she tell him to spend his last day there with Gianni? Had he been nothing more than a pawn in some sort of twisted game between her and Gianni? Or had she grown repulsed by his stub? Or was he just not good enough for a princess? It didn't matter, he decided, as a combination of humiliation and anger swept through him.

"Good morning, everyone. God has certainly given Jean Pierre a beautiful day," Andre announced as he and Francine joined them.

Ethan took the opportunity with Andre and Francine drawing everyone's attention, and he slipped out of the vestibule.

When he reached his suite, he grabbed the telephone. It was his own damn fault, he told himself as he punched in his butler's extension. He'd been reckless with her. He'd let his guard down. "Could you arrange a ride for me to the airport?" he asked when the extension was answered.

"Yes, sir. Your ride will be right up. Shall I come for your luggage?"

"No. I can manage," he replied and set the receiver down. He made a mental note to have his secretary send a message when he got back to Victor and Andre apologizing for his hasty departure, along with a gift thanking them for their hospitality. That would be the last he would have anything to do with Dominique. She and Monteaux would be behind him.

CHAPTER TWELVE

Bruno noticed after Jean Pierre's funeral that things had settled down. He hid behind his camera outside the palace walls, focusing the powerful zoom lens on the grounds inside. He reached in his pocket, retrieved a small notebook, and took a few notes.

"Are you a reporter?" He spun around when he heard a cheery voice behind him.

"No, a tourist." He looked the gentleman over and gave him a nod.

"Pretty fancy camera for a tourist."

"It's a hobby."

"Taking pictures of pretty ladies?" he asked with a chuckle.

"Landscapes, mostly." He dropped the camera, let it dangle around his neck, and took out a cigarette.

"Ah, you'd appreciate the palace gardens. I hear they're pretty remarkable."

"Have you seen them?" he asked, his interest piqued. He struck a match, touched it to the cigarette, and then tossed it to the ground.

"No, but my friend has. He works for the king."

"Doing what?" He kept his voice nonchalant, almost disinterested, and led the gentlemen down the street with a casual stroll. Maybe I can learn something from him about the palace security, he thought.

"He's a groundskeeper. He tends the gardens. That's how I know so much about them."

"How come he's never taken you to see them?" He took a

long drag, then exhaled it.

"I'm not that interested. I'll listen about them over a beer but waste my time to see them. That's another matter. But I bet I could get him to show you if you're interested."

"Oh, yeah?"

"Probably, but not for a few weeks. The princess just got back from a trip a couple of weeks ago. Someone tried to kidnap her, so security's going to be tight at the palace, I'm sure."

"Really?"

"Didn't you read the papers? It was in the papers."

"Yeah, I did read something about that. Did they catch the kidnappers?"

"No. I don't think they have a clue."

"That's too bad." He smiled to himself and took another drag from his cigarette.

"So, are you going to be around for a few weeks?"

"Maybe." He paused a moment not to seem eager. "I'm touring at my leisure, so my schedule's not really rigid. I could still be here."

"Well, if you are, come by and see me. I work here," he said.

They stopped outside of a small café, and Bruno made a mental note of the name.

"I'll see if I can get you in."

"Okay. If I'm still around." He flicked his cigarette, slid his hands in his pockets, and continued his stroll.

"My name's Gerard. What's yours?" the gentleman called after him.

"John," he called back, allowing the grin to slide over his face.

"You've been back for almost three weeks now, and I've yet to see a smile on your face since the soiree."

Dominique watched Lidia strut across her office, then draw open the heavy drapes. A burst of sunlight shot across the room.

"That's much better."

"There's not much to smile about." Dominique's frown deepened as she flipped through a stack of invitations. She had fallen in love with Ethan. She couldn't recall the exact moment. It had happened so quickly. Then just as quickly, her heart had broken into a million little pieces. She remembered that vividly. It was the moment she had watched him walk out of the vestibule the day of Jean Pierre's funeral. "You might as well decline these invitations." She sighed as she dropped them on the edge of her desk.

"Well, let's see." Lidia picked them up and began shuffling through them. "Perhaps we can offer to have some of these events here at the palace."

"Whatever you think." She really didn't care one way or the other.

"Oh, Dominique, I hate to see you so miserable." She allowed Lidia to brush a tress of hair from her face. She heard the sympathy in Lidia's voice and knew it was sincere, but there wasn't a thing Lidia could do to ease her pain. "I'm sure it won't be long before the police find out who's after you or the necklaces. Then you'll have your freedom back."

"I suppose." She'd have her freedom, but she would never have Ethan, she reminded herself, then pushed away from her desk. She strolled over to a settee, sat down, and stared out the window.

"Maybe I could talk to your father. Perhaps I can persuade him to make an exception. We could have *Lantham Boutique* stay open a few extra hours and have Frederique secure the building so you can shop. It'll cheer you up to buy some new clothes or shoes or maybe a new handbag."

"I appreciate your trying to cheer me up, Lidia, but I don't feel like shopping."

Lidia sat down next to her, and she placed a hand over hers. "What is it, Dominique? What's bothering you? I know you well enough to know it's not just being confined that has you so upset."

"I don't want to talk about it." She gave Lidia's hand a little squeeze. "It's not that I don't trust you. You know there's nothing I can't talk about with you. It's just that it doesn't matter."

"Does it have anything to do with Major Moore?"

"What makes you think that?" She kept her voice even, but she knew her eyes betrayed her as she felt the unhappiness swell behind them.

"Dominique, I've known you for twenty-five years. I saw the sparkle in your eyes when you looked at him. There was a glow around you . . . an aura . . . whenever he was in the room with you. Since he left, you haven't had a happy moment."

"Oh, Lidia," she drew her hand back and raked it through her hair. "I think I fell in love with him. I tried not to, but it happened anyway."

"Sometimes love just happens no matter how we try to fight it. There's nothing wrong with that."

"There is when it's me it happens to."

"What makes you say that?"

"I've been standing beside my father for almost twenty years. My royal duties consume at least ninety percent of my time. And the last time I was in the public eye with a man, things went horribly wrong. The press published terrible things about me that weren't even true, and people held it against me for a long time. They lost respect for the family. My father was ashamed, embarrassed, and disappointed. It was a terrible scandal. If I step out with a man again, the entire thing will be revisited in the press, and there's no telling what new stories they would come up with."

"I must admit that the burden on you is not fair. Now that Andre and Francine's children are older, perhaps they should share more in the royal obligations."

"Even so — "

"There is no *even so*," Lidia interrupted. "The press is always going to print unflattering and sensationalistic stories. Unfortunately, that's what sells. And some of the people who read those stories will believe them. You cannot let that control your life, Dominique. And I think you misunderstood your father's reaction. He was angry with Luis for saying such lies about you and with the tabloids for printing them. He wasn't ashamed, embarrassed, or disappointed with you. He was upset watching what it was doing to you. Your father only cares what is printed about the family when it hurts his children."

"It doesn't matter, anyway. I ended things badly with Ethan. I hurt him. That's why he left so abruptly."

"I thought he left for an emergency."

"I made that up to avoid having to explain what happened."

"Do you want to talk about what happened?"

"It was Gianni," she began, "she left me no choice," she continued as she explained everything to Lidia.

"I see why things look so grim to you, but we'll figure all of this out. I promise you."

Lidia had always been there for her, but she didn't see what anyone could do to put the pieces of her heart back together. She should never have let her guard down. It didn't matter that she had been in a foreign country or miles above Earth or within the palace walls. She had made a mistake, and she was paying for it. She just hoped that Ethan's anger was worse than the pain she had seen in his eyes. The anger would dissipate much more quickly than pain.

"Damn," Ethan muttered as he shoved the keyboard aside and leaned back in his chair. It had been over a month, and he still couldn't shake Dominique from his mind. She was all he had thought about since he had returned from Monteaux.

He wondered how the police there were progressing with their investigation. His friend with the military police hadn't found any good prints on the pistol before he'd had it shipped to Monteaux. The palm print on the grip was too smudged to be of any use, and the serial number had been ground down, so there was no way to trace the gun. The GPS dot hadn't provided any clues either. His car had been found but had been torched, destroying any evidence that might have been left behind.

"Hey, boss? Got a minute?" He looked up to see a tall, lanky figure poking his head in the doorway and nodded. He couldn't remember his name though he remembered he was one of the young college graduates he'd hired a year ago. He'd grown fond of him. He was intelligent, persistent, and hardworking. "Yeah. Come on in, uh . . ."

"Lance. My name is Lance," he said, and as he strolled in, Ethan took note of his cocky smile, which seemed to widen with each stride. When he reached the desk, he dropped a picture in front of him. "I think I got a match on the dead guy. What do you think?"

"How'd you do that? I thought our security cameras had managed to snag only partial photographs of the asshole that attacked me."

He stared down at the photograph and studied it. A pair of dark eyes deeply set in a crusty face peered at him from under two bushy brows. Thin lips beneath a wide nose grinned at him. He smiled back and raised his gaze to his Lance. "That's him. How did you get this?"

"I superimposed all the photos our cameras snapped of him, and then I tweaked them using an old photo software program I had on my computer at home. I came up with enough detail to be able to run it through our system. It matched him with a photo on an internet dating service site. The guy is on a dating site. Can you believe that? He listed his name, age, hometown, interests. Listen to this," he said with a chuckle. "I am a gentle pussycat looking for a kitten. Yeah, right, when he's not stalking princesses and beating up—"

Ethan lifted a brow.

"Uh, sorry. Didn't mean that he beat up . . . I mean, I'm sure he looked a lot worse."

"I'm the one who's still breathing," Ethan reminded him. "And good work, by the way." He looked back down at the picture and mumbled as he read the report under it. "Peter Dempster. Frankfurt, Germany. He was a long way from home."

"I got an address and phone number for him from the system. I called the number a few times. No answer. He must have lived alone. I also ran a search on him. No criminal record. And not much of anything else on him. He wasn't listed as a passenger on any commercial flights from Frankfurt around the time the princess arrived here either." He shrugged. "Want me to send this to that detective in Monteaux?"

He thought for a moment as he stared at the picture again, recalling what Lidia had said about her grandfather. He was killed in Poland by the Germans during World War II. The asshole was from Germany. There might be a connection there, he mused, then decided to see if he could get a little more information before turning his identity over to Laroche. "How's your German?" he asked, glancing up at Lance.

"*Ein bisschen rostig, aber nicht schlect,*" he said with a smirk.

"A bit rusty, but not bad," Ethan repeated in English.

"Sounds good enough to me."

"Good enough for what?"

"How would you like to go to Germany?" He set aside the photograph and leaned back in his chair.

"You're kidding!"

"I'm quite serious."

"Awesome." Lance's smirk turned into a full-blown smile as he tossed his arms in the air and did a little shuffle. "I'll book myself on the next flight, boss. Just tell me what you want me to do."

"Above everything, stay safe. I don't want you taking any chances."

"Stay safe. No chances. Got it."

"I want you to go to Germany and check out the address you got. Watch it for a day or two first. Then call me, and we'll discuss where to go from there."

"I'm as good as there." He turned to leave.

"Not so fast, Agent Bond. I want you to take a laptop that will give you access to our system. Program five levels of security. While you're getting that set up, I'll get a list of what else you'll need to take with you."

"Yes, sir," he replied and then hurried from the office.

Ethan tilted his chair back a bit further. He wondered if anyone had missed Peter Dempster yet and wondered for a second if he was sending Lance into any danger. He'd be fine as long as he did as he was told, he decided. He wasn't going to have him do anything that would even remotely put him at risk. As soon as he got a little more information, he'd give it to Laroche. Then Dominique would be safe, and he could get on with his life.

CHAPTER THIRTEEN

Dominique had been stuck inside the palace perimeter for over a month with no end in sight. A person can only take this confinement for so long, she thought as she stared out the window over Monteaux. In the distance, thousands of people moved around the streets, most of them nondescript under their little straw hats sheltering them from the bright sun. They looked like an army of ants, each indistinguishable from the other. A perfect disguise, she thought, as the idea struck her.

She walked over to her closet and rummaged through her clothes, selecting a pair of capris and a short-sleeved top. A perfect tourist's outfit, she told herself. After changing, she grabbed her camera and draped the strap around her neck, then reached for one of her straw hats and a pair of sunglasses. Perfect, she thought, surveying herself in the mirror, and satisfied, dialed the housekeeping extension.

"I don't feel comfortable doing this," the housekeeping assistant told her as she pulled her car to the curb at the end of an empty alley.

"No one will know," she assured the assistant. "I will meet you here in two hours," she reminded her and then stepped out of the car.

As the car pulled away, Dominique walked out of the alley and onto the sidewalk. She continued past the storefronts inspecting the various displays of goods. A walk in the park by the lake would end her excursion, she decided, then she'd head back to the alley.

"Stop complaining," Bruno told his cousin as they sat under the hot sun on the sidewalk patio of the café.

"What difference does it make if I complain?" Gunther replied.

"Just study the map," Bruno grumbled. "It's going to be your job to get us out of here." He flipped through his photos of the palace, his sketches of every entrance to and exit from the palace grounds, and his notes of every person and vehicle that had gained entrance to the palace over the past few weeks. I'm proud of my research, he thought, and I should be. My life depends on its thoroughness.

"Don't worry about me, Bruno."

"I better not have to," he warned. Seeing the waitress approaching their table, he tucked the papers inside his folded newspaper.

"Here are your sandwiches, gentlemen," she said and set two plates on the table. "How are your beers?"

"They're fine," Bruno answered with a dismissive wave.

"But thanks," Gunther added.

She nodded, then hurried on to another table.

Bruno wrapped his mouth around the sandwich and tore off a generous bite. "Not bad," he mumbled as he followed it with a swig of beer.

"Oh, yeah," Gunther agreed. "Look at those legs," he added, nodding toward a tall, slim figure across the street.

Bruno followed his gaze to the figure, narrowed them, and studied the woman. Her gait was smooth and flowing. She moved like a swan over a lake of glass. Her posture was poised and dignified. Her hand rested gracefully over the camera hanging around her neck. She was a classy broad, he concluded. He frowned at the fact that her face was hidden by the giant hat that flopped down around her shoulders.

"She must be a model," Gunther commented. "I wonder if she's famous."

Bruno watched as a couple rambled down the cobblestone walk toward her. When they neared her, she turned away and lowered her head, the brim of her hat dipping to further conceal her face. After they had passed, she turned back, lifted her head, and continued along the sidewalk before stopping in front of a small store with an array of porcelain boxes in the window. She lifted the brim of her hat and lowered her sunglasses to the tip of her nose to inspect a box more closely.

He fumbled for his camera. Snatching it from under the table, he lifted it to his face and squinted through the viewfinder. He slid his fingers around the zoom lens and focused it on the reflection of her face in the window. Then he lowered the camera to his lap and scanned over the block. There wasn't a guard in sight. She must have snuck out, he figured. The unexpected smile that erupted across his face surprised him as much as finding the princess right in front of him did.

"Looks like our job just got easier." He flung the back of his hand against Gunther's arm. "Go get our things from the inn, then go to the van and wait to hear from me."

"I'm not done with my sandwich," he complained.

"Take it with you," Bruno ordered. "We got a change of plans."

"What the —"

"It's her," he said under his breath, cutting Gunther off. "Now go."

Without another word, Gunther crumbled his map and tucked it under his arm. He grabbed the rest of his sandwich and disappeared down the street.

Bruno picked up the newspaper and shoved it through his belt behind his back. He slid the camera strap around his neck and tossed a few bills on the table. He tore another bite from his sandwich and kept his focus on Dominique.

He watched her push her glasses back up her nose and let her hat fall back down over her eyes. She sauntered past the next few stores and then stopped beside the cart of a street vendor. The vendor handed her an ice-flavored drink and accepted her payment, appearing to not recognize her. "Dumbass," Bruno said under his breath. All the better for me, though, he thought. She might get spooked and run back to the palace or call someone if she thought she'd been recognized. She strolled toward the end of the street, and as she approached the corner, he stood, slid his *Panama* hat down over his brows, and headed after her, careful to keep a reasonable distance.

Arriving at the corner, he saw her peer down the street. The lake park was just a few blocks away. He knew from where she was standing she would be able to see the sun shimmering across the water in the distance and wondered if she'd take that direction. "Here we go," he said aloud to himself when she stepped off the curb.

He followed her to the park and watched her slip out of her sneakers at the edge of the grass, then make her way to a spot midway between the park's edge and the water. It offered a generous view of most of the lake. When she sat down on the lawn, he took a seat on a bench near enough to have an unobstructed view of her. After a few minutes, he snatched his cell phone from his pocket and punched in Gunther's number. He answered on the first ring. "Did you get our things?"

"Yes. I'm ready," Gunther replied. "Where are you?"

"At the park. Drive along the street on the west side of the lake. Then sit and wait to hear from me," he instructed, then tucked his phone back in his pocket. He scanned the park, mulling over a new plan. They would be too exposed, and there were too many people in the park to make a move there. He would be patient. He'd follow her and wait for a better opportunity.

The park was beginning to thin out as the hour passed. He still couldn't believe his good fortune and hadn't taken his eyes off of her. He wasn't going to fail this time. She had practically fallen in his lap.

He felt his back stiffen when he saw her slide her feet into her sneakers. When she stood, he stayed vigilant but didn't get up. Instead, he watched her cut across the park toward the south side of the lake. When she reached the sidewalk, he got up, tapped Gunther's number into his phone, and followed her.

"I see her," Gunther said. "What do you want me to do?"

"Stay on the line and wait for my order."

Bruno kept pace with her and kept aware of their surroundings. An occasional car passed in either direction, and even fewer pedestrians walked at that end of the lake. The opportunity was nearing. He could feel it. When she approached an entrance into the cemetery and quickened her stride, he followed her inside. There were just a few visitors at that time of the day, and it was peaceful. Once inside, he issued orders to Gunther. "Drive to the northeast side of the cemetery. Hurry. As the princess comes out that end, call her over and ask her for directions."

"Got it." He stayed on the phone and heard the engine crank up and then shift into gear. When he heard the engine die a few minutes later, he assumed Gunther was at the entrance.

"Are you in place?" he asked.

"Yes, I am here," Gunther replied. "I don't see the princess."

"You will shortly. Get your map and get out of the van. Open the map and look like you are studying it," he instructed.

"Okay. I'm doing that now."

His camera bounced heavily against his chest as he increased his pace to narrow the distance between them. "Damn," he cursed to himself when he saw Dominique glance over her shoulder. He wondered if she recognized him. His question was answered as he watched her take off in a sprint. They were at least halfway through the cemetery, he estimated, and she was now outrunning him. By his estimation, she was about three or four seconds ahead of him. With Gunther at the entrance, a few seconds was nothing.

Hopefully, she'll tire as she gets to the gate, he thought, watching her pull away while he sucked in each breath with every step. He had lost the distance he'd gained before she spotted him and was getting winded. At least he was managing to keep her in his sight. One foot in front of the other, he told himself as he maintained his pursuit.

She was at the entrance. He could see the van, and there was Gunther. He was leaning against the van reading the map. He watched as she burst through the gate. Gunther looked up at her but didn't move. He appeared confused by her. Good boy, Bruno thought. I'll be there in a few seconds.

With his next few strides, he could hear her voice. "Please, help," she pleaded. She was gasping for air. That was good, Bruno thought. She had tired. She wouldn't be able to put up much of a fight.

"What do you want me to do?" Gunther asked.

"Drive!" she shouted, snatched the map from his hands, and then circled to the passenger side of the van.

Gunther opened the driver's door.

She threw open the passenger door and leaped inside. "Go! Hurry!" she screamed just before Gunther slammed the driver's door shut as he bolted through the gate.

The engine fired up as Bruno yanked open the back door and leaped inside. He slammed the door shut behind him just as the van shot away from the curb. In half a second, he had an arm wrapped around her throat. He jerked her backward out of the seat, and Gunther tossed him a rag. He muffled her scream with the rag, and she went limp in his arms.

"Hey, boss, you won't believe where I've been." Ethan heard the excitement in Lance's voice tumble off his words.

"What are you talking about? You are supposed to be watching Dempster's apartment." Ethan glanced at his watch and calculated the time in Frankfurt. It would be three in the afternoon there.

"I was in his apartment. It was so easy. I can't believe it," he rattled on. "I was actually in Dempster's apartment. Only —"

"What?" Ethan cut him off as the anger sliced through him. "I told you to watch his apartment and not to do anything else until we talked. You're there alone. That means that you have no one watching your back. What if someone had walked in on you? What would you have done?"

"It's cool, boss. It's cool. I got in and out with no trouble. I'm fine."

"No, it's not cool. These people have murdered. I need to know you're safe, and the only way I'll know that is if I know you're following my orders."

"I know. I'm sorry, but I had to seize the moment."

"What's that supposed to mean?"

"Well, I was checking out the mailboxes, trying to figure out where Dempster's apartment was in the building so I could keep an eye on it. I saw he had some mail in his box, so I tried to jimmy the lock. Some guy came up from behind me and started cursing and complaining that Dempster was past due on his rent and wanted to know what I was doing there."

He listened, growing angrier by the minute at himself for sending him to Germany. He didn't need some overly zealous kid dying to play spy going off half-cocked halfway around the world. Lance's blood was going to be on his hands if anything happened to the kid, and he wasn't going to be able to live with that.

"All of a sudden," Lance continued, "the words started spilling out of my mouth. I told him that I was a friend of Dempster's and that he had asked me to come by and pick up some things to send to him. I told him that since Dempster was out of town, he couldn't give me the key but told me to go see the landlord and get him to let me in and pay his rent for him while I was at it. I paid the guy his rent in cash, and he was happy to let me in Dempster's apartment."

"Damn it. He knows what you look like. What if someone else comes around and Dempster's landlord tells him about you and what you look like? Don't go near that building again," he ordered. "I don't want you anywhere near that neighborhood. Do you understand?"

"Yes, fully. I won't go near there. Sorry, boss. Really."

"I never should have sent you there."

"It was worth it, boss. Totally. And I promise I'll follow your orders strictly from now on to the letter."

"You better or you're fired. What do you mean *it was worth it*? Did you find something?"

"I did. The dead guy also goes by Knapp. Edgar Knapp. I ran his name through the system. He's a small-time crook. Convicted of a few burglaries, assaults, disturbing the peace, those sorts of things. He worked at a vineyard as of about two months ago."

"What's the name of the vineyard?"

"Van Dousen Vineyard and Winery. It's not too far west of here, near Koblenz. I was going to check it out tomorrow. Take a tour. Ask a few discreet questions. Of course, if that's all right with you," he added. "What do you think?"

"I'm thinking about telling you to get your ass back here."

"I can take the tour *and* be on a plane back tomorrow," he offered. "I promise I'll check in with you every few hours, and I won't seize any more moments. It might lead us somewhere."

He was right about that, but he'd gotten enough information. The kid had put himself at risk, and he wasn't going to put him at any additional risk by letting him stay a moment longer. "No," he replied. "Get on the next flight back. No detours. Understood?"

"Understood," he answered. "Boss, am I fired?"

"Just get your ass back here."

Lidia rang Dominique's room one more time. There was still no answer. She finished sorting through Dominique's mail, setting aside the invitations she'd have to decline, and strolled over to the window. She looked out across the expansive grounds. There was no sign of her. She glanced down at her watch. It was dinnertime, and she hadn't heard from her since she had told her she was going to take a nap and didn't want to be disturbed. That was over five hours ago, she calculated.

"Poor thing," she mumbled to herself with a heavy sigh. She strode over to the doorway, slid her fingers over the light switch, and closed the door to her darkened office. As she started toward Dominique's suite, she spotted one of the household assistants. "Have you seen the princess in the last hour or so?" she asked.

"No, ma'am. I haven't seen her all day."

"Thank you," she replied and continued down to the end of the hall. She climbed the two flights of stairs to the fourth floor and headed down the east wing. "Dominique?" she called out as she knocked on the door to a small gym. She opened the door and looked inside. It was empty. When she got to the next door, she did the same. It was empty, too. She continued to the end of the hall and knocked on the door to her suite. "Dominique? It's Lidia. Are you awake?" She waited a moment for an answer before knocking again. "Dominique?" she called, then hesitated before tapping her fingers over the keypad and entering the suite.

It was dim in the foyer. "Dominique?" She glanced around and then checked the other rooms. Finding they were all empty, she lifted the receiver and dialed down to the kitchen. The phone was answered on the first ring. "This is Lidia. Is the princess down there?"

"No, mademoiselle. We haven't seen her since breakfast. She didn't request lunch today."

"Thank you." She frowned as she set the receiver down, then lifted it back up again and dialed the chauffeurs' quarters. One of the drivers answered. "This is Lidia. Did the princess call for a car today?"

"No, Lidia. We haven't heard from Her Royal Highness today. We understood she wouldn't be using our services until further notice, which we haven't received."

"Thank you." She dialed Dominique's cell phone next. The ring pierced the silence, and, startled, she jumped as she turned to see the cell phone sitting atop a credenza. She disconnected the call and punched in the number for security.

"This is Frederique."

"Frederique, this is Lidia. I can't find the princess." She could hear the anxiety in her own voice. "Could you please send some men to search the palace and the grounds? I've already checked her suite. She's not in the kitchen either."

"When's the last time you spoke with her?"

"About five hours ago. She said she was going to rest and asked not to be disturbed."

"Okay. I'll get on it."

"I'll be with His Majesty. Please call his suite and let me know when you find her."

"Of course. I'll call you the minute we find her."

She dropped the receiver and lifted her hand to her lips. "Dominique, please don't have done anything foolish," she whispered to herself.

She hurried down the hall to Victor's wing. As she started down the next hallway, she could see that the door to his office was open. She was almost out of breath when she reached his office and was glad to find him alone. He was seated behind his desk, reviewing some papers. As was her habit, she closed the door behind her after she entered.

"Ah, Lidia," he said with a smile as he glanced up at her. He slid off his reading glasses and rose to greet her. As he circled his desk, his smile dissolved. "What is it?" He slipped his fingers around her arms. "Are you all right? You're as pale as a ghost. Maybe you should sit."

"No, I'm fine. It's Dominique." She lifted her hand to his arm. "I can't find her anywhere. She's not in the east wing. She's not in the kitchen with Jacques." Her fingers tightened their grasp around his arm, and the desperation in her voice grew. "I'm worried, Victor. I think she is gone."

"The palace is enormous, Lidia." He took her hand in his. "You're like a mother hen with Dominique. Perhaps we should have security search for her before you start getting so upset."

"I've already called them. They're searching now. Frederique will call us here, but I think we should call Inspector Laroche."

"Let's wait to hear from Frederique first." He placed his arm around her shoulder and started with her toward the sofa. "She's got to be here somewhere. No one could possibly get past the guards to her here. The palace is sealed."

"She always lets me know where she is during business hours if she's not in the east wing so I can get in touch with her, and she always checks in with me before the end of the day." She sat down on the edge of the cushion. "She told me she didn't want to be disturbed for a few hours. She said she was going to take a nap. She would have called me when she awoke. She—"

The sound of the telephone ringing interrupted her. She sprang to her feet and rushed to the phone. Snapping up the receiver, then pressing the speaker button, she said, "His Majesty's office."

"Lidia, it is Frederique."

"Have you found Dominique?" she asked.

"No. It appears she is not in the palace. Shortly after noon, the exterior security cameras show the princess leaving with a household assistant through the northwest entrance. The cameras do not show that she has returned. I've sent some men out on the streets to look for her."

"Have you spoken with the assistant?" Victor asked.

"Oh, Your Majesty, I'm sorry I didn't know you were on the line. I have not. She is not here."

"Call Inspector Laroche, have him come over, and then meet me in the drawing room," Victor ordered. He took the receiver from Lidia and set it down. "That's just a precaution. No need to worry yet," he said, taking her hands. "Dominique may have left on her own volition and may be on her way back as we speak." He slid his arms around. "We will find her."

CHAPTER FOURTEEN

He must have fallen asleep in his chair, Ethan figured. The dream felt so real. Damn, he thought as he ran his hand through his hair. He was never going to be able to shake Dominique if his subconscious kept letting her in. He got up and paced his office. It was close to three in the morning. There was no point in going home. He'd get a second wind with a cup of coffee. He'd see how much he could find on the Van Dousen enterprise and then head home.

He roused his computer, and the screen lit up. As his fingers flew over the keyboard, information spilled onto the screen. Helmuth Van Dousen owned the vineyard and winery. He scrolled over a series of pictures of him. In one, he was standing in front of a stack of oak barrels. In another, he was sitting in the middle of a row of grapevines. In another, he was sitting at the head of a long table holding up a glass of wine, and in yet another, he was standing among racks of bottles of wine. "Interesting," he murmured, studying the man. In each photograph, Van Dousen was draped in jewelry, colorful, ostentatious, and ornate. He looks like a human Christmas tree, he thought, amused.

His appreciation for jewelry wasn't enough to accuse the guy of kidnaping, he figured as he read more, at least not with his reputation. The system reported that he donated generously to a number of charities. He was also a major benefactor of the arts. He contributed heavily to a number of museums and institutes. He funded the construction of a building at a university. He owned a tour boat company in Greece. That's odd, he thought. He must have more connections there, he assumed, and clicked into another database. Van Dousen owned another company in Greece that owned another company that owned a Greek island. It's under a lot of layers for just a vacation home, he thought.

"What's this?" he muttered to himself as he clicked on an item for more information. A Polish World War II survivor claimed that one of the paintings Van Dousen had loaned to a museum for a special exhibit had been stolen from her family during the war. Van Dousen claimed that the painting had been in his family for years and that he had inherited it. The information was several years old but noteworthy.

He clicked back to the personal information on Van Dousen. Based on his date of birth, he wasn't born until about ten years after the war had ended. His father, Hans Van Dousen, certainly would have lived during the war. "Let's see what we can find on you, Hans," he mumbled.

Information rolled onto the screen when he entered his name. Served as a commander in Hitler's army. Led German units into Poland. If my memory of World War II history serves me correctly, he thought, Hitler authorized his commanders to kill *without pity or mercy all men, women, and children of Polish descent or language*. Hundreds of Polish community leaders were executed in public while much of the leading class was sent to concentration camps, where they later died. "No doubt Hans was responsible for the killing of thousands of Poles," he surmised aloud. And perhaps collected some of their valuables along the way. Among them Lidia's grandfather's? "Maybe it wasn't such a stretch," he said to himself.

"Mr. Van Dousen, sir." The voice outside of his study door drew Van Dousen's attention.

"Come in," he replied and watched as his butler pushed open the door just enough to step inside. He closed it behind himself and stood ramrod straight, his white-gloved hands at his sides.

"I apologize for interrupting you, sir, but you have visitors," he announced.

"Visitors?" he asked, annoyed. He glanced over at his right-hand man. He knew he understood the subtle, unspoken message his eyes conveyed when he shifted in the chair and slid his hand just inside of his shirt over his sidearm. He turned back to his butler. "I am not expecting any guests. Who are they?"

"Bruno is here with a woman," he replied. "Shall I show them in?"

"You may." He looked at his right-hand man as his butler stepped from the study. He flashed him a satisfied grin. "How convenient for us, Remus, that Bruno came here."

"He probably picked up a wife somewhere and brought her here to help him beg for mercy," Remus replied.

"Yes." He laughed. "Now, you'll have to kill them both." He turned his gaze as Bruno strode into the study. He saw Bruno's hand gripped around the woman's arm and his grin dissolved. He pushed himself up from his chair with such force it sent his chair slamming into the credenza behind him.

"Mr. Van—"

"Bruno!" His roar cut Bruno off before he could finish saying his name. He slid his gaze to Dominique and allowed a smile. "Your Royal Highness," he said, calming his voice. "There appears to be a terrible mistake here, and I apologize for any inconvenience you may have incurred."

He observed her as she pulled her arm from Bruno's grasp with a slight stumble. She appeared disoriented and light-headed. He wondered if Bruno had drugged her either to kidnap her or to get her there, or both. "Mistake? If this is all a mistake, I suggest you return me to Monteaux, and I will over-look this . . . inconvenience," she managed. He detected a slight slur in her words. Yes, he concluded, Bruno had drugged her.

"Of course," he replied. "But I'm sure your journey here was exhausting for you. Why don't you get some rest, and we can discuss things in the morning." He signaled to his butler. "Please show the princess to a guest room."

"I do not," was all she managed to say before his butler whisked her out and the door closed.

"Mr. Van Dousen, now we can get the necklaces," Bruno said, a bead of sweat dripping, his hands fidgeting. He was nervous as hell, Van Dousen noted, as the damn idiot should be, he thought.

"Oh, Bruno," he replied with a shake of his head. "What am I going to do with you?" he asked as he lowered himself to his chair. "Sit." He gestured to a chair.

"We can continue with the plan," Bruno answered and sat down.

"Continue with the plan," Van Dousen repeated. "And what plan is that?" He heard the irritation in his voice increase despite his effort to restrain himself. "What plan called for the princess to be brought to my home? What plan called for the princess to see my face, to hear my name?"

"I thought—"

"You thought?" His voice exploded as he slammed his fist on his desk. Bruno had gotten on his last nerve. "Who told you to think?"

"I-I'm sorry. I-I'll fix it," he stammered.

"The damage is done," he told him, calming his voice again. "Now, we'll deal with it."

He watched Bruno lift his fingers to the collar of his shirt. He tugged on it and then swallowed hard. He could see that Bruno knew what was coming. He had warned him not to think. He had told him to only follow his orders. "How?"

"I don't know yet," he said as he thought aloud. "But for now, it appears that the only option we have is to take advantage of your . . . miscalculation. We'll make a demand for the necklaces."

"Do you want me to contact — "

"You will do nothing further," Van Dousen ordered. "The plan has changed since you brought the princess here. She was never supposed to know that I am involved, let alone meet me."

"But there was to be an exchange. The princess for the jewels."

"An exchange is no longer possible, thanks to you."

Dominique tugged at the knob, but the door didn't budge. She concluded that the double key bolt must have been locked from the outside, then glanced around the room. A delicate lace scarf was draped over the canopy of the bed, matching the lovely lace coverlet below it. A full-length oval mirror, beautifully carved with roses and cherubs, stood in a corner. She had no intention of being there long enough to use either, she decided, and she did her best to cross the room to the set of French doors on the other side.

As she yanked on the levers and the doors sprung loose, a glimmer of hope tangled with the fear that gripped her. The hope disappeared just as quickly when she stepped onto a balcony and peered over the railing. Beneath, a veranda spanned across the grounds. She was certain the unforgiving marble would do more than break just her fall if she were to jump. In the distance ahead, she saw an armed man walking along a cliff, and beyond him, the sea. She scanned the horizons on both sides. Beyond the property was just more water. Small islands emerged from the sea while boats of various shapes and sizes bobbed on top of it. An island, she guessed. No one would ever think to look for her on an island.

Nausea churned inside her like simmering lava. Breathe, she told herself as she stumbled back into the room. She lowered herself to the edge of the bed, struggling to think. She was too faint. She needed rest, and then she could figure things out, she decided, and she fell backward onto the bed.

A knock on the door startled her awake, and as she blinked away the fog, the fear settled back in. She listened as the knocking continued, unsure if she should answer it.

"Miss?" the timid voice of a man called from just outside the door. "Miss, you okay?" he asked. He spoke in broken English with what she thought was weighted with a heavy Asian accent. She thought she heard a hint of alarm in his voice and decided to answer.

"What do you want?" she asked, wondering how long she had been asleep.

"May I come?" he asked.

She pushed herself up. "You may."

When the door opened, she saw a slight man dressed in a starched white uniform enter the room. With him was a serving cart, and as she looked it over, she noticed a display of assorted fruit, bread, and cheeses.

"For you," he said with a cursory bow.

"Thank you, Monsieur . . ." she asked, taking measure of him. He appeared meek, humble, definitely not aggressive, she concluded. He was more likely a servant than a guard.

"Chen," he answered. He dropped his gaze and turned to leave.

"Wait." She ventured a few steps toward him. When he turned back, she spoke. "Monsieur Chen, would you kindly tell me where I am."

"I cannot say," he answered, then turned again to leave.

"Am I on an island?"

He paused but did not turn back. "I cannot say."

"Please," she allowed the desperation in her voice, hoping to elicit some sympathy from him and some answers. "I must know where I am."

"I am sorry, miss. I know nothing. I am the cook." He stepped from the room, closing the door behind him. She heard a bolt snap shut and then listened to footsteps fade into the distance.

CHAPTER FIFTEEN

"Andre Beauvais is on line one," Ethan heard his secretary announce. "Isn't he the Prince of Monteaux?"

"Yes, he is," he replied, snapping up the receiver. "Andre, to what do I owe this pleasure?" He slid his keyboard aside.

"Ethan, thank goodness I am able to reach you," he said. Ethan heard the urgency and what he discerned as worry in his voice. "I wish this was a call of pleasure."

"What's wrong?" he asked, hoping the answer was not what he was thinking. "Has something happened to Dominique?"

"She's gone. She's been taken."

The words wrapped around his heart like a vise.

"We just received a ransom note. You were right. They want Lidia's necklaces. All of them." He listened as Andre's sentences spewed out in rapid succession. "Inspector Laroche has been here. He's taking control of the situation—"

"Andre, slow down." He interrupted him as he tried to collect himself. He was going to need his wits about him if he was going to be of any benefit to Dominique. And he was going to need to get as much information as he could. "How long has she been gone?"

"Yesterday. Since yesterday afternoon."

"Does Inspector Laroche have any idea who took her?"

"None. Or at least he's not saying. I'm not sure. I think he's wary about telling us too much if someone inside the palace is involved with this. Frederique was supposed to be looking into that, but he hasn't come up with anything."

"What's Laroche's plan?" One step at a time, he told himself. Slow Andre down. "Do you know that much?"

"At this point, it is to do what Dominique's kidnappers want. To exchange the necklaces for her return. My God, Ethan." He heard Andre's sigh as he paused. It was filled with desperation. "She's my baby sister."

"When is the exchange supposed to happen?"

"From what I understand, it is not simultaneous. We are supposed to deliver the necklaces tomorrow morning. If we do as we are supposed to, then we will get instructions on getting Dominique back. Ethan, I'm not sure I trust Laroche's strategy on this, and I sure don't trust the word of Dominique's kidnappers. I need to know if you have been able to find out anything more."

He hesitated a moment while considering whether to give Andre the information he'd obtained on Van Dousen. The rules of the game had changed now that Dominique had been taken. He didn't know much about Laroche's skills, and if Laroche was careless, he could endanger her further. He couldn't risk Van Dousen finding out he was under suspicion if he was the one behind her abduction. He decided it was too risky to give Andre the information. Besides, this was his specialty. This was one of the things he had been trained to do, and very few soldiers, if any, were better than he at executing missions. He couldn't leave Dominique's rescue up to Laroche.

"Ethan, don't hold out on me. My sister's life is at stake here." He noticed the increasing anxiety in his voice. "If you know anything, I need to know."

"I don't know anything," he replied. "How was the ransom note delivered?"

"Someone paid a kid to deliver it here. He told the kid to wait two hours, then to take the note to one of the guards."

"How are the necklaces to be delivered?"

"I don't know. The delivery is going to involve a series of instructions. The final drop-off point is not known to us."

"Who's going to deliver them?"

"Lidia's nephew, Brian."

"Why Brian?"

"He volunteered."

"The note didn't specify a carrier?"

"No. Do you think that's unusual?"

"I don't know. Did Laroche think it was?"

"He didn't say. Ethan, why do I get the feeling you know more than you're saying?"

"You're desperate, Andre. You'd like to think you have other options."

"Do I?"

"I'll keep trying to come up with something. The more information you can give me, the more I'll have to go on." He was going to need Andre to keep him informed. He was going to need to know what Laroche was doing. "I'll call you tomorrow. Give me a secure number I can reach you on."

"You can reach me on this line. It's secure." He glanced at the number on his phone and entered it into his contacts. "Ethan, if you come up with another option, I want in. You know I'm an expert marksman. I'd be an asset."

"I'll keep that in mind, and I'll keep in touch." He hit the button to his second line and punched in the number to Lance's cell phone.

"Hey, boss," he answered. "I'm boarding now. In line as we speak, in fact."

"Well, get out of line," he instructed. "I want you to exchange your ticket for one to Greece."

"No way. Did you get a lead on someone else?"

"No. Right now, Van Dousen's all we've got to go on, and we've got to move fast."

"What do you want me to do?"

"Fly to Athens. Van Dousen owns an island somewhere in Greece. Work on finding out which one. It's under a lot of layers."

"Boss, aren't there like a couple thousand islands down there?"

"Something like that, but only about two hundred or so are inhabited. That should narrow your search."

"Uh-huh. I don't suppose you happen to have any other information that might narrow my search a little more?"

"I do. Van Dousen's island is in the Ionian Sea, west of Greece, on the Italy side."

"Isn't that where Onassis's island is, Scorpios?"

"Yeah. I guess you can eliminate that one."

"Okay. One down. I'll get right on it."

"He also owns a tour boat company and may have a boat he uses exclusively to get him to the island. Find out if he does, what kind of boat it is, and where he docks it at the mainland. Then get us a couple of rooms at a hotel near the port where he docks it. Oh, yeah, after you find out which island he owns, find out what kind of security is in place, get a map of the island, and copies of the blueprints to all the buildings on the island. Then wait to hear from me."

"Got it, and I'm on my way."

"Good." And so was he. He'd call Smitty and Mike from the road, he decided. He could use a couple buddies with their training and expertise to help him out in the event he was right. He knew they'd be willing. He just hoped they were available.

Dominique walked out onto the balcony and stared out at sea. Swimming to freedom was out of the question, she concluded, even if she could somehow manage to get out of her room and past the guards. She'd probably drown from exhaustion. The closest island she could see was too far away.

She studied the guard patrolling along the cliffs. He walked the entire length of the island, mostly watching the sea. The sun had risen over the horizon a few hours before, telling her that she must be facing east. The sea was already dotted with boats of every sort and size.

A sound outside the room interrupted her surveillance. Closing the balcony door behind her, she stepped inside.

"Miss?" She recognized Chen's voice. It was followed by a soft knock.

"You may enter," she replied.

A key slid in the lock, and the door sprang open. "Your breakfast," he said, avoiding eye contact and rolling a cart into the room.

"Monsieur Chen?"

"Yes?" he replied with a slight bow of his head, his gaze cast down.

"Would it be possible for me to have a change of clothes delivered and perhaps some make-up? Maybe a tube of lipstick?"

"I will ask."

"Would you please also ask if I may stroll the grounds?"

"Yes."

"Thank you."

With a nod, he turned and left.

She looked at the mirror. At least she had a plan.

Ethan booked a reservation on an evening flight leaving for Greece from Dulles International Airport. It gave him enough time to get to the bank, exchange some dollars for Euros, and then pick up some extra clothes and supplies. Mike told him he was going to catch a flight out the next day. He figured he'd pick up the rest of the supplies he anticipated needing once he got to Greece while he looked for a boat, scoped things out, and waited for Mike to arrive. He hadn't been able to reach Smitty, but Mike was going to try before he left.

He tried to convince himself that he wasn't crazy as he turned onto the Beltway and headed toward the Dulles toll road. It had to be Van Dousen. There were too many coincidences. The dead German guy he employed. His interest in jewelry. His father invading Poland during WWII at the same time Lidia's grandfather was trying to escape from there. The artwork purportedly stolen from the family of a Polish survivor. And a private Greek Island buried under layers of ownership, an ideal place to hide things.

"Hell," he muttered. On the other hand, he could be wasting his time. And Mike's, too, he thought. Van Dousen could have no connection to whoever had kidnaped Dominique, and even if he did, it would be quite a risk for him to keep her at one of his residences. What in the hell was he doing? He should call Lance and tell him to get on the next plane home, he told himself, and call Mike and tell him to stay home.

He should get off the next exit for Tyson's Corner and just loop around. He'd be back on the Beltway heading home. And he should let Inspector Laroche do his job. According to Andre, the kidnappers were going to release Dominique once they got the necklaces. Dominique could be back safely at the palace before he even found Van Dousen's island.

He didn't need to be playing soldier, either. That part of his life was over. There was a reason he had been benched after his injury. He had a new career now. He had a business to run, and he had a responsibility to his employees. He shouldn't be running off half-cocked halfway around the world looking for trouble.

"Shit," he mumbled as he swerved onto the ramp, nearly missing the turn.

Chapter Sixteen

"Brian, you don't have to go," Lidia implored. Inspector Laroche was growing impatient with Lidia. She was wasting time arguing with the young man. "It's much too dangerous."

"Lidia, everyone agrees. We can't take a chance by sending an undercover police officer or a member of our security. The instructions warned against that." Laroche heard the evenness in Brian's voice. If he was nervous, there was no sign of it. He's doing fine, he thought. "Besides, the necklaces are a part of our family. It wouldn't be fair to send anyone else to deliver them."

"He will be under constant surveillance by the best of my men," Laroche interrupted to assure her and to get things moving.

"Yes, and the instructions warned against that, too," she reminded him, "and against any kind of tracking device. What if they spot one of your men or find the tracking dot?"

"They will not recognize any of my men, and the dot is well hidden in the lining of one of the boxes. It will not be discovered," he replied, injecting a touch of agitation in his words, which he hoped she'd pick up on. He didn't want to be rude to a staff member, especially one that appeared to be close to King Victor, but they needed to get moving.

"Lidia, come." He was relieved that King Victor intervened as he watched him urge Lidia toward the door. "I'm sure Inspector Laroche knows what he is doing. We must let Brian leave now, or he will be late for the first stop."

Thank goodness, he thought, when he saw Prince Andre and his wife follow them from the room. Now, he could get on with his job.

"Is everyone in place?" Laroche asked, adjusting the voice transmitter on his headset.

"Check. Team one," a voice in his earphone responded, followed in sequence by nine other voices through the last of ten teams.

"Brian, go now," he commanded and walked him to the front entrance of the palace. "And remember what I told you. Do not look around for my men. Do not try to signal them. Do nothing that might inadvertently give them away."

When Brian nodded in agreement, he handed him the black briefcase. He watched him walk from the palace. He was looking straight ahead as he proceeded to the car parked at the bottom of the steps. That's good, Laroche said to himself. Eyes straight ahead. Don't look back. He kept his focus on Brian while he entered the car and then pulled away.

"Team one," he uttered into the microphone as he hurried back to the drawing room that he had set up as a command post. When he entered the room, he was glad to see the four uniformed officers in their places, one at a computer tracking the briefcase in Brian's car, one at a large map outlining the positions of his men in the field, one monitoring communications over a radio transmitter, and one to help coordinate and assist the other three.

"We have a visual," a voice responded.

"Stay put," he ordered, following the location of Brian's car on the computer screen displaying a global positioning satellite map. The car traveled two miles down the road, then turned left.

"We no longer have a visual," the voice of team one responded after the car's turn.

He nodded and cleared his throat. "Team one, proceed."

He watched Brian's car take three more turns. Brian was traveling the route he had mapped out for him. He lowered himself to a chair beside the officer tracking the briefcase, his gaze never leaving the screen. The vehicle stopped for two traffic lights and a stop sign as it inched its way through town.

"Team two."

"We have a visual."

"Team two, stay put," he directed. He calculated from its position that team two would be able to keep Brian in sight for about two and a half miles.

He reached over to a tray of sandwiches and lifted the top slice of bread off of a sandwich.

"Turkey or ham," the officer working the map mumbled.

He grunted, dropped the slice of bread back onto the sandwich, and snatched it from the tray. He leaned back, focused back on the monitor, and took a bite.

"He's passing by the Plaza," the officer at the computer advised.

"Yeah, I see," Laroche replied, swallowing his bite.

"Must be a little bit of traffic there. He seems to be slowing."

"Team two," he said into his microphone.

"We still have a visual. He's stuck in traffic."

A couple of minutes later, the car started picking up speed, and he listened when team two reported in. "He's moving again."

He motioned to the officer keeping track of the teams' positions, and the officer tossed him a bottle of water. He twisted off the cap and downed half the bottle.

"He's on the motorway," a voice from team two reported. "We no longer have a visual."

"Wait ten minutes, then proceed," he instructed. "Team one."

"We're on standby."

"He's now outside the limits of Monteaux, about two miles south of you. Hang tight," he advised the team. He paused as he watched the screen, then continued. "He's about twenty minutes from target. Stay alert. He'll be in the city in a few minutes."

He was silent for a few minutes while the car continued, then directed the team. "Team one, go ahead."

"Affirmative."

"Let me know when you get a visual. He should be upon you in about three minutes," he reported as he checked his watch. He guzzled down the rest of the water, ran the back of his hand over his lips, and sank further into the chair, feeling the nerves starting to kick in.

Three minutes later, team one checked in. "We have a visual."

"Okay. Everyone, stay alert. We're about fifteen minutes from point one."

He tilted forward in his chair and pushed himself up. He paced over to the map and studied the positions of his teams. The first contact point was surrounded by the east, south, north, and west, with teams two deep. The first line of teams was on foot, the second in vehicles. A helicopter was positioned on a roof a block away, and the two teams in transit would be available as backup.

"It's warm in here," he grumbled, tugging on his collar. He loosened the top button of his shirt and then wandered back over to the table. He reached for another bottle of water, twisted off the cap, and pulled down a mouthful.

"Where's Brian now?" he asked, squinting at the monitor as he stood over the officer.

"He's making good time. He's getting off the exit."

"Team one, what's your location?"

"We're about two blocks ahead of the car."

"Okay. Keep your distance."

"We have a visual," team three reported. "He's changing lanes, making his way over. He's in lane two. He just put his signal on and is turning into the garage. He's pulling a ticket . . . the gate is up, and . . . he's in."

"Team four?"

"We're going into the bar now."

"Team three?"

"He parked on the first level. We pulled in about ten spots over. We're with him."

He sucked in a deep breath, dropped back into the chair, then blew the breath out. He listened to the silence in the room and over the air. He watched the monitor as Brian made his way on foot.

A few minutes later, team three checked in. "He's in, and we're going back to position."

"We've got him," team four reported. "He took a seat at the bar."

"Team five?" Laroche asked.

"We're in the alley. It's quiet back here."

He tapped his fingers on the table. He was feeling the tension grow. He removed a pill from his pocket and placed it under his tongue. He took another drink of water and then waited as he listened to the silence and watched the stillness.

Ten minutes passed. It's the waiting that's the worst, he thought. The waiting made him wonder what was happening that he and the team couldn't see. It gave him time to think about what could go wrong.

"Team four, anything?"

"Negative. He's still at the bar. Alone."

"Any exchange with the bartender?"

"Nothing out of the ordinary. Brian ordered a drink. The bartender delivered it."

"Anyone paying particular attention to him?"

"Doesn't appear to be. Wait a minute."

"What? Don't tell me to wait a minute. What's going on?" he demanded.

"The bartender just slid the phone over to him . . . he's taking a call . . . he's nodding . . . he's hanging up . . . he's leaving . . . with the briefcase."

"Team six. Heads up," he ordered.

"We've got him. He just came out. He's headed south."

"Stay on him," he ordered as he watched the screen. "How's he doing?"

"Good. Looking good."

"It looks like he's going back to the garage," he commented. "Team six?"

"That's an affirmative."

"Keep your eyes on him and the briefcase until they are back in the car."

"Yes, sir."

"Team five, get in position to follow him once he gets out of the garage," he instructed as he leaped from his chair and took two quick strides over to the map.

"We're on our way."

"Team seven, I want you three blocks to the north of the garage."

"Check."

"Team eight, three blocks to the south."

"Check."

"Team nine, three blocks to the east."

"Check."

"Team ten, three blocks to the west."

"Check."

As he spit out orders, he made sure the officer covering the map moved the push pins into their new locations.

"Team one, team two, team three hold your positions. Team six, report."

"Brian and the briefcase are back in the car. He's moving."

"Team six, team four, get to your cars and hold position."

"On our way," team four responded, echoed by team six.

"Team five."

"We have a visual. He's paying for his ticket."

He wiped the sweat from his brow and studied his men's positions. "Damn, it's hot in here."

"He's headed east," team five reported.

"Team nine."

"We have a visual."

"Pick him up. Team five, head south a block and then turn east and parallel him."

"Heading south now."

"Team ten, turn around and head east. Team seven, head east parallel to him. Team eight, the same."

"On our way."

"We're moving."

"He just turned left. He's headed south," the officer at the monitor reported.

"Team nine, stay with him," he ordered as he stepped back for a wider view of the map. "Team seven, location."

"He just passed through the intersection. We can pick him up."

"Go ahead. Team nine, back off. Team ten, team eight, head south. Team four, get on Chateau and head south. Team six, get over to Blanc and head south." He popped another pill into his mouth and strode over to the monitor. He watched over the officer's shoulder as Brian's car continued south. "He's slowing down. Team seven?"

"Traffic. It's getting congested. There's construction going on, but we're still on him. Damn."

"What?"

"A bus just cut us off. We lost visual."

"Team eight, team ten, get over to Olivier and get on him." His gaze bore into the monitor. "It looks like he's turning.

He's heading west. Damnit! Does anyone have a visual?"

"Shit, we just passed him," team seven reported. "He pulled into a parking garage. It's the parking garage to the Hotel Farber. We're going to have to circle around."

"Team ten, report."

"We're about twenty seconds from target."

"Team eight?"

"We're stuck in traffic about four blocks away."

"Team ten, when you get to the hotel, I want a man inside pronto." He swiped at the beads of sweat forming around his brow. "He just parked. Team seven, where the hell are you?"

"Still circling, sir. Traffic's thick."

"We're here," team ten responded. "We're going inside."

"All other teams, form a perimeter around the hotel. Teams seven, eight, and nine, I want you on foot. The rest stay in your cars, staggering within two blocks of the hotel. Check in when you're in position." He groped his pocket for his pills, pulled one out, slid it into his mouth, then chomped down hard on it. "Team ten, anything?"

"He's not in the lobby. He may not be in from the garage yet. We're going to check the elevators."

"Someone damn well better get a visual," he ordered between clenched teeth.

"Team eight, reporting. We're in position. We're covering the garage exit."

"Team seven, reporting. We're out front. We'll cover the hotel entrance."

"Team nine?"

"We're headed inside the garage now."

"He's moving," he reported, his attention focused on the monitor. "He's there somewhere."

"Team ten, reporting. We have a visual. He's heading into the lobby."

"Does he have the briefcase with him?"

"Affirmative."

He released a long, relieved breath. This job is going to kill me someday, he thought. "Keep your eyes on him."

"He's going out the front entrance."

"We have a visual," team seven reported. "We're with him."

"Team eight, follow him from across the street. Team ten, follow him behind team seven. Team nine, stay with the car. Everyone else, stay in position. Do you have everyone accounted for?" he asked the officer mapping the teams' locations.

"Yes, sir."

"Good. Toss me another water. It's damn hot in here."

"Yes, sir."

He unscrewed the cap and guzzled the entire bottle before settling his gaze back on the monitor. "He's not moving. What's going on?"

"He's at the corner, waiting to cross," one of the teams replied.

"Do you see anyone following him?"

"Negative. Not that we can tell."

"Excuse me, Inspector." He recognized the king's voice and looked up to see him in the doorway. Just what I need, he thought, to be interrupted by the king when things are getting critical.

"Yes, sir?" he answered and stood up.

"I thought I'd come in for an update. Has Brian delivered the necklaces yet?"

"Not yet. As far as we can tell, he's headed to a second point of contact as we speak." He glanced down at the monitor, then raised his gaze again to the king. "I'll report to you as soon as something happens."

"Very well," he replied and turned from the room.

"Well, what did he say? What's happening?" Andre asked his father when he returned to the parlor. Victor stared down at Andre. He was perched on the arm of the chair Francine was sitting in. He could see the stress on his son's face.

"Nothing yet." He shook his head as he lowered himself to a chair and tried to convince himself that everything was going to work out, and Dominique would soon be safely returned to him. "Brian still has the necklaces. He's waiting to be contacted again."

"I don't have a good feeling about this." Andre's words sliced through Victor like a cold, steel knife. He didn't need that kind of negative talk. He watched Andre slide off the arm of the chair and walk over to the liquor cabinet. Two bottles of *Macallan* scotch were sitting on the marble countertop. He watched him pour a generous amount from one of the bottles into a glass. "Anybody care to join me?"

"Father?" he asked when no one answered.

"No, not now." That was the last thing he needed.

"I don't know why Laroche insists that we stay out of the drawing room," Andre remarked, strolling over to the door. He watched Andre look down the hall in the direction of the command post, then swallow half the contents of his glass. "Other than that he doesn't want us to see him bungle things."

"Andre, you're making the rest of us more nervous with remarks like that," Francine said.

"Tell me, son, how would you handle things?" Victor demanded, aware that his nerves were wearing and his patience was thinning. Francine's right, he thought. Andre's remarks are just putting everyone more on edge.

"Well, Father, for starters, I would not be turning over all of the necklaces at once. Laroche is giving away all of our leverage."

"The instructions called for all of the necklaces to be delivered at once. To do anything other than that would put your sister's life in jeopardy." He knew he was defending his own decision, since he had approved Laroche's strategy, and he was aware that decision was weighing on him. But he'd had no choice, he reasoned. Laroche was the expert in these matters. He had to rely on him.

"It's already in jeopardy." Andre knocked back another gulp and finished what was left in the glass. "And I would have demanded proof that Dominique is safe."

"And how would you have done that?" He heard the anger in his own voice and knew better than to let Andre's words provoke him, but it did no good knowing it. "You would have picked up the telephone and called whom?"

"I don't know," Andre snapped back. "I'm not an expert at these things."

"None of us are," Lidia said. "And I think that's why we all feel so helpless."

"Lidia's right. We have no choice but to trust that Laroche knows what he is doing." Saying it aloud didn't make it any easier to accept than thinking it, he decided. He had to admit, he didn't like having to trust Laroche any more than Andre did at this point.

"I wish I could, Father. I just don't like feeling that I'm at the mercy of Dominique's kidnappers."

"None of us do." He lifted a hand to his face, stretched it across his forehead, and pressed his fingers against his temples. "I can't stand this waiting," he said, softening his voice. He stood up and crossed over to the window. He sighed as he brushed aside a heavy panel of drapery and stared at the grounds outside.

He felt Lidia touch his arm with an affection only he would sense. Her touch was discreet. They were both always cautious with their affection when others were present. "Victor,

I'm so sorry," she whispered, and when he looked at her, her eyes were brimming with tears. "I had no idea asking Dominique to wear the necklaces would put her in danger. I should never have asked her. It was unprofessional of me to do so."

"Nonsense." He glanced back at Andre and Francine, and satisfied that they were too involved in comforting each other to notice anything else, he slid his hand over Lidia's. He stroked hers between his fingers, then raised it to his lips and kissed it before lowering it back to his arm. "No one could have known there was someone out there who wanted those necklaces so desperately they would kill for them. And knowing my daughter the way I do, I'm sure she was honored to wear them." He placed his fingers under her chin and lifted her face to his. "I feel blessed that your love for my daughter runs so deeply. You have given her things that I could never give her. Her mother died when she was much too young to be without one. You filled the absence left by her death. If you think doing that is unprofessional, then you are wrong. I consider such devotion a gift and one for which I am very grateful."

"She's easy to love, Victor, and don't think that I was the only one filling a need. Dominique has enriched my life in so many ways, as well." She drew her hand from his arm and pulled her gaze from his. "I feel like I've failed her."

"I don't want to hear another word like that." His voice carried across the room, drawing the attention of Andre and Francine. "You are not responsible, and no one is blaming you."

"Lidia, how could you have possibly predicted the actions of a madman?" Francine asked, frustration surfacing in her voice. "It is as much a waste of energy for you to blame yourself as it is for Andre to be so aggravated, and it will accomplish nothing. We all need to be positive and alert so that when Inspector Laroche comes in here and tells us what our next options are, we can make intelligent decisions."

"I agree. We should be making the decisions," Andre said, slamming his empty glass down on the table beside Francine and shooting to his feet, "not sitting here like a bunch of moronic imbeciles blindly taking orders from someone with absolutely no personal stake in the matter."

"Andre, where do you think you are going?" Victor called after Andre, seeing him sprint from the parlor. "Do not distract Inspector Laroche," he ordered, marching after him. "I forbid you to interfere with what they are doing."

"Andre," Francine called from behind him.

Andre stopped in the doorway to the drawing room. When Victor reached him, he saw that Francine and Lidia had left the parlor and had caught up to them. He turned when he heard Laroche's voice spitting out orders over the splattering of voices booming from a radio. Laroche was dripping in sweat with his tie dangling under the opened collar of his shirt. His hands were clenched in fists as he paced feverishly from a map to the radio, to a monitor, and then back again.

"He's crossing in the middle of the street," a voice reported, "right in front of a bus. We lost visual. The bus is blocking him now."

"Team ten?" Laroche spit into his microphone.

"No visual, the bus is blocking him."

"Team eight?" Laroche asked next.

"No . . . wait . . . okay . . . we've got him. He's on our side of the street now."

Laroche stopped long enough to exhale before resuming his frantic pace back over to the monitor. "What direction is he headed in?"

"None. He's not moving."

Victor continued watching and listening to the activity from the doorway. The officer on the monitor nodded, and there was an abrupt silence for about ten seconds before a voice cracked over the radio.

"East. He's moving east again."

The officer at the monitor nodded.

"Team seven, I want you a half a block in front of him, then cross over to his side."

"Affirmative."

"He's crossing over to Fleur, still heading east," a voice from the radio advised. "He's got two blocks before he has to change course. Fleur ends two blocks up."

"Team seven, head south at the end," Laroche instructed. "Team four, I want you a block to the south. Team five, a block to the north."

"He stopped," someone over the radio reported. "He's not moving."

"What do you mean? He's still heading east," Laroche responded.

"Negative. He's not traveling."

"Does he still have the briefcase?"

"Affirmative."

Laroche studied the monitor. "He's got to be moving. The signal shows he's still heading east," he insisted.

"That's impossible, sir. There's a building blocking easterly travel."

The officer at the monitor looked up at Laroche and shrugged. "The signal shows that the briefcase is still traveling east."

"What's Brian doing now?"

"Nothing. He hasn't moved."

"He's got to be moving!"

"Negative, sir."

Victor stepped into the drawing room and positioned himself where he could see the monitor.

Laroche raked his fingers through his hair, then squinted

down at the monitor. "How can that be?" Laroche muttered. The dot Laroche was following was moving to the east. Laroche jogged over to the map and dragged his finger across Fleur. Sure enough, the map showed Fleur Street stopping at a dead end. Laroche raced back to the monitor. The dot was still traveling east.

Something was wrong, and he fought to push the fear aside when Laroche turned and looked at him, his eyes saturated with confusion.

CHAPTER SEVENTEEN

Ethan walked down the long, winding street from the hotel that led to the fishing village and then rambled along the waterfront. He'd had to come to Greece. He'd come largely on instinct, but he had always trusted his instincts. He had fallen in love with Dominique, and he knew if Van Dousen was behind her kidnapping and she was there, he'd never be able to live with himself if he did nothing. And if she was there, he was going to put his fist down Van Dousen's throat and rip his organs out one by one.

He was smart enough to know nothing would become of him and Dominique. She had made that clear. He just wanted to make sure she was safe. Then he could get on with his life. Besides, Andre had asked him for his help. And, he had a score to settle with Van Dousen. If he was behind things, it was his men who had tried to kill him. Twice.

"Yeah," he said, answering a call from Lance.

"Boss, I was researching the security network on the island, and you were right. I was able to get the system to hack into it." There was no mistaking the excitement in Lance's voice. Ethan had heard it before. "I just wanted to let you know, I saw the princess. I saw her. She's there. She's on the island."

"Good work, kid." The exhilaration of knowing she was there and within his reach rolled through him as he shoved his phone in his pocket. Game on, he thought to himself, grateful he had relied on his instincts and hadn't wasted any time getting there.

He walked past the quaint shops and cafes that lured tourists to their doors with their local goods and rich, savory aromas without so much as a glance. He had no interest in the tourist attractions. He needed to find a watering hole where the locals hung out. Since there were certain supplies that they were going to need that he hadn't been able to bring with him on the plane, the seedier the bar, the better.

He stared out over the boats. Even after much modernization, most of Greece's fishing fleets consisted of relatively small boats, and by late morning, many of them had already set out to sea for the day. Those that remained behind dotted the harbor with splashes of bright colors.

He figured they'd be far less conspicuous motoring around the island in a fishing boat. They'd blend right in with all the other fishing boats that scattered themselves around the islands. He'd planned on spending at least a full day studying the island once they found it, familiarizing themselves with the geography, learning the occupants' routines, and of course, hopefully seeing Dominique in the flesh.

The sound of boisterous, drunken laughter spilling out into the waterfront and the scruffy duo stumbling from the doorway following it drew his attention. He stopped to watch the two men. They staggered their way down one of the docks, slapping and shoving each other along the way. His lips cracked into a grin as he watched in amusement — one of the men tripped and fell backward onto a boat. The other man howled until he saw someone on the boat come out of the cabin, shout at them, then grab the man that had fallen. The man on the dock launched himself off the dock and onto the two men.

For a minute, all three men wrestled among themselves on the floor of the boat. He strolled toward the boat to get a better view of the scuffle. The man who had been on the boat was the first to get to his feet and got in a few decent jabs as the other two men struggled to upright themselves. Once vertical, though, the two drunkards overpowered the other man. He received a sharp blow to the stomach from one of the men and a solid punch to the kidney by the other. That must have hurt, Ethan imagined, grimacing.

It hardly seems fair for the poor sucker who had been on the boat minding his own business to be getting such a beating, he thought, and no one seems the least bit interested in intervening to help the poor guy. Maybe if he gave him a hand, he'd return the favor. The boat was a pretty good size, bigger than most, he figured, as he sized it up over the tussle. It looked a little tired and worn, though. At the least, maybe the guy knew someone who might be able to help him get what he needed. What the hell, he thought as he leaped onto the boat. It was worth a shot.

He grabbed the man who had delivered the shot to the kidney by the back of the collar and spun him around. The surprise on his face was met with a set of knuckles to the nose. As he stumbled backward, Ethan helped him over the back of the boat with a foot to the gut. He hit the water with a whale-like splash. A second later, the second man sailed past him over the back of the boat headfirst into the water. Both men slapped and kicked at the water as they swam away in a storm of yelling and cursing.

Ethan turned to a bronzed, leathery face that looked as if it had been touched too many times by the sun. The man's young, well-toned frame left no doubt, though, that he wasn't as old as his complexion suggested. He was just a little older than Ethan was, he guessed.

The man's gaze followed a crow that flew above them. He muttered under his breath. "*Sto kalo, sto kalo, kala nea na me feris.*"

"Go to the good, go the good and bring me good news," Ethan repeated in English.

The man looked at him and nodded. "You understand Greek. You know that crows are a bad omen?"

"You speak English," Ethan replied. "I know it's an old Greek superstition. Ethan Moore." He extended his hand to the man. "I take it they weren't friends of yours."

The man paused before he took his hand and long enough for Ethan to know he was taking measure of him. "Nikko Pappasopolous. And no, I wouldn't consider them among my friends."

Ethan bent over and scooped up Nikko's fisherman's cap, which had flown off during the fight, and tossed it to him. Nikko slapped it against his leg, snapping it back in shape, combed his fingers through his dark, wavy locks, and set the cap in place.

"Thanks," he said and turned to go back inside the cabin.

"I take it you're a fisherman?"

"What's it to you?" he asked before stopping and turning back to Ethan.

"Actually, it's your boat I'm interested in." Ethan took a step back and leaned against the side of the boat. Then making himself comfortable, he crossed his arms over his chest.

"And what's so interesting about my boat?"

He sensed an uneasiness in his question despite the coolness in Nikko's voice.

"Nothing other than it's a fishing boat, and I'm looking to charter one for a few days."

"I don't do fishing charters," he said.

"I'm not looking to fish," Ethan replied.

"Then what do you need a fishing boat for?"

"I need to get to an island."

"There are ferries and hydrofoils that do that."

"I'm not planning on disembarking right away."

"There are yachts you can charter. They're much more comfortable than this."

163

"I'm looking to be . . . inconspicuous in an unostentatious sort of way."

Nikko lifted a hand to his chin and strolled over to him. He stopped in front of him and raised an eyebrow. "What is it exactly you are planning to do?"

"Let's just say I'm trying to find a certain woman, and I'm willing to make it worth your while to help me find her. Of course," he continued as he glanced over the boat, "the boat's got to be seaworthy, and its captain needs to know his way around the islands."

Nikko tossed his head and laughed. "A woman." He yanked loose the bowline that was securing the boat to the dock and motioned to Ethan. "Come," he said as he ducked inside the cabin. Ethan followed him and listened to the engine cough and sputter when Nikko turned the ignition key. On the next attempt, the engine turned over. "We can talk privately away from here. There are too many nosey people around."

Ethan glanced around the inside of the cabin as Nikko guided the boat from the harbor. The engine knocked and banged as it pushed the boat wearily through the water.

"I know the islands like the back of my hand," Nikko shouted over the clatter of the motor. "My grandfather was a fisherman. He fished all of these seas. He used to take me out with him all the time when I was little."

Ethan shook his head with a frown. "When was the last time you had the engine serviced?"

Nikko grinned and shrugged.

A mile out, Nikko turned the ignition key off, and with a loud clank, the engine died. It was silent for a moment except for the lapping of the sea against the boat and the buzzing of motors in the distance. Then Nikko pressed a button. Like magic, the engine effortlessly turned over and purred like a kitten. "My backup engine," Nikko said with a wink.

Ethan raised a brow.

"Let's just say I didn't exactly follow in my grandfather's footsteps."

Nikko eased down on the throttle and the boat skimmed over the water. Ethan assumed he was showing off when he steered to the left and then cut to the right and followed up with a few slick maneuvers. When they were clear of the path of other boats, Nikko cut off the engine and let the boat drift.

"Now, we can talk," Nikko said and stepped out onto the back deck. Ethan followed him. The sun was warm. "Ah," Nikko said, filling his lungs. "There's nothing like the smell of the sea." He pulled a pack of cigarettes from his pocket and offered one to Ethan.

"No thanks. I don't smoke," he said, stepping onto the deck. He cast his gaze over the sea, wondering if any of the islands visible from the boat were holding Dominique.

"Good thing. Nasty habit." He struck a match, then touched it to the end of the cigarette and took a draw. "Tell me about this woman. Just how much is she worth to you?"

He studied Nikko. He figured whatever Nikko was into, it probably wasn't entirely legal. Not that it mattered, as long as he didn't attract any unwanted attention, and he seemed careful not to. He was sure he could handle Nikko, and as long as either he, Mike, or Lance was around to watch him, he could trust him. "It's a little more complicated than simply motoring up to the island and picking her up."

Nikko chuckled. A puff of smoke swirled from his lips, then floated away. "Things usually are more complicated when a woman's involved." He took a pull on his cigarette and continued. "I take it she doesn't want to leave the island?"

"Something like that." He'd inform Nikko on an as-needed basis, he decided. As far as he was aware, Dominique's kidnapping hadn't hit the papers yet, and there was no need to tell Nikko about it. He didn't need to know all the details.

"Her host won't be too happy to see her leave. Things could get a little . . . sticky."

"I see. So you'll need some . . ."

"Firepower," Ethan finished for him. He slid his hands into his pockets and leaned against the side of the boat. "Is that something you can handle?"

"Not a problem. Tell me what you need." He took one last drag of his cigarette, then dropped it to the deck and stamped it out.

"Pistols, semi-automatics will do, rifles preferably with scopes, knives with sheaths."

"Will you have . . . help . . . or shall I recruit—"

"I have a team."

"And when are we leaving?"

"Tomorrow morning. Five o'clock."

Nikko nodded. "Okay, my friend. It sounds like we have a lot to do before morning. Let's get down to business."

By the time Ethan returned to the hotel, Mike was there and already studying maps and photographs of the island. Lance was supplementing the blueprints with what he could observe from the security network and downloading videos and photographs of the interior of the structures.

"The island is less than three square miles. It looks like there's a cove on this side," Mike said, running his finger along the map. "We might be able to get a boat pretty close to it. Looks like there's a forest of trees obscuring the view on this side of the island. Since there's a cliff here, there's a chance they don't even patrol this area. The drawback is that we'd have to scale the cliff to get on the island."

"How far is it to the buildings from there?" Ethan asked, hovering over his shoulder and studying the map.

"Looks about three-quarters of a mile, maybe a little more."

"How secure are the buildings from a wiring standpoint?"

"Not very. They're solar-powered. We can interrupt the

power, but there's a generator for backup. We'd have to disable the security network before the generator kicks on."

"You'd think he'd feel secure enough just being on an island."

"You'd think, but it looks like he's got a vault in the main building. Look," Mike said, pointing to a dense square. "It looks like it's temperature controlled."

"It could be for wine. After all, the man's a winemaker."

"Look how thick the walls are. And look here," Mike continued. "Look how thick these walls are. He's protecting something in that room."

"Hey, boss," Lance cut in. He was sitting cross-legged on one of the beds with his computer in his lap. "You got an e-mail from the office. It says you got a call from Andre Beauvais. He left a message saying it was urgent that you call him."

"How long ago did he call?" he asked, backing off of Mike. He tugged his cell phone from his pocket and strolled over to the window. He pulled back the curtain a crack and peered out, then let it drop.

"Uh ... let's see ... with the time difference ... that's about ... about ... four hours ago. He left a number. Do you want it?"

"Yeah, give it to me."

Lance rattled it off, and Ethan compared it with the number Andre had told him was a secure line. The numbers matched. He punched it in and waited. An anxious voice answered almost instantly. "This is Andre speaking."

"Andre, Ethan here. I just got your message."

"Thank God you called. Have you been able to come up with anything?"

"What's going on there? Did something happen?"

"We've lost the necklaces. The kidnappers got them without Laroche's men noticing."

"How did that happen?"

"Brian was crossing the street and someone popped up from a manhole and switched the briefcases. Laroche's men didn't see the switch. The person took the jewels out of the briefcase and then sent the briefcase floating down the sewer under the street. By the time the briefcase floated under a building and Laroche's men noticed and retrieved it, then figured out what happened, there was no trace of anyone or the necklaces."

"And Dominique?"

"We've heard nothing. No instructions on where she is or where to pick her up or when she'll be returned. I can't just sit here and do nothing." Ethan heard the crack in his voice as he continued. "I have to do something. Tell me if you have any information that might help us find Dominique. I don't care if it's confirmed or not."

"Hang in there, Andre. I'm working on things."

"To find Dominique? When I called your office, they said you were out of the office for a week. Does it have anything to do with Dominique?"

"Like I said, I'm working on things." As much as he wanted to ease Andre's anxiety, there was no way he was going to risk telling him anything. He was too close to getting Dominique from Van Dousen, and he had no intention of jeopardizing his mission.

"Ethan, we need your help."

"I understand. Call me if you hear from the kidnappers. In the meantime, trust me. I'll call you when I have something."

"All right. I will. I do. Thank you, Ethan."

Ethan tossed his phone on the dresser and released a slow breath.

"Was that her father?" Mike asked.

He shook his head. "Her brother."

"It didn't sound good from this end of the conversation."

"It's not. Van Dousen got the necklaces, and they, as we

know, didn't get Dominique." He looked over the equipment spread across the floor. Binoculars, cables, ropes, a tarp, wetsuits, scuba tanks, waterproof containers, and a myriad of other items. "Let's start packing, shall we? We've got an early boat to catch."

The night was still as Dominique stared out over the quiet sea and thought about her family. She knew they were furious with her for sneaking out of the palace and frantic with worry. She vowed to never complain about her royal duties if she ever saw them again. She had gotten much more than what she had bargained for with Ethan, and she would be grateful for it.

She clutched the tube of lipstick in her hand, walked over to the bed, and set it on the nightstand. It had been delivered with the few items of clothes she had requested. It was red. That's good, she thought.

CHAPTER EIGHTEEN

Nikko was right, Ethan thought, pleased that he'd managed to find him as easily as he had. He knew the islands like the back of his hand and had found Van Dousen's island with little effort. The generous-sized yacht moored to the dock with the name *Precious Gem* blazoned across the stern confirmed it. According to Lance, the yacht was registered under the most recent name that Van Dousen had used to purchase the island.

They circled the island once with no sign of Dominique but had been able to determine that only two men patrolled the island in the morning.

"Looks like they mostly stick to the inside perimeter of the trees," Ethan observed through binoculars as Nikko slowed the boat and cut the engine quite a distance away.

"Yeah, and they look pretty bored," Mike added, peering through another pair of binoculars. "Not like they're expecting any visitors."

"That'll work in our favor," Ethan remarked.

"I hope she is worth it," Nikko said. When Ethan glanced over, Nikko allowed a lovesick grin to spread over his face.

"Just do your job," he said, ignoring the grin and lifting his binoculars. "Look like you're doing something."

"Boss, are you in love with her?" Lance asked. Ethan heard the amusement in Lance's voice and didn't bother to look over.

"Why else do you think he flew halfway around the world and dragged our asses out here?" Mike asked.

"Damn," Lance replied. "That hadn't occurred to me. How'd I miss that?"

"That's enough speculation about my motives." Ethan lowered his binoculars. He needed a break. "As it happens, I'm doing this strictly as a favor to her family."

"Of course." Nikko agreed, but Ethan saw the wink he tossed to Lance. "And as we all know, pigs fly, too," he added before erupting into laughter. "That's all right, my friend," he said as he calmed his laughter and slapped a hand on Ethan's shoulder. "We've all been put under the spell of a woman at one time or another. And if Aphrodite or Eros had a hand in your affliction, you cannot blame yourself for your weakness for this woman or for any chaos that may surround her. The gods can be mischievous in their adventures into the lives of mortals."

Ethan shrugged off his hand and his comments without a word, assuming the less he said, the sooner the subject would be closed.

"Aphrodite? Eros?"

"Ah, Lance, you have much to learn about the Greek gods," Nikko began. "Aphrodite is the goddess of love. It is said that her father's genitals were cut off and tossed into the sea. The immortal flesh eventually spread into a circle of white foam, and from this foam, Aphrodite was created. According to most legends, Eros is her son, the god of love. He harnesses the force of love and directs it into mortals."

"Nikko, when you're finished giving Lance his mythology lesson, how about a snack?" Mike asked. "It looks like it's going to be a long day. I need to stay nourished."

"Ah, yes," he replied. "We did start early today."

"Maybe she isn't allowed outside," Lance offered. Ethan watched Lance kick off his sneakers and tilt back on the small box he was using as a chair.

"*Skorda!*" Nikko rushed over and righted Lance's sneakers

and then spit on them three times. This is going to be an interesting mission, Ethan thought, waiting for Lance's reaction.

"Hey, what the hell are you doing, dude?" Lance shot back, bouncing forward on the box.

"Never leave your shoes on their sides, Lance," Ethan said with a chuckle.

"That's right. You'll bring bad luck on us all," Nikko warned.

"So, did you have to drop a loogie on them?"

Nikko nodded. "It helps to ward off evil spirits."

"I hope you're not planning on warding off spirits from our snack," Lance retorted.

"Only if you request it," Nikko replied with a laugh.

"Maybe I'll help you with our snack," Lance suggested, rising from the box.

"Whatever you want," Nikko replied as he flipped up a bench, revealing an icebox built into the boat underneath the bench.

Lance surveyed its contents, and a smile spread across his face. Ethan turned back toward the island, lifted the binoculars, and resumed his recon. "Wow," Lance remarked, "this thing's full of shit. Drinks, cheese, olives, meats, bread. It's like a little deli in there. And here I thought we'd be roughing it."

"This is nothing," Nikko replied. "If I throw out a net, we can have fresh fish for lunch and dinner."

"Mike, do you see that?" Ethan asked.

"Yeah. A new guard." He looked at his watch. "Is he relieving him for a break, or is his shift over?"

"We'll see," Ethan replied. "But that makes five so far. Two guards per shift. Two shifts so far. Lance, you got that?"

"Yeah, boss, got it," he replied.

"Here. You slice the tomato," Nikko said.

"I can do that," Lance replied. "Nikko, what is it you do?"

"You mean, like a job?"

"Yeah."

"A little of this. A little of that."

"And what is this and that, exactly?" Ethan grinned at Lance's persistence. Not a bad thing, he decided, as long as it doesn't get him into trouble.

"Why do you want to know?"

"Just curious."

"There is a problem in Albania," he began. Ethan listened as Nikko's voice trailed off. He assumed Nikko went into the cabin to make their sandwiches or whatever it was he was going to make. The boat was small enough to hear Nikko from the deck while he continued. "Albania is a rich source for women and children trafficked for sex or labor. They are forced to prostitute and beg. Sometimes they are tricked into leaving Albania. Sometimes they are abducted. Sometimes they are sold by their families."

"I had no idea," Lance said. "And they are brought to Greece?"

"Largely. Often they are then shipped on to other countries."

"What do you have to do with it?" Lance asked.

"I find the children and the young girls that are put to work in Greece or those that are brought here before they are sent on. I steal them back and return them. There are people in Albania that reunite them with their families. Or, in the case the children were sold by their families, they take care of them."

I'll be damned, Ethan thought. He would have never figured that was what Nikko was up to.

"Did you hear that?" Mike asked under his breath.

"Yeah," he replied.

"I would have never guessed," Mike remarked.

"Me, either," Ethan agreed. "I have to admit. I'm impressed," he added, then continued listening.

"Dude, I'm surprised. That's really —"

"Shh! Do not say it," Nikko warned. "The evil eye. No compliments."

"The evil eye? Should I spit on you?" Lance offered. Ethan grinned when he heard Lance gurgle up a mouthful of saliva.

"No. And it is not a slimy spit. It is just *ptew*. Like that," he said, demonstrating.

"Got it. *Ptew*," Lance repeated. "So, do you work with someone?"

"No."

Ethan lowered his binoculars and turned to Nikko when he heard him step from the cabin onto the deck.

"I hire when I have money. Otherwise, I do this myself. Even if I save only one at a time, it is one less life that will suffer."

Ethan took the plate Nikko handed to him and set it down beside him.

"So, how do you make a living at that? These people in Albania pay you?" Lance asked from behind Nikko, then set a plate down beside Mike.

"Sometimes they pay me," he said with a shrug. "Sometimes I steal from the people who exploit the children."

Ethan bit into the pita, then raised his binoculars back to the island. A fusion of rich, spicy flavors burst inside his mouth. He had to hand it to Nikko. He knew how to make a hell of a pita.

"It must be dangerous."

"Yes, but I am a cautious man."

"He's back," Ethan said between chews. "See that, Mike?"

"Yeah. Twenty minutes precisely. Must have been a break."

"Nikko," Ethan said and lowered his binoculars.

"Yes?"

"Let's circle around to the other side of the island," he said. "Slowly."

"Whatever you say," he replied and ducked back inside the cabin.

Lance took a seat on the small box he had claimed previously, snagged a bite from his plate, and picked up a pair of binoculars. "I can take watch now," he offered.

"Okay," Ethan replied. "Mike, why don't you take a break?"

"Will do," he agreed.

Ethan studied the island as they circled, making mental notes and refining the details of the preliminary plan they had worked over the evening before. When they approached the other side, he looked at his watch and nodded. "Good," he muttered. "No guard in sight."

Lance lowered his binoculars and scribbled down some notes.

Ethan kept his binoculars to his eyes as the boat motored along the length of the residence. "What the . . ." he murmured as he caught a flash of light. He steadied his binoculars and waited. Another spark caught his gaze, and he narrowed his sight on a balcony on the second floor. His heart gave a little kick as he saw a figure holding what he guessed must be a mirror. "I'll be damned," he said as the glass lit up under the sun's rays. They were too far out to be able to see any detail, but he knew it was Dominique. He could feel it.

"Lance, do you see that?"

"What, boss?" he asked.

"The mirror. The signal. Halfway up, two-thirds in."

"Uh . . . hold on. I was taking notes. Let me see . . . Yeah. I see it. We're too far away. We have to get closer."

"Nikko," Ethan called out.

"Yes?" he answered.

"Get us in closer."

"How much?"

"About a mile," he estimated.

"Ah," he replied. "Then we will go trawling."

Ethan joined Nikko in the cabin while they motored closer toward the island. Mike helped him unfold and spread out photos and blueprints of the island and buildings while Lance hid the equipment that had either accumulated on the deck or had never been stowed. He looked over when he heard the engine stop and then watched Nikko move onto the deck with Lance and set the net. When Nikko returned with Lance, he jockeyed for a comfortable position in the tight space while Mike and Lance did the same and Nikko started the engine.

He kept his eyes on the residence while Lance fumbled with the photos and blueprints beside him. He heard Mike curse from somewhere below. They had been cruising for what felt like hours in the cramped space when he decided to take another look. He lifted the binoculars to the balcony and saw Dominique standing in the doorway. She appeared close enough to touch, and his heart gave an unexpected jolt as a smile unfolded from his lips. She was holding a mirror. Down the length of it, the letters HELP were painted in red.

"This is good, Nikko," he said. Nikko turned off the engine and then walked onto the back deck. He leaned over the stern and tugged on the net, then he twisted it and tugged on it again, giving the impression to anyone watching them that he was repairing or untangling it. He pulled part of it from the water and took his time as he threaded it through his fingers.

"What's going on?" Mike asked as he emerged from under the front of the boat.

"We know where she is," Ethan answered with a nod and tossed him a pair of binoculars.

Mike lifted them to his eyes. "Yep. I see her."

Ethan reeled off specifics of the location of the balcony

while Mike confirmed and Lance marked them on the photographs and the blueprints. When he was finished, he checked the location of the guard. He was making his way back up the side of the island toward the residence. He jerked the binoculars back to the balcony. Dominique and the mirror were gone. She must have been watching the guard, he figured, relieved. She had left the doors open, but it was too dark inside to see.

He focused back on the guard just as he was raising a pair of binoculars.

He grabbed Lance and pulled him down while Mike snatched the blueprints and photos off the counter and dropped to the floor. "Nikko," he called out to him. "We're being watched."

"No problem." Ethan peered over the deck. Nikko's back was to the island, and he continued fumbling with the net. "We will give him nothing of interest to look at."

Ethan felt the boat drift in the afternoon wind and saw the stern began to turn toward the island. "Nikko, we're turning," he called to him.

"I can see that."

"Well, get your ass in here before he gets a clear shot into the cabin."

"I'm on my way." Ethan watched him thread the rest of the net through his fingers and toss it back over the stern. Enough with the superstitions, he thought as Nikko spit into the net before finally returning to the cabin. "I see him. There are two guards. Wait," Nikko said. "One of them is walking toward the building. The other one is continuing along the cliff."

"Lance?"

He checked his watch. "Got it, boss," he said, and Ethan tossed him his notebook.

"Nikko, let's go back out and circle around again," he instructed.

Nikko nodded and guided the boat away from the island.

He had him circle the island from further out a few more times as he and Mike gathered more information. Evening was approaching. The wind had picked up, and the sun was beginning to set. He noted that the *Precious Gem* hadn't left the dock all day, and he hadn't received any messages from Andre.

"I think we make our move tonight," he announced, lowering his binoculars to his lap. "It doesn't look like Van Dousen plans to honor his part of the deal to return Dominique. I'm afraid the longer we wait to make our move, the greater the risk he'll dispose of her."

"I'm good with that," Mike agreed. "Let's find a place to go over everything and check our gear," he suggested. "Nikko?"

"I know just the island," he said. "The accommodations aren't great, but it's private."

CHAPTER NINETEEN

The conditions couldn't have been better suited for a midnight mission, Ethan concluded. The moon was barely a sliver, allowing them to blend in with the darkness of the night. The wind was as gentle as a baby's breath. Even the sea offered little resistance.

He and Mike kept the portable underwater motors in place while the propellers urged the boat forward. All Nikko had to do was steer the boat. They crept into the cove, the hum of the motors muffled by the sea. When he saw the anchor begin to sink, he knew Nikko had signaled to Lance to lower the first anchor into the water. He nudged Mike, and they cut the motors and crawled onto the boat. He saw Nikko release the second anchor into the water.

They proceeded in silence according to the plan. He and Mike peeled off their wet suits and slid into camouflage trousers and shirts. Next, they pitched their lines atop the cliff with impeccable accuracy and secured them. He watched Lance attach lines to the boat while Nikko set out their weapons and equipment. He and Mike strapped, tied, and clipped the weapons and equipment to themselves one by one. When they were finished, Lance inserted an earphone into each of their ears and pinned a microphone to each of them. Then Lance slid on his headset and tapped his microphone. Ethan and Mike nodded, then tapped their microphones. Lance nodded in return.

He was ready to make the climb onto the island and signaled Mike. As they reached for their lines, Nikko lifted his hand and gestured to them to wait. He reached into his pocket, removed something, and divided the contents of what he had removed in his hands. He then offered a hand to Ethan and one to Mike. They held out their hands, and he set something into each one. Ethan stared down at the bat bones Nikko had placed in his hand. They were a talisman, an old Greek superstition meant to bring good luck. He smiled and nodded to Nikko, then tucked them into his pocket. He was sure Mike didn't know what Nikko had given him, but when Mike slid them into his pocket and gave Nikko a grin, he knew Mike understood their meaning.

It took no time for him and Mike to scale the cliff. Within minutes, they were on the island. He glanced down at the boat just as Nikko slithered over the side and into the water. Lance looked up and shrugged. Ethan frowned as he checked his watch. He had no time to worry about Nikko. The guards would be down at the dock for only ten minutes. They would use six of the minutes to get to the residence. He motioned to Mike, and they began making their way through the forest of trees.

He went over the blueprints of the main residence in his mind. Dominique's room was the second one from the right on the second floor. That was his destination.

Dominique slid the wire hanger under the door and under the carpet, then dragged it back toward herself. She had heard Chen drop the key when he had come to retrieve the cart after dinner. Then she had watched under the door as he slid it under the carpet.

On the second attempt, the wire snagged the key. She hoped it would be as easy to replace when she returned. Tonight, she would explore the house, see what was on the other side of the island, and try to find something to use as a weapon. Tomorrow night, she would find a boat or some other way off the island.

She held a nervous breath as she inserted the key and turned the lock. When the deadbolt slid back, she released her breath. She pulled open the door and peered into the hall. It was empty and dark. A whisper of moonlight filtered down from the skylights, but it was enough to cut through the darkness. Barefoot, she slipped from her room and closed the door behind her. She slid the key back under the carpet. If she got caught, she would say Chen had forgotten to lock the door.

She drew another breath and released it. Then she crept along the wall, keeping in the shadows. When she reached the steps, she stopped at the top stair. Her heart plunged as she studied the streak of green that passed over the bottom step. She stepped from the shadows, leaned over the railing, and surveyed the floor below. Hundreds of green laser beams hovered above the floor, crisscrossing in all directions.

She studied the pattern of beams. Without warning, her body stiffened as it sensed someone behind her. Her heart pounded to keep pace with the adrenaline rushing through her veins.

She tried to move, but she was frozen in place, her hands glued to the banister.

The rough hand of a man clamped over her mouth while he slid his other hand around her waist. The force of his pull ripped her hands from the railing as he dragged her back into the shadows.

She would rather endure the wrath of her kidnapper than to be molested by one of his men. She struggled to scream, but the force of the hand over her mouth made it difficult to even breathe. She tried to wrestle free, but he kept her pinned against the wall. The weight of his body crushed against hers made it impossible to move.

She tried to yank herself free, but he was a mountain of

power and strength. She was sure he could snap her neck with little effort. She felt like a mouse trapped in the claws of a lion. Each ounce of resistance she exerted was met with a ton of pressure. He was impossible to fight.

Ethan could taste her fear, and it increased as he defeated her resistance. If he was going to keep to the timetable, he had to get moving. The guard would be on his way back up along the cliff behind Dominique's balcony, and they would have to make their escape from another side. He needed for her to see his face so she would know it was him and stop struggling.

Keeping his hand planted over her mouth and with his other hand binding her arms behind her, he jerked her around to face him in one swift movement. He had complete control over her and held her firmly against him as he pulled her with him from the shadows. He saw the terror in her eyes. Then he saw the flicker of recognition in them, and with that, he felt her body yield. When she nodded, he released her wrists. He lifted a finger to his lips, and when she nodded again, he dropped his hand from her mouth.

He pulled her back into the shadows with him and took her hand. He led her to the stairs and smiled. It was dark. The maze of beams had disappeared. Mike had done his job. He would be waiting for them just inside the tree line where they had split up.

He led her down the steps without a sound, guiding her into the darkness below. With the blueprint of the residence etched in his mind, he led her in the direction of a service entrance. Once outside, they would cut across the back and duck into the shelter of the trees. From there, it would be an easy escape back to the boat.

He kept them close to the walls as they slinked along their escape route. Halfway down the last hallway that led to the service entrance, he felt her stop and her hand slipped from his. He whipped around, ready to attack, thinking someone had grabbed her from behind. She was only inches away, staring at someone in the middle of the hallway a few yards behind them. It was a small figure standing motionless just outside of an opened door. His arms hung still at his sides.

Ethan slid his knife from the sheath and took a cautious step forward, his mind calculating. He had to resolve the threat and get them out of the residence before anyone else noticed that the solar power had been shut off and before the generator kicked on. The clock was ticking.

Dominique took a step back toward him and shook her head. He advanced another step. The figure remained motionless in the deafening silence. Before he could advance further, she extended an arm across his path, blocking him.

"Where are you? You've got about twenty seconds to get your asses out of there," Mike whispered over his earpiece.

Slowly, the figure lifted an arm and raised his hand. He put a finger to his lips. Then, without a sound, he turned and disappeared through the opened door.

Ethan snatched Dominique's arm and spun her around with such momentum that she slammed into his chest. He locked his gaze on hers. Hers told him that whoever it was wasn't a threat. He shoved his knife back into the sheath.

"C'mon, Ethan. Where are you?" Mike whispered again.

"On our way," he whispered back as they hurried down the hall.

"You better haul ass."

They were no more than thirty feet from the exit. He had a tight grip on Dominique, and she was keeping up. He quickened their pace and studied the door as they neared it. There were no deadbolts to turn, no locks to pry, no knobs to twist. All he had to do was slide two bolts through their guides, lean into the door, and it would open. It was so easy a monkey could do it.

He reached for the first bolt and tugged on it. It slid through the guide. They were almost there. One more bolt and then a dash around to the back and into the woods. He tugged on the second bolt. It slid just as easily as the first.

"Too late," Mike whispered. "The guards just turned the corner. Find a way out the back."

He scanned the corridor behind them. It was still clear. He tightened his grip on Dominique and kept her close as they hurried back up the hallway. Based on the blueprints, the closest way out the back from where they were was through the foyer.

"They haven't noticed the beams yet." He knew Mike was still at the rendezvous point just inside the tree line and concealed by low-lying brush. It offered a good vantage point to watch the guards without being seen. Mike was going to have to be his eyes on the outside while he figured out how to get through the inside. "Oh, shit. At exit four."

Instinctively, he shoved Dominique behind him as they entered the foyer, lifting his hand to his pistol, readying for a confrontation. He could see a faint light outside through one of the windows that flanked the doors. He leaned into Dominique and took a step back. He pulled the pistol from its holster and took another step back.

"False alarm," Mike whispered. "Cigarette break."

He released a long, quiet breath and slid the pistol back into the holster. They were lucky, but he was sure it was just a matter of time before the guards noticed the absence of the green glow that should be radiating just inside the window from where they were standing. They had to get out and fast. He reached for Dominique, and she slid her fingers around his. They stepped back into the foyer and into a white light, their sight blinded. The clicking of a bullet falling into a chamber warned him against reaching for his pistol.

"Going somewhere, Princess?" a voice from somewhere behind the white light asked.

"Shit," Mike snapped. "You've got two more coming," he warned just as Ethan heard the guards out front blow through the front door.

"She's coming with me," he answered for her, drawing her close. He raised a hand to shield his eyes from the direct beam of the light.

"Then I'm afraid she's going nowhere," the voice said. "I do hate being awakened in the middle of the night. Now, what am I supposed to do with you two?"

"If I were you and your men, I'd start running for cover." A bluff was worth a try, he figured. At the least, it would give him time to assess the situation and adjust their plan. "In about ten minutes, the island's going to be surrounded by authorities."

"Really," he replied with a chuckle. "And what are you? The first battalion?"

"Well, you can take your chances," he replied with a shrug. "But maybe your men don't want to," he suggested, glancing behind him. He confirmed that both of the two men were behind them, but with the light in his eyes, he still couldn't make out how many were in front of them.

"Don't insult my intelligence," the voice snarled, his anger revealing itself, "or my men's loyalty. We all know if anyone else knew the princess was here, soldiers would be dropping from the sky and washing up from the sea."

"Two more are on their way," Mike whispered.

"How do you know they're not?"

"Escort the princess and her friend into my office," he ordered to the men behind them, then turned, ignoring the question. "And for God's sake, take his gun."

He felt a tug on his pistol as his gun was snatched from the holster.

The light beam turned and illuminated a path through the foyer. Ethan stepped aside, so the light shining from behind them fell on the men facing them. He recognized Van Dousen from the pictures and made out just one guard with him. There were three guards in all so far. Three-to-one. Not bad odds, he figured, not including Van Dousen.

He shrugged the hand of one of the guards from his shoulder as it shoved him from behind and slapped away the hand of the other guard before it could touch Dominique. Her hand trembled in his as they followed Van Dousen and the guard with him. Van Dousen wasn't much of threat himself, he figured, as long as he didn't have a weapon. He was short, stubby. Most likely couldn't move very fast. He could flatten him with one strike. The guard was on the lean side. Average height. It wouldn't take much to take him down.

"Are the authorities really coming?" she whispered in French.

"I have back up," he replied in French.

"Lance, you got this?" Mike asked.

"I'm on it," Lance replied.

"Ethan, in addition to the two guards that stormed in on you and the two on the way, how many more are there?" Mike asked.

He coughed once.

"Okay. Six-to-two, including Van Dousen." He heard Mike draw a slow, even breath. "I'm coming. I'll let you know when I'm in place."

They followed Van Dousen into his office. The guard with him lit four gas lanterns placed around the perimeter of the room. Van Dousen shuffled to his desk, adjusted his robe, dropped to his chair, then cleared his throat. He tapped his chubby fingers on the desk.

"Sit," he ordered, and he and Dominique were shoved onto

a sofa by the guards behind them. The guard that had accompanied Van Dousen lowered himself to a chair across from them. He aimed the barrel of his gun at him, then slid it to Dominique. A sneer sliced across his face.

Ethan kept an eye on the two other guards who took positions flanking the sofa. Two more coming, he thought as the two guards Mike had warned him about stormed into the room, rifles tucked under their arms.

"Find his boat and sink it," Van Dousen ordered the rifled guards, "along with anyone on it."

Without a word, they spun around and hurried from the office.

"Oh, hell!" Lance's panicked voice exploded in his earphone. "What do I do? What do I do? Nikko's not back. Where the hell did he go? Is he with you?"

"Lance." Mike's voice, cool and steady, flowed over the earphone.

"Mike?"

"Take a slow, deep breath, Lance."

"Okay. Okay. I can do this. What do I do?"

"All right. Lance, now I want you to pull up the anchor from the bow."

"The bow?"

"The front of the boat."

"What about Nikko?" Terror laced his voice, and it tore at Ethan. Walk him through it, Mike, he thought. Stay with the kid. Keep him alive.

"Don't worry about Nikko."

"Okay. The anchor. The anchor," he repeated. Ethan heard sounds in the background. He was moving around the boat. That's it, kid, he thought. Do what Mike tells you. "I got it. I'm pulling it up now."

"That's good," Mike assured him. "Let me know when it's out of the water."

"You're an American." Ethan heard Van Dousen's voice and turned in his direction. "Do you work for the palace?"

"I don't work for anyone."

"What is your connection to the princess?"

"We're old friends."

"I'm afraid being evasive won't help you," Van Dousen warned, then leaned back in his chair and studied him. "You are causing me such an inconvenience."

"Mr. Van Dousen." Ethan turned to see a man dressed in a perfectly pressed suit and wearing white gloves standing in the doorway. Must be some sort of butler or valet, he figured. "Your clothes are packed." The odds against them were increasing. Seven-to-one. But hopefully, he thought, that guy's not going to put up much of a fight. He looked like the type to leave the dirty work up to the guards.

"Good." Van Dousen rose from his chair. "Now pack everything in the vault. All of it."

"Very well, sir," the butler replied and strutted over to a set of pocket doors. As he slid them apart, a light flickered across a metal vault door.

"Make sure they don't go anywhere," Van Dousen ordered as he rounded his desk and strode from the office.

"It's out of the water, Mike," Lance reported, his voice still an anxious tangle of nerves. "Now what?"

"Now pull up the anchor at the stern and let me know when that one's up."

"Right. Okay. Is that the back of the boat?"

"Affirmative, yes."

"Ahhhh." Lance's cry erupted in his ear, followed by what sounded like a thud. Ethan swore his heart was going to jump out of his chest as he fought hard to keep from reacting.

"Shh." He strained to identify the soft, hissing sound that had replaced the scream.

"Geez. You scared the crap out of me." Lance's whisper

sent shockwaves of relief through him. "Where the hell have you been? They're looking for us. They're going to sink us. We have to get out of here."

"No problem," Nikko whispered. Then a minute later, he heard the roar of an engine in the distance. He listened to the familiar sound of Nikko's boat starting up and then the low, steady hum of its engine.

He didn't need the earpiece to hear the sound of the gunshots just before the line went silent and communication with Lance was severed. He prayed that Lance and Nikko were all right.

"What is that?" Dominique asked.

"The death of your cavalry," the guard across from them answered with a sneer.

"It sounds like they're getting away," Ethan said for Dominique's benefit because, in truth, he couldn't tell if the howl in the distance was one engine or two.

"I doubt that."

"Where is the fat guy going?" he asked. Distract him from everything outside this room, he told himself. Mike is on his way.

"That's none of your business."

"Is he taking you with him?"

"I go where he goes."

"So you're packed, too?" His lips curled up at the corners as the guard shifted. He could almost see the wheels of his mind spinning at the realization that he might not be going with Van Dousen.

"Keep an eye on them," the guard snarled as he got up, then hurried from the office.

"What about you two?" he asked, tossing the guards flanking them a glance.

"Shut up," one of them answered.

"I'll take that as a no," he muttered.

"I said shut up," the guard repeated, raising the barrel of his rifle.

Before he could strike, Ethan grabbed the rifle and, in the blink of an eye, shoved the handle upward, catching the guard under the chin and sending him flying backward. With the same lightning-quick motion, he flung the rifle over Dominique's head, smacking the other guard flat against his temple. The guard flew over sideways and hit the floor with a thud. He leaped over the back of the sofa, grabbed the first guard by his throat, and drew back his arm to deliver a blow to the jaw.

"That's enough," Van Dousen's voice crackled through the office at the same time Ethan felt the blunt butt of a pistol smack against the base of his skull, sending him to his knees.

"Stop!" Dominique screamed as he saw her leap onto the back of Van Dousen's guard and circle his neck with her hands.

"Bitch," the guard howled and thrust himself backward against the wall, slamming her against it.

She dropped to the floor, gasping for air, the wind knocked out of her. Ethan crawled over to her, his vision still blurred from the blow he'd received.

"Deep breaths," he whispered, shielding her with his body.

"Try that again, and you'll die a long, slow death," the guard warned, standing above them with his pistol cocked and aimed.

"Nice try, bad timing," Mike whispered. "Next time, wait for me, buddy. I'm in the house."

Nikko looked over his shoulder and out onto the deck. He grinned at the sight of Lance clinging to the side of his boat. He guessed that was where he had landed when the boat had launched out of the cove like a rocket and soared over the wake of the yacht.

It had taken only seconds for him to get them in the clear, and they were far ahead of the yacht and widening the distance. He drove them further out into the sea, leading the yacht into the darkness. He saw it plowing through the water behind them, struggling to keep up. He steadied his speed and motioned to Lance, then watched him inch his way to the cabin.

"That was close," Lance said when he reached the cabin. "Where did you go back there?"

"To take care of business," Nikko answered.

"What business?"

"You'll see," he said with a grin.

"Where are we going? How can you see?"

"I don't need to see to know where I am going."

"What if we hit something?"

"We won't." Nikko glanced over his shoulder. The running lights on the yacht were steady behind them. "It won't be long at this speed."

"What won't?"

"You'll see."

"What are we going to do?"

"Nothing."

"Nothing? We don't have a plan?"

"Oh, we have a plan," Nikko assured him. He placed his hand on Lance's shoulder and turned him around. "Keep an eye on them."

"Mind telling me what our plan is? They're slowing down," he said. "They're slowing down fast. I think they're giving up."

"They are not giving up," Nikko replied and lifted the throttle.

"Yes, they are. Look. They're stopping," Lance insisted.

"Yes, but they are not giving up."

"Do you think it's a trap?"

"It is not a trap. They are out of gas." He tossed his head and laughed.

"Is that what you were—"

"What did you think I was doing? Going for a midnight swim?" He slapped a hand on Lance's shoulder. "Now, what do you say we see how your friends are doing?"

"Come." Van Dousen motioned to the two guards.

Ethan kept his focus on him and the guards.

"Carry these cases to the helicopter," Van Dousen ordered as his butler stacked the last of the steel cases outside the vault.

Ethan took a quick count, then slid his gaze back to Van Dousen.

"And hurry." He strolled over to the chair previously occupied by his guard and sat down. He crossed his legs, slid his fingers down the crease of his immaculately pressed trousers, and let go of a long sigh. "Thanks to you, Princess, I now have the missing pieces to my collection. It's just unfortunate how things have ended up for you."

Ethan felt Dominique twitch at the words. He was planning on killing them. "Don't think for a minute, Van Dousen, that you're going to get away with anything," he warned.

"I'm right around the corner, buddy," Mike whispered.

"You're hardly in a position to level threats," Van Dousen replied with a chuckle. "Incidentally, how did you find out the princess was here on this island?"

"Her father told me where to find her."

"Still playing that hand, are you? Your problem, young man, is that you don't know when to fold. A bluff is only good when you can fool the other player."

"Why would I bluff if I'm holding a royal flush?"

"Mr. Van Dousen." The butler appeared in the doorway with the two guards and drew Van Dousen's attention. "We are ready."

"Very good." He pushed himself up from the chair and dropped his gaze back to Ethan. "Lock them in the safe. In a half-hour, take them out to sea and dispose of their bodies."

The guards nodded and pushed into the room.

"Sir, we don't have the combination to the safe," one of them said.

"GEMS. 7 . . . 5 . . . 13 . . . 19," he said and then turned to leave. "Let's go," he called over his shoulder and strutted from the room.

"Here's one for the road," Van Dousen's guard snarled at Ethan, then delivered a quick kick to the gut. Ethan doubled over with a moan. "And I owe you one," he added, drawing his arm, the back of his hand poised to strike Dominique.

"You heard Mr. Van Dousen. Let's go," the butler said and caught the guard's arm mid-swing. Lucky son of a bitch, Ethan thought, unclenching the fist he was going to thrust into the guard's balls.

"Don't tell me what to do," the guard shot back, shoving past the two other guards and following the butler from the room.

"Get up." One of the remaining guards nudged him with a foot to his side. "I said, get up," he repeated, glaring down at him.

"We're even now, buddy," Mike whispered. "Two-to-two. I'm almost there."

"Look, we won't try anything," he said, struggling to his feet and taking more time and more effort than required to give Mike some time. "There's no need to lock us inside the vault."

"Don't worry. I'm sure you'll be quite comfortable in there," one of the guards replied.

Ethan lowered his hand to Dominique and helped her to her feet.

"Now get moving," the other one ordered.

The sound of the helicopter blades rotating in the distance filled the room.

"I'm at the door," Mike whispered. "In one."

Ethan assessed their positions. He was at the vault with one guard to his right and Dominique on his left. The other guard was next to Dominique. He was closest to the door. That was the one Mike would take. He smiled to himself when he heard Mike's voice. "You take the one to your right."

He nudged Dominique with his elbow, curled the fingers of his left hand into a hard fist, then waited for Mike's count. He knew Mike was waiting until Dominique was in the clear.

She took his cue and stepped into the vault. Mike's voice signaled. "One." Ethan heard the crystal vase shatter with an ear-splitting pop when something hit it.

Instantly, both guards spun toward the vase, their rifles surging upwards. With a split-second reaction, he swung his left arm with the weight of a major league batter behind it, slamming his fist into the guard's face. He could feel the bones in his nose crumble against his fingers as the guard released a curdling scream and dropped his rifle. He finished him off with an uppercut to the jaw, which sent him flying backward, smashing through a window. The guard came to a rest halfway over the sash of the window.

Mike had the other guard grappling with the belt twisted around his neck, gasping for air. A swift bang of his head against the foot-thick vault door assisted by Mike stilled him. He fell to the floor like a sack of potatoes.

Dominique sprang from the vault, ready to pounce, then stopped when she spotted the guards taking a nap.

"Let's put them in the vault for safekeeping," he said and yanked the guard back through the window. Mike slid his hands under the shoulders of the one on the floor and dragged him into the vault while he hauled the other one across the room.

Dominique spun toward the sound of the helicopter lifting from the pad. "They're getting away," she yelled as she scooped up one of the rifles before she tore out of the room. Ethan knew she was going after the jewels.

"Shit." He tossed the limp body of the guard into the vault and took off after her. She was already beyond the hallway by the time he flew out of the office. He heard the front door bang against the wall, and within a second, he heard the first shot.

By the time he reached the front door, she'd gotten off three more rounds. "You're going to draw fire," he yelled, but his words were too late. He saw the flash from the first shot fired from the helicopter as he ran toward her. He dove at her in a storm of gunfire as the assault against them continued. He slammed into her hard, taking her to the ground with him. He held her down, shielding her body with his. It sounded like the front line of a war zone.

CHAPTER TWENTY

The explosion of gunfire ceased, and all Ethan could hear was the sputter and cough of the engine as it fought to keep the helicopter level and airborne. It bucked like a bronco as whoever was piloting it wrestled with steering it back over the island.

He jumped to his feet and snatched up Dominique, not yet sure whether she had been hit and equally unsure whether the helicopter was going to career out of control and crash on top of them. He could feel her trembling in his arms and the fear whipped through him.

Mike raced over toward them, his rifle aimed to cover them if the gunfire resumed. "Are you all right?" Mike hollered over the ruckus as he raked his gaze over him.

"Yeah," he yelled back as he turned, swooped Dominique off her feet, and tore back toward the house. "Come on," he shouted to Mike.

"I'm okay. You can put me down," Dominique said once they had all crossed into the foyer.

He set her down and looked her over to make sure for himself. The relief spilled from him like water from a broken spigot, and with it, the anger. "What the hell were you thinking running out there like that? You could have been killed."

Before she could answer, a loud crunch sent vibrations fluttering under their feet and had them racing back to the door. They stopped in the doorway, watching as the helicopter teetered at the edge of the cliff. It balanced tenuously as the blades atop it wound down to a halt. It looked as if the mere flick of a finger would be enough to send it crashing to the sea below.

They stood speechless, their gazes fixed on the helicopter perched on the rim of the cliff, hanging in the balance. Its engine quieted, and its lights dimmed. It sat silently except for the crunching of loose rock under the skids as the helicopter rocked back and forth.

"What do you think?" Ethan asked. "Is it going over?"

"A hundred dollars says yes," Mike replied.

"We have to get the cases," Dominique insisted. "Lidia's jewelry is in them."

"I think it's too late," a voice said from behind them.

Ethan turned to see Nikko peering past them through a pair of binoculars and a two-way radio hanging from his hip. "A crow," Nikko said with a chuckle.

"Where's — " Ethan began.

"He's fine. He's on the boat, waiting to hear from me. It landed . . . and there she goes," Nikko said, and Ethan watched the helicopter tip downward, the skids grinding on the gravel beneath it as if clinging for one last chance, until finally, it disappeared below the cliff.

"No," Dominique screamed, running toward the cliff.

The helicopter hit the water with an enormous splash.

He raced after Dominique and caught up to her at the edge of the cliff. She was staring down into the darkness. Nikko stopped beside them and aimed the flashlight into the abyss. The helicopter was sinking fast.

"Nikko, where are the other guards?" he asked.

"They are drifting around out at sea headed toward Africa."

"Where's your boat?"

"About a quarter-mile out. I'll call Lance and tell him to pick us up at the dock," he offered, twisting the radio loose from his belt loop. "If you are ready to go, that is."

"Call him," he ordered. "And let's see how deep it is down there," he added as he turned and started down toward the dock.

"This should be fun," Mike muttered.

"It has been so far," Nikko replied as he raised Lance on the radio.

"I want to dive down with you to retrieve the cases," Dominique said, catching up to him.

"You're not going," he said.

"It's only fair that—"

"You're not going," he repeated. "Look, I'm trained to do this." He softened his voice. There was no reason to be angry at her, he decided. She was safe, and that was all that mattered. That was the purpose of the mission and he had accomplished it. "But I won't be able to concentrate if I have to worry about you down there."

"All right," she agreed.

He glanced down at her, surprised she had given up so easily, and annoyed with himself when he felt the tugs. Damn, he wanted her, and the sooner he got her back to her father, the sooner he could put her out of his life, he reminded himself as he pulled his gaze away.

"Mike, what the hell took you so long?" he asked. "I was beginning to think we were going to end up as fish bait."

"We accounted for five guards. We had figured there were seven based on three shifts. I had to stop by the smaller residence first and take care of them. And what the hell took you so long to get to the service entrance? That's what screwed the plan up."

"We ran into someone in the hallway," Ethan told him. "He caused the delay."

He looked at Dominique. "Who was he?"

"Chen. He is the chef."

When they approached the dock, from the look on Lance's

face, he figured Lance was on at least his third attempt at trying to maneuver the boat close enough to the dock to tie up. Gauging the distance between the boat and the dock, he wasn't sure Nikko was going to land on the boat when he sailed past him off the dock.

That must have hurt, he thought with a grimace when he saw Nikko smack hard on the side of the boat and then tumble into it. "At least he made it," he said as Mike chuckled.

Once on the boat, Ethan slapped an affectionate arm around Lance's shoulders and then pulled him into a tight embrace before letting him go. He had made a mistake bringing the kid along, and it was one he would never make again. He'd grown fond of him and he'd almost lost him. He knew it would haunt him for the rest of his life if he had to bring him back in a box. "I'm glad to see you in one piece. You had me worried after we lost communication."

"Thanks, boss. I was worried, too. I kinda figured you for a goner, as well. Nikko saved my life. He really knows how to handle a boat."

"Batten down," Nikko called from the cabin as he eased down on the throttle and the boat pulled away from the dock.

"I'll get the scuba gear ready," Mike volunteered and ducked into the cabin.

"I'll help you," Lance offered and followed him.

Ethan rummaged through one of the duffle bags until he found his cell phone, then stepped away from Dominique and dialed Andre's number.

He answered on the first ring. His voice was an anguished mix of exhaustion and grief.

"Andre, Ethan here."

"Ethan, there's been no word yet on Dominique. I've been waiting for your call. Have you found any information to help us? We're desperate, I—"

"I found her, Andre. She's safe. She's with me now." He

wasn't going to waste another second letting him know that Dominique was no longer in danger.

"What? Ethan, how? Where—"

"I'm sorry I couldn't tell you anything when we spoke last. I didn't want to take any risks, and I wasn't even sure where she was until a day or two ago. I was just operating on a hunch."

"My God, Ethan." The line was silent for a second, then Ethan heard him laugh or cry. Or maybe it was both. He waited until he spoke again. "Thank you. I can't believe it. Where is she?"

"She's in Greece. How soon can you fly into Preveza Airport? I'll have her there so you can take her home."

"We'll leave now. We'll be there in four hours. Ethan, how can we ever thank you?"

"No need. Here, I'll let you talk to Dominique." He handed her the phone, then joined Nikko in the cabin.

"I think the helicopter went down right around this corner," Nikko said, squinting up toward the cliff and easing up on the throttle.

Mike dragged two tanks past him, followed by Lance, who was schlepping out a big duffle bag. He followed them onto the deck. He picked up a flashlight from the deck and flicked on the light. He cast the beam over the side of the boat where Nikko figured the helicopter had sunk.

The engine quieted, and Nikko stepped from the cabin and began lowering an anchor. "What the—" Nikko started before a smile spread over his face, followed by a roar of laughter. "Lance, drop the anchor at the stern," he called out.

He directed the beam of light past Nikko over the water. Stainless steel cases were bobbing in the water and more were surfacing. He shined the light over the starboard side and reached down and plucked one up. Mike reached over the port side and yanked one up, and Dominique grabbed one off the stern. Nikko leaned over the bow with a boat hook and pulled one in. Lance lifted another from the water near the stern.

"They're locked," Mike announced. "We need combinations."

Ethan looked at Dominique, and her smile met his. "Try the numbers that correspond to the letters G . . . E . . . M . . . S," she said.

Nikko brought the case he'd retrieved from off the bow and joined them on the deck. Lance took a few strides closer to Mike, and Dominique lowered herself to the ice chest. Soon, all eyes were on Mike. He sat down on a box, placed the case on his lap, and flipped the dials on the lock. It opened on the last number. Ethan watched him lift an item from the box and unwrap it from the soft cloth protecting it. What looked like a large silver stein glistened under the beam of light. Mike turned it over in his hands, studying it. It bore two different crests.

"Boss, I think I saw a picture of that on the history channel about a month ago. I was watching a show on old artifacts that were stolen and never recovered," Lance said. "If that's the one on the show, it dates to the sixteenth century. It was stolen about a decade ago."

"Why doesn't that surprise me?" he remarked.

He looked at Dominique, and she was sliding her finger over the dials on the case in her lap. When she opened it, he saw that it contained dozens of small velvet boxes. None appeared large enough to hold a necklace. She pulled one of the boxes out of the case and snapped open its lid. A set of garish gold and diamond cuff links twinkled under the light. She closed the box and pulled another one from the case. It held an ornate emerald broach. Another box contained an elegant diamond and sapphire tie clip. She returned the box to the case and closed it. He could read the disappointment on her face.

He opened the case in his hand. It contained an assortment of large, polished gemstones. He didn't know a lot about rocks, but he recognized diamonds and emeralds when he saw them and was willing to bet they were worth a fortune.

They retrieved the rest of the cases that had surfaced. Case after case was unlocked and its contents examined. He noticed that most of them contained jewelry, but according to Dominique, none of it was Lidia's. Others contained small sculptures, some small paintings. He watched Lance open the last of them and unwrapped the cloth from one of the items. It contained a number of items, but the most impressive was a stunning amethyst pendant of a winged scarab the size of his hand.

"Wow," Lance gushed. "This is . . . beautiful."

"Must be from Egypt," Mike remarked, examining it as Lance held it under the light.

"And probably stolen," Ethan added.

"There have to be more cases," Dominique said, ignoring the latest find.

"Maybe Van Dousen didn't keep what you're looking for in the vault," Mike suggested.

"He had to have kept them in there," she insisted. "Why wouldn't he?"

"There are fifteen cases. I countered them when they came out of the vault," Ethan announced. "How many do we have?"

"Eleven," Nikko replied. "I've been keeping track." He hefted up a spotlight and rested it on his shoulder. The beam shot out over the stern onto the sea. He turned toward the port side, dragging the shaft of light over the water. Ethan scanned the water for more cases among the broken pieces of helicopter that had floated to the surface and littered the water.

Nikko skimmed the light back over the stern to the starboard side. "The sea is still tonight. If there are other cases, they should be here," he said.

"There's something behind that boulder over there," Ethan heard Lance say, then saw him pointing to a massive rock jutting up from the water a few feet from the side of the cliff. "I can't make it out. Maybe it's a case."

"It's too far to reach with the boat hook," Nikko said, aiming the light at the rock.

Ethan stripped off his shirt and dove over the side of the boat. He surfaced near the rock and reached behind it, pushing the object loose. A case floated out from behind the rock. He grabbed it and tossed it toward the boat. It landed a few feet from the boat, and Mike pulled it in with the boat hook. He handed the case to Dominique. "Try this one," he said to her. "I hope it's what you're looking for."

She set the case on her lap and set the dials to the combination. Ethan grabbed the side of the boat and hoisted himself up halfway out of the water. He saw her close her eyes and knew she was making a wish or saying a prayer. He just hoped that either way, the Lord would answer it. He knew how much finding Lidia's jewels meant to her.

Nikko whistled when she opened the lid. "Holy cow," he added, looking over her shoulder and staring down at the large denomination of Euro bills filling the entire case. Ethan felt Dominique's disappointment.

She handed the case back to Mike. He flipped through the stacks of bills. "Must be close to half a million here."

Ethan grabbed a flashlight and pushed off the boat. He sucked in a deep breath and dove under the water. He searched beneath the boat for the helicopter. There were three cases unaccounted for. They were either still in the helicopter or stuck somewhere around it.

He guessed he was about sixty feet or more down when he

spotted the helicopter. He swam between the blades and peered into the cockpit. Four bodies were still strapped in, all of them dead. Apparently, the schmucks weren't prepared for a water landing, he thought and kicked hard enough to get himself to the side of the helicopter. He had to work fast. He knew he was going to have to release his breath soon.

The door was all the way open but it was dark that deep down. He had to rely on his flashlight to see. He aimed the light inside and spotted a case stuck partially under a seat. He pulled it loose, and feeling the pressure of it rising, shoved it out the door and released it. He directed the light across the floor. Nothing. He moved the beam between the seats and over the bodies. No cases. He was going to have to release some air or surface. He decided on the former and allowed some air to escape his lungs. As the bubbles floated up past his eyes, he jerked the light to the roof. Two cases were clinging to the ceiling. He reached for one and thrust it out the door. He grabbed the other case and pulled it with him as he pushed away from the helicopter. When he let it go, he followed it to the surface, releasing the air left in his lungs.

When he broke through the top of the water, his chest heaved as his lungs sucked in air, then forced it out. Mike was already pulling the last case out of the water. Dominique was staring down at him, relief visible in her eyes.

She reached for him as he lifted himself over the side of the boat. "Why didn't you tell someone you were diving down there?" she asked. He swore he heard a hint of irritation in the question, followed by a chuckle from Nikko.

He shrugged and dragged a hand through his wet hair. "I wasn't planning on going that deep. I just wanted to try and see how far down the copter sank." He paused when he felt the mild annoyance. "Is there a problem?"

"No." She shook her head. "Thank you for finding the rest of the cases."

"We were all beginning to worry, buddy," Mike said. "You were down there a long time, even for you. I was ready to go in after you."

"Hmm." Mike was right. He had been down there a long time, and he knew that it was much longer than an average person could have lasted under water because of his training. A smile crossed over his lips. So that was it, he concluded. The worry in her eyes was for him. Well, maybe in part. "Sorry, man."

"See anyone down there?" Mike asked as he opened a case and handed one to Dominique.

"Yeah. They're all dead."

"*Opa*," Nikko said, staring at the ruby necklace in Mike's hand.

"Is this what you're looking for, Princess?" Mike asked, holding the necklace up.

"Yes," she answered and shot Ethan a look. He recognized the necklace. It was the one she had been wearing the night of the concert.

Mike wrapped it in the cloth that had held it and placed it back in the case. He removed another piece and unwrapped it. "Would you look at this?" he remarked. "A matching bracelet."

Ethan was staring at Dominique, and when she looked up at him, he winked. She answered with a smile, and he knew she understood. Not only had they recovered the stolen ruby necklace, but the matching bracelet as well. He was sure the last cases completed the collection Stanislaw Kaminski had crafted for his wife.

"Let's put these cases and the rest of this stuff inside," Ethan said as he tossed his shirt over his head, "and get the hell out of here." He picked up a rifle and pistol and passed them to Nikko. Dominique confirmed that Lidia's jewelry was accounted for in less than fifteen minutes, and they hoisted up the anchors.

He was standing on the deck at the back of the boat as Nikko pulled out of the cove. He had changed out of his wet camos and into a pair of jeans. Dominique strolled over to him and rested against the side of the boat next to him. Her mere proximity alone kicked started the tension in his gut. The fact that he could have her in his arms with little more than a flick of his wrist drove it into gear. Put the brakes on and back up, he warned himself. You know where that road leads. Turning, he put a couple feet of distance between them, leaned against the boat, and tapped into his resolve. "I booked a hotel room and picked up some clothes for you. You should have enough time when we get back to shower and get to the airport in time to meet your plane."

"You won't be accompanying me back to Monteaux?" she asked.

"There's no need. Your security team will be coming to Greece with Andre to accompany you back."

"All right." She nodded. "I would like to properly meet your friends and to thank them personally. Will there be time for that?"

"You can do that now if you'd like," he offered.

"Yes, please," she replied.

"I'll be right back." He took a few strides to the cabin and returned with Mike and Lance. "Mike." He raised a hand to his shoulder. "Lance," he said with the same gesture. "I would like to formally introduce you to Her Royal Highness, Princess of Monteaux, Dominique Beauvais."

"Mike Dunn," Mike said, extending his hand to Dominique with a nod. "It's an honor to be formally introduced, Your Highness."

"Please, you may address me as Dominique," she replied with a warm smile, accepting his hand. "I wanted to be sure to have the opportunity to thank you personally for risking your life to rescue me."

Lance stepped forward and offered his hand. "Lance Fortney," he said with an awkward courtesy. "I'm honored to be of service to you."

"What are you doing, Lorraine?" Ethan teased with a laugh and a soft slap to the back of his head.

"Men don't courtesy," Mike added with a howl. "They bow like this," he said, demonstrating with a slow nod.

"I'm sorry," he replied. "I didn't know. I thought you were supposed to curtsy to a royal lady and bow to a royal man."

"That's quite all right, Lance," Dominique said, taking his hand. "It's a pleasure to meet you. Thank you for coming for me. It was courageous of you, and I am very grateful to you."

"You're welcome, Your Majesty."

"Please, I prefer my friends to call me Dominique."

A smile beamed across his face. "Okay," he replied with a nod. "Dominique."

"I would like to invite you all to Monteaux as my special guests—"

"Thank you, but that's not really necessary," Ethan cut in.

"I'd like to accept your offer, but this trip was last minute, and I've got things I've got to get back to," Mike said. "But thank you. I hear Monteaux is a beautiful place. Perhaps another time. I'd love to come visit and bring my wife with me," he finished and then strolled toward the cabin, stopping midway and lowering himself to a crate.

"I, uh, I have to get back, too," Lance replied, glancing at Ethan. "But if that's an open offer, uh—"

"All right, Lance," Ethan interrupted, "don't you think you've seen enough of Europe for a while?"

"Yes, sir," he answered, then bowed to Dominique. "It's nice meeting you," he said and headed back to the cabin.

"I would like to do something special to express my appreciation," she said.

"There's no need." He looked down at her as the wind whipped through her hair. He wanted to reach out and brush it from her face. She was so damn hard to resist. In less than a second, he could have his lips on hers. And in less than a second, he could lose all his free will, he reminded himself.

"Well, then, I will assume that Andre and my father agreed to compensate you all very well."

"You needn't be concerned about that. Now, if you'll excuse me for a minute, I'd like to go over something with Mike." He took the few strides over to Mike, as much to put a halt to the rumbling in his gut as to discuss what they should do with the cases. The ones containing Lidia's jewels would be delivered to Andre along with Dominique so she could return them to Lidia. If Mike concurred, his thought was to turn the other cases containing the gemstones, artifacts, and other jewelry over to the authorities, assuming that most of what was in them had been stolen. He'd leave the task of finding their rightful owners to the authorities. As for the case containing the Euros, he was sure Mike wouldn't object to his plans for that case.

It wasn't long before he heard the steady hum of the engine quiet when Nikko cut it off. It was close to sunrise, and as far as he could tell, they were still better than a mile from docks. "Cover your ears," he said to Dominique. She looked up at him, and a little line of confusion formed between her brows. Before he could warn her any further, the other engine clanked, coughed, and sputtered before settling into a steady knock and bang.

He watched as heads lifted when they puttered into the harbor and then lowered just as quickly when Nikko eased the boat into its slip. It was too early for most of the shops to be open, and the fishermen scattered around the docks appeared too busy to be concerned with Nikko beyond a quick glance.

"I will help you with your bags," Nikko offered.

"Thanks, Nikko, but we can manage," Ethan said, tossing a duffle bag over his shoulder. "We're taking the cases and only some of our equipment with us."

"Where would you like me to send the rest of the equipment?" he asked.

"We have what we need. You keep it." He offered him his hand. "Thanks for everything. You have my number. Call me if you ever need anything."

"You are welcome, my friend," he replied, drawing Ethan into him and slapping an arm around him. "I hope she is worth it," he whispered before turning to Lance. "My boy, I give you this," he said, removing a chain from his neck. It held a blue charm with an eye painted into the middle of it. "It will ward off the evil of the eye."

"Thanks, Nikko," Lance said, turning it over in his hand, then returning the gesture with a healthy hug.

"Take it easy," Mike said with a slap to Nikko's shoulder.

"I will, and you, my pretty lady," Nikko said, turning to Dominique, "you have a wonderful life."

"Thank you, Nikko. I wish the same for you," she said.

Ethan waited while Dominique, Mike, and Lance climbed onto the dock, then turned back to Nikko. He lifted the case containing the cash and tossed it to Nikko. "This one's for you," he said. "Maybe it'll help those kids of yours," he tossed over his shoulder as he stepped off the boat.

A grin erupted across Nikko's face as he caught the case. "May the gods be kind to you, my friend," he returned.

They made it to the hotel with enough time to spare for showers before Dominique and Lance had to start out to Preveza. Ethan managed to repack the contents of the cases, except for Lidia's jewels, into three duffle bags. He arranged for the Greek authorities to accompany Lance and Dominique to the airport, and he was able to get in touch with Andre on his way to Preveza. Andre assured him that he would be more than happy to give Lance, along with the duffle bags, a lift back with them. Ethan had also arranged for Interpol to meet Lance at the airport in Monteaux and relieve him of the bags.

"The escorts for Dominique and Lance are here," Mike said as he walked into Ethan's room. "The guards posted at Dominique's room are waiting for the okay."

Ethan pulled the blinds aside and glanced down into the street. A motorcade of police cars lined the street. Curious onlookers had already begun to congregate, but blockades were in place keeping them at bay. The police had gone all out for Dominique. He was confident that she and Lance would make it to Preveza with no trouble. He dropped the blinds and strolled over to the bed. He lifted a bag from the bed and tossed it over his shoulder.

"Boss, would it be all right if I crashed for a day before I catch a flight home?"

"Why don't you take a few weeks?" he suggested. It wasn't a completely selfless gesture. He'd nearly gotten the kid killed. Giving him a paid vacation to tour some of Europe would help ease his guilt. Besides, the kid earned it, he figured. None of what he'd done was exactly within his job description. "You can use it to see a little more of Europe. Just charge what you need to the company."

"Wow. Thanks, boss."

"You're welcome, kid. Mike, are you ready?" They were going to fly back together from Athens. It would give them some time to reminisce and put some much-needed distance between him and Dominique. He had just about paced a hole in the carpet, trying to wear down the temptation to break down her door during his shift before the police guards arrived.

"I'm ready. Nice meeting you, kid," he said, extending his hand to Lance. "You did a great job out there with us. You should be proud."

"See you in a couple of weeks, buddy," Ethan said as they stepped into the hallway. He gave a nod to the guards. "You can escort them down in five minutes." It would give him and Mike enough time to catch their ride and make it through the blockades. There was no point in saying goodbye to Dominique. He wouldn't be seeing her again. A few less words between them wouldn't make a difference.

CHAPTER TWENTY-ONE

"Lidia, why do you suppose Dominique is still so depressed?" Victor's voice revealed as much sadness as it did perplexity. "It's been over a month since she's been home. Do you think she was . . . mistreated on that island?"

"No, Victor." She reached over and squeezed his hand to reassure him. "She was adamant that she was not. And I believe her."

"Perhaps she is experiencing some sort of lingering stress from it all." He got up and paced as she knew he often did when something bothered him and required serious thought. "Maybe we should hire a psychiatrist for her, discreetly, of course."

"I'm not sure that she is suffering from the stress of the ordeal. She seems over it, especially since Van Dousen's death has been officially confirmed." She lowered her head. "I should have never kept the necklaces in the palace."

"We've been over this, Lidia. You've done nothing wrong. You must stop punishing yourself."

"I'm afraid that's easier said than done." She set her cup of tea down on the saucer and watched him. She loved him with all her heart and had for so many years. Yet, she had caused him so much worry and pain because of the necklaces. They seemed almost like a curse instead of a symbol of love.

"Well, it needs to be done. I need you to help me with Dominique. I don't understand her. Now that this whole thing is over and I've lifted the restrictions, she is free to come and go as she pleases. She's no longer confined to the palace.

Everything is back to normal. She should be happy."

"She is free within limits, Victor." Only in Victor's salon, alone as they usually were at the end of the day, did she have the privacy to be candid with him about matters of a personal nature.

"What do you mean by that?" He stopped and stared down at her.

"Victor," she began. "I know it was difficult for you when Queen Adeline died. Apart from the deep loss of losing someone you love, I realize that simply because of the role of the Queen, the fact that many of your royal duties, particularly the public ones, were performed together made it even more difficult for you to bear her loss. An enormous void was left in your life when the Queen died."

"Yes, that is all true, but what does that have to do with Dominique?"

"I think more than you appreciate, perhaps." She rose to her feet. It was her turn to pace. "Please don't take this the wrong way. I don't mean to imply anything negative about how you have raised Dominique. You know I believe you have always been an outstanding father to Dominique."

"Just say what you have to say." He took her hand and turned her to him. "You know you can be frank with me, Lidia."

She nodded and drew him down beside her as she lowered herself to the sofa. "Well, since Dominique's tenth birthday, you've had her serve beside you, accompanying you to every official and unofficial event, gala, and function hosted by the palace and which you attended as a guest. She's even attended some in your place without you. It's almost as if . . .well . . ."

"As if what?"

"As if you've imposed the responsibilities of the Queen on her all these years."

"But she's never complained."

"You know she wouldn't, Victor. Dominique has always striven to make you proud. She was more devastated by how upset you were with all the news reports than how hurt and betrayed she was when that actor used her to advance his career."

"I wasn't upset with her," he explained. "I was upset by how those reporters were exploiting the situation."

"I know, but she interpreted that as disappointment."

"I didn't know that, and you're right." He released her hand. "Dominique would never complain." He shook his head. "I've used her to fill the empty seat beside me, and in so doing, I've kept her from enjoying her life. What kind of a father am I?"

"An exceptional one, Victor. A caring and loving one. And you've raised a beautiful, compassionate, and loving daughter."

He lifted his hand to her cheek. "Not alone, Lidia. You've helped me raise her. You deserve credit, as well. Possibly more than I."

"Don't be so hard on yourself." She took his hand and lifted it to her lips, touched them to his fingers. "And, I would not say that Dominique has not enjoyed her life. I would say that she has enjoyed it immensely."

"Then what has changed? Is it that she will be turning thirty soon?"

"That may have something to do with the situation, but I don't think that's entirely it," she said with a warm smile.

"What else is it, then?"

"She's in love, Victor."

"What? Oh, no," he said with a frown and pushed himself up from the sofa. "That's not good, Lidia."

"How can you say that?"

"Look at what happened last time. I couldn't stand to see

her go through that again. It was tough for her to keep her head up and pretend like she wasn't being degraded by the press and crucified by the public."

"I know how painful it was for Dominique, and I know how painful it was for you to watch her go through that." She hesitated a moment before she continued. Then she rose from the sofa and walked over to him. "But the fact is that she loves you, and it was that she thought she had disappointed you that hurt her the most."

She had silenced him with those words.

She lifted an affectionate hand to his arm. "Surely you can appreciate the real cost to Dominique of discouraging her from finding love, can't you? Besides, don't you think the risk should be her decision?"

"Damn it. Why does everything you say make so much sense?" He took her hand, and she followed him back to the sofa. When he sat and drew her down, she sat next to him. "Who is this young man she is in love with?"

"Major Moore."

"Ah," he said with a nod. "Of course. He's saved her life twice. At least I know she is safe with him. And does he love her?"

"I am sure of it though there seems to be some obstacles they have to work out."

"Why does love have to be so complicated at times? Like ours. I don't know why you insist on keeping ours hidden."

"We've been over it dozens of times, Victor." She touched her hand to his face and brushed her fingers along it. "No one wants to see the king marry the help. People would lose confidence in your judgment. Besides, my priority has been Dominique. I was retained to care for her, and she still relies on me."

"I disagree with you. I've been king for over forty years and have served the people of Monteaux exceptionally during that time. I highly doubt that they are going to fault me for the selection of my wife."

"I am happy, Victor. Aren't you?"

"Yes, my love, I am. But I would be a great deal happier if I didn't have to restrain myself around you and engage in this . . . this . . . facade."

"Enough about us. You are changing the subject. What are you going to do about Dominique?"

"What do you suggest?"

"I've given this a lot of thought. I think you should relieve Dominique of her royal duties and let her step back, so she is not constantly in the public eye. I'm sure she will want to continue with some of her duties, such as her charities, but I think she should be less burdened so she can pursue a relationship with Major Moore. The successor to the crown is Andre. With all due respect, perhaps he and Francine should start getting involved a little more with the responsibilities of the family. It would also help take the focus off of Dominique."

He lifted a brow. "What would you do if Dominique were free of her obligations?"

"If she no longer needs me, I suppose I would . . . I would . . . I don't know. I haven't thought about it."

"You would marry me. Dominique would no longer be an excuse."

"Victor, Dominique was always only one factor in the equation. Even if I would no longer be in your employ, it doesn't change the fact that I have been for twenty-six years. I would still be thought of as nothing more than the help."

"My God, Lidia. You are a highly educated and intelligent woman, and you are worth millions with those jewels you own. I will not stand here and allow you to talk like you are some illiterate pauper we took off the streets and hired. And another thing, it is not up to the people of Monteaux who I marry."

He tossed his hands in the air, and she watched him pace the length of the room, then stop and lift a bottle of *Hennessy Ellipse* from a tray. He poured himself a glass and started back across the room, downed the glass, then turned around to refill it. She knew the second glass he would sip and concentrate on his thoughts.

"Victor—"

He shook his head. "I'm thinking."

She started toward him.

"Sit down. Please," he said and continued to pace and sip the glass of cognac.

She waited, and after about ten minutes, he spoke.

"I have a proposal to make to you." His voice was firm, a tone not often used with her.

"A proposal?"

"Yes." He sat down across from her and set his glass on the table between them. "I'm going to give Dominique her freedom on the condition that she relieves you from her employ. After all, she will no longer need your services."

"Very well. I—"

"I'm not finished. You will loan to the Monteaux Royal Museum all of your jewelry, and it will be prominently displayed in the museum under a state-of-the-art security system, except, of course, when you are wearing it. The Museum will pay you the greatest of three independent appraisals of the value of your collection for the exclusive right to display your jewelry. You will never have to work another day in your life unless you choose to do so. If you wish, you will also be appointed a member of the Monteaux Annual Gala Committee, which will require you to circulate with some of the world's richest and most famous people. That should afford you enough wealth and social standing to be worthy of marrying me."

"Victor—"

He lifted a hand and continued. "And you will marry me before the end of the year. The details of the wedding will be your choice, but it *will* take place."

"To create a false persona for me by paying me money and surrounding me with the rich and famous so that I will marry you makes my concerns seem so shallow and ridiculous, quite frankly. Perhaps I have not given you or the people of Monteaux enough credit." She rose and strolled toward him, and he stood. "One of the things I love about you is your integrity. I'm sure the people of Monteaux see that in you, as well." She slid her hands up his arms and circled her fingers around them. "I will not accept your proposal. But I will marry you on the condition that you allow me to display my jewelry at the Monteaux Royal Museum without compensation. And, of course, assure their security."

He slid his arms around her and pulled her into him. "There are going to be a lot of changes around here," he whispered.

"Gianna Parducci is on the line for you."

"Tell her I'm not in," Ethan instructed his secretary. He'd read in the papers that her father would be performing in the DC area and assumed her call involved some sort of an invitation. Not only was he not interested in Gianna, but he also wasn't interested in being reminded that he had been handed off to her like a hand-me-down. "Tell her I'm out of the country."

"She'll know I'm lying," his secretary replied. "You told me an hour ago to say you were in a meeting."

"All right," he said. "I'll take it." He disliked putting his secretary in the middle of things more than he despised the idea of talking to Gianna. If she was planning on coming to DC with her father, he would have to deal with her sooner or later anyway.

"Ethan Moore here."

"You sound so formal. You do remember me, don't you, Ethan?" she purred. "We met in Monteaux a few months ago."

"Yes. Leonardo Parducci's daughter. I remember."

"We really didn't get a chance to spend much time together. As I recall, we were . . .interrupted."

"Listen, Gianna, I—"

"There's no need to explain, Ethan," she interrupted, "I know everything Dominique said about you was a lie. I know it was all a ruse so she could be with you."

"I don't know where you got that idea, but—"

"Don't be coy with me. I know she snuck into your room after getting me out of the way."

"Look, Dominique is not a topic I am going to discuss with you." Or anyone else, he thought. It had been hard enough trying to get her out of his mind since he'd returned from Greece. He certainly wasn't going to have a conversation reminding him of the night he'd spent with her.

"I can understand that. I had to threaten to tell the tabloids that she snuck into your room to get her to back off of you so we could spend some time together."

"What?"

"The press is her worst nightmare. They weren't really kind to her when they found out she'd made a sex video."

He remembered the barrage of bruising articles written about her and the alleged sex video when he'd run her name through his system. The last thing she had wanted, he figured, was to face something like that again and to have Jean Pierre's funeral turned into a paparazzi feeding frenzy. "You know just where to strike." Now he understood the reason Dominique had distanced herself from him the morning following the soiree.

"Anyway, it was unfortunate that you had to leave so abruptly. We didn't get our chance to get to know each other better if you know what I mean."

"I know what you mean, and there's no need to waste your time. I'm sorry, but I'm not interested." He dropped the receiver and leaned back in his chair. What an idiot, he thought. He was sure Dominique hated him, and she had every reason to. He was insensitive, and as she had said, arrogant and rude. He'd add stupid to the list himself.

CHAPTER TWENTY-TWO

A knock on Dominique's door had her moaning. She wasn't in the mood to talk to anyone. It had taken every ounce of energy she'd had to get dressed, paste a smile on her face and be charming for every appearance, appointment, event, and visit she had accompanied her father to since she'd been back.

"Dominique? It's Lidia. May I come in?"

"Yes, just a minute." She dragged herself out of bed and tossed on her robe, assuming Lidia probably wanted to go over her schedule. "I'm sorry I'm not dressed, Lidia," she said, opening her door.

"I understand." She stepped in, closed the door with an elbow, and then walked over to a table in her office. "I thought you might like some tea," she said, setting down a tray.

"Thank you, but you shouldn't have gone to the trouble."

"Dominique, what can I do to help you get out of this terrible depression?" Lidia poured a cup of tea and handed it to Dominique. A compassionate smile graced her face. It was a smile Dominique had seen many times. "Try some. It won't hurt."

She took the cup and sank into a nearby chair. "Nothing. Really, it's just something I have to work through myself."

"Why don't you call him?" Lidia suggested.

"Who?"

"Ethan."

"Oh, Lidia. He hates me. He hardly spoke to me after I was safe. Then he just left without saying a word."

"He also flew halfway around the world to search for you," she reminded her. "Then risked his life to save yours. A man doesn't do that unless he's in love."

"Yes, a man does that if the price is right. Just how much did my father pay him anyway?"

"What are you talking about? Your father didn't pay Ethan."

"Yes, he did," she insisted. "Ethan told me Andre called him and asked for his help."

"That's true. Andre did call him. He called him several times, in fact. And Andre begged to hire him, but Ethan declined his offer."

"What are you talking about? He didn't decline Andre's offer. He came to Greece."

"The first time Andre called Ethan, it was to tell him that you had been kidnaped and to find out if Ethan had been able to obtain any information about your captors." She sat in a chair across from Dominique as she continued. "The second time Andre called Ethan, it was to hire him to find you. Ethan declined and didn't tell Andre that he was already in Greece looking for you. After Ethan rescued you, he called Andre to tell him you were safe and to explain that he had refused to give him information or let him know he was already looking for you out of concern that your captors might somehow be alerted. Andre offered to pay him again, but Ethan refused any payment, even for his expenses."

"I had no idea." Andre hadn't said a word to her about his conversations with Ethan. "But I'm not sure it matters, Lidia. He's angry with me because I treated him so poorly. And how would any relationship ever work? I have obligations here, and he has a business to run in the United States. We are on different continents separated by an ocean."

"If it were possible, do you love him enough to go to the United States to be with him?"

"The measure of my love is not a question, Lidia. The circumstances of my life preclude a relationship with Ethan, and that's assuming he is not angry with me. I'm not sure he would forgive how I treated him."

"Dominique, I've spoken with your father. He's agreed to relieve you of your royal duties if it's something you want."

"I don't understand. Why would he do that? He's relied on me all these years to stand beside him."

"He realizes that your duties all these years have far exceeded those expected of a princess. He realizes that you have been filling the obligations of your mother, and he understands that if you continue to do so, you will have sacrificed a great deal in doing so."

"Who is going to help him if I don't? What will he do without me?"

"Andre is next in line to succeed your father. He and Francine will have to raise their visibility, and with that, they will be expected to take on more responsibility." There was a hesitation before she continued. "And I would accompany your father to events. He's asked me to marry him."

"Oh, my gosh!" she erupted as she shot up and threw her arms around Lidia. "Lidia, that's wonderful. I knew there was something special between you and Father. Neither of you keeps your feelings for each other hidden very well. I am so happy for you and for Father, and I must say it's about time."

"Thank you. I'm pleased you are happy about it. I was hoping you wouldn't think I was overstepping my bounds."

Dominique pulled back and looked her in the eyes. "Lidia, you've been like a mother to me for the past twenty-five years. I love you. This feels perfect to me."

"All of this was decided only last night. I'm still trying to get used to the idea. But enough about me. You are going to miss out on your own life if you don't stop moping around and get out of bed," she warned.

"This will make it much easier now that we have a wedding to plan."

"This is not just about me, Dominique. You can step away from the public eye and enjoy more privacy in your life. And now that you will no longer be consumed by royal obligations, you have no reason not to call Ethan."

"It's been a month since I've seen him last. What if he's gotten over me?"

"Then you'll just have to remind him of what he is missing."

CHAPTER TWENTY-THREE

"Bailey, I can't just show up on his doorstep," Dominique explained. She had been in DC for a week and hadn't been able to work up the nerve to see Ethan. Even if he did love her, and she wasn't convinced that he still did, the fact hadn't changed that she had hurt him. And as far as she was aware, he hadn't forgiven her. "What would I say?" She sipped the last of her coffee and got up to clear the table. "I just happened to be passing by?"

"Sit," Bailey insisted and took her empty cup. "You made breakfast. I'll clean up, and no, you tell him the truth."

"The truth?" She stacked the dishes on the table, scooped up the silverware, and followed Bailey to the sink. "That I'm in love with him and thought I'd come to his house on the chance that he might be in love with me, too? I can't. That would be awkward."

"I don't see what's wrong with my dinner party idea. He comes over, and you just happen to be here visiting. . ."

"It's too obvious. He'll know the whole thing was arranged. I don't want him to feel tricked." She paused for a moment and felt the mountain of frustration. "Maybe I shouldn't have come here. I didn't really think this whole thing out properly."

"Well, you're here, and I'm not letting you leave until you see Ethan." She helped Bailey finish loading the dishwasher, then snapped it shut and leaned against the counter.

"I think I need some time to figure everything out," she said, reaching for a dishrag. "My coming here was on pure impulse."

"And impulse is based on instinct. And instincts are usually right."

"Perhaps." She thought for a moment before she spoke again. "I think I need to find a place to live."

"As in here? In Washington?"

"Yes." Her lips lifted into a smile. "That's exactly what I need. If I have my own place to live, my coming here won't appear so presumptuous. It won't look like I came here expecting Ethan to sweep me up in his arms and take me into his life."

"Aren't you?"

"That would be terribly romantic," she said with a wistful sigh. "But maybe a bit unrealistic."

"Well, I like the idea of your living here. Can I help you look for a place?" Bailey asked, catching the dishrag Dominique tossed to her. "It'll be fun."

"I'd love your help. And I think we should look for a house in Saint George. I should probably get to know the place."

Ethan couldn't shake Dominique from his mind no matter how hard he tried, and he knew it was making him cranky around the office. His secretary had let him know and warned him that if he didn't lighten up, she would need to take a week of vacation just to get away from him.

A weekend of fishing is just what I need, he thought, as he headed back home from the bait shop. He was going to enjoy the sweet little boat Victor had replaced his old one with after his return from Monteaux and couldn't wait to get back and get it out on the water. It was a sunny day, and people were already out enjoying it, he noticed as he glanced over at the vegetable stand. Damn, he cursed to himself, glancing a second time in his review mirror. There's no way that was

Dominique, he told himself. That's the last straw, he thought, slapping the palm of his hand against his steering wheel. He had to do something to get her out of his mind. He was starting to hallucinate now. He was sure he still had Andre's direct telephone number. He'd give him a call, he figured. He'd ask him how he was doing and then casually bring up the subject of Dominique. If things were back to normal for her and she had gotten back to her life, he would know there were no loose ends. There would be no unfinished business between them, and he could move on himself. Yeah, that was what he needed. Closure.

When he got home, he tugged his cell phone from his pocket, scrolled down to Andre's number, and pressed the call button. Andre answered after the second ring.

"Hello, Andre." He dragged a stool out onto the deck, straddled a leg over it, and sat down. "This is Ethan."

"It's good to hear from you, Ethan."

"I hope I didn't catch you at a bad time." He was already regretting calling as the embarrassment crept in. He felt like a love-sick teenager.

"Not at all. I'm glad to hear from you. How are you doing?"

"Fine, and you?"

"Excellent. Things are getting pretty exciting around here."

"Oh?"

"There's going to be a wedding. The women are just inundated with the planning of it all."

Dominique was getting married. The blow was sudden and swift. He just hoped his voice wouldn't disclose the shock. "Really?"

"I'm sure you will be on the guest list. It'll be grand to see you again."

"Yes . . . yes, it will." He slid off the stool and took a step to the edge of the deck. He couldn't imagine having to watch

Dominique walk down the aisle with someone else. He should have called her after his call from Gianna. He'd been an idiot to have let enough time slip between them to lose her and allow someone else to sweep her up.

"How does that news strike you? Pretty incredible, huh?"

"It does seem a bit quick." He wasn't going to ask any questions, he decided. He'd rather not know. The purpose of the call was served. If that wasn't closure, he didn't know what was.

"What's the matter? You don't sound happy for the betrothed couple."

"I am." If he didn't know better, he'd swear Andre was enjoying himself at his expense. "Please, tell Dominique I wish her all the happiness in the world."

"Why don't you tell her yourself? I'll see if I can get her on the phone."

"No need," he quickly responded. "I imagine, like you said, she's inundated with planning everything. I wouldn't want to interrupt her."

"I wish I could keep this up," Andre said, bursting into laughter. "You do sound somewhat pitiful. I'm sorry to say I am rather enjoying it."

"What are you talking about?"

"Just a little payback for letting me dangle by the last thread of my sanity while you were in Greece."

"I explained my reason. It was for the protection of your sister. And what do you mean by *payback*?"

"Dominique is not getting married. My father and Lidia are the ones getting married."

"Dominique isn't getting married?" The heaviness started to lift, and the relief began to settle just in saying the words.

"No, she isn't. But I am glad to know Francine and Lidia were right about one thing, though?"

"What would that be?"

"You."

"Me?"

"Yes. They insist that you're in love with Dominique."

He pondered Andre's words and slid back onto the stool, wondering if he'd been that transparent.

"Are they right?"

"Your sister is not that easy to resist, Andre."

"Well, then there's something you need to know." His voice dropped to just above a whisper. "I've been sworn to secrecy, but this is one promise that I feel is better broken than kept. I think you and Dominique need to stop tiptoeing around each other, clear the air, and get on with things between you two. Quite frankly, I'm getting a little impatient."

"I'm listening."

"Dominique is there in the United States. She left about a month ago and is living somewhere near you. Apparently, some business about you and her and Gianna has her worried that you're angry or otherwise upset with her, so she's been apprehensive about visiting you. I don't know the details about any of that, but apparently, it's making her uncertain about how to approach you."

"Where is she exactly?"

"I'll tell you, but you've got to swear not to tell anyone I told you."

"You have my word."

"Dominique, you've come up with every excuse to put off calling Ethan," Bailey complained. "First, you had to find a place to live so you wouldn't appear presumptuous. Then you had to lease the restaurant so he wouldn't feel pressured or obligated to you since you're here. The restaurant's opening is tomorrow night, and you still haven't called him. What are you going to come up with next? That you're too busy running the restaurant to have time for him?"

"Not a chance," she assured her. "That's why I hired two chefs. I'm training them so I can work when I want to work. Besides, the restaurant has given me a plan."

"Am I supposed to believe that you've finally worked up the nerve to call him? Even my dad is getting tired of keeping your secret." Dominique read the doubt in her gaze and her arms folded across her chest confirmed that she wasn't convinced.

"I sent Ethan a special invitation from the restaurant to come to dinner on Sunday evening under the guise that we're hosting a private dinner for select Saint George residents, but no one else is coming. When he gets here, I'm going to surprise him."

"Has he RSVP'd?"

"Not yet. I may need to enlist your help if he doesn't."

"Be sure to let me know. If I have to knock him out and drag him here myself, I will."

"Dominique, look." She turned toward the pretty young girl she'd hired to work as the hostess and saw a delivery man carrying an enormous bouquet of roses into the restaurant. "Where should I tell him to put them?" she asked.

"Just put them on one of the tables for now," she said, heading over.

"This is just one of twelve, ma'am," the man said. "You're going to need more than one table."

"Okay. Use as many tables as you need. I'll decide where to place them later."

"Here's the note," Baily said, handing her a tiny envelope. "Who are they from?"

"I don't know," she answered, reading the card. "It just says *Congratulations on your opening. I look forward to seeing you tomorrow night.*"

"Have you looked at your reservation list? Is there anyone

on there you know?" Bailey asked.

"No. I haven't looked at it."

"I'll get it for you," the girl offered and reached behind the small maître d stand.

She handed the reservation sheet to Dominique, and she scanned the list of names. "I don't recognize any names." She handed the list back. "I guess I'll find out tomorrow night."

"Who's going to sign for these?" the delivery man interrupted, setting down the last arrangement.

"I will," the girl volunteered.

"Wow," he said, looking around while he waited. "You guys really revamped this place. From hick with plastic tablecloths to classy with real linens. Quite an upgrade."

"You should taste the cuisine," the girl answered, handing him the delivery receipt.

"Aren't you curious about who sent all these flowers?" Bailey asked. "Someone's got an eye on you. If whoever it is thinks he's going to slip right in —"

"No chance of that happening, Bailey. Not in a million years."

"Is everyone ready?" Dominique asked, standing in the middle of the kitchen surrounded by her hostess, two chefs, wine steward, busboy, dishwasher, and four waiters. She had gone over everything with each employee, every aspect of their jobs, down to the tiniest detail. There wasn't so much as a wrinkle in even the busboy's crisp white shirt.

"Absolutely," was the unanimous answer echoed around the group.

"Then, places everyone."

After a few hours, Dominique allowed a minute to observe the dining room. The evening had started out smoothly and had continued without a hitch. The guests showed up pretty much within ten minutes of their reservations, and between the direct compliments and the snippets of conversations she picked up, it seemed that the patrons of Beau Jardin were quite pleased with the new restaurant in town. She was proud of her staff. She stepped into the kitchen to let her chefs know there was one more party expected.

"This is so exciting," her hostess gushed, popping her head through the kitchen door after her. "So far, everyone who made reservations showed up, except for the last party. I'll let you know when they arrive," she said, letting the door swing closed behind her.

"Has anyone claimed responsibility for the flowers yet?" one of her chefs asked.

"No one has mentioned them," Dominique replied, lowering the flame under a pot of bouillabaisse. "Maybe the last guest sent them." She had to admit that she was mildly curious and a bit nervous at the possibility that whoever had sent them might have discovered her identity. As far as she was aware, no one in Saint George had a clue that she was a princess, except for her wine steward, who wasn't impressed and promised he wouldn't disclose her secret.

"What a night," one of the waiters remarked as he pushed through the door. "I don't think there were any cancellations or no no-shows. That's pretty good, considering our advertising was minimal."

"Maybe that's why. Maybe people were intrigued," one of the chefs said.

"That could be, but it's going to be our food and service that keep them coming," Dominique reminded them.

"I wonder if there were any critics here tonight," the waiter commented.

"Maybe this last party's a critic," one of the chefs speculated.

"I doubt he'd be so conspicuous," the other chef replied.

"And I don't think critics send flowers to restaurants, particularly before they've eaten there."

"Two chocolate mousse," a second waiter announced as he walked into the kitchen and took two cups and saucers from the beverage corner. "By the way, the couple with the last order just asked if they could have their meal wrapped up. They said they have some sort of babysitting emergency." He filled the cups with coffee, then loaded the sweeteners and cream on a tray and hurried back toward the door. "What should I tell them?"

"Tell them we would be happy to accommodate them. Can you handle that?" Dominique asked one of the chefs as she took off her apron and slid it onto a hook by the door. "I'm going to take a break before our last guests arrive." She needed one. She'd hardly gotten any sleep since she'd devised her plan to see Ethan. She'd played the scenario over in her head a million times. She had every detail worked out down to the sterling silver candlesticks and the music that would be playing in the background.

"Yeah, I'll take care of that."

She stepped out the back door and into the warm night. Although the heat of the day had relented, the humidity still hung thick around her. She leaned against the railing of the steps and let her mind wander forward again to Sunday. Her pulse quickened at the thought. She pictured him entering the restaurant and looking around, puzzled at first because the restaurant would be empty of any other diners. Then he would see her. She would be standing in the dim flicker of the soft candlelight. There would be no trace of hurt or anger in his eyes, and he would be pleased to see her. The pull between them would be impossible to resist, and he would take her in his arms. No words would be necessary. The heat between them would be communication enough.

"Dominique?" one of the waiters asked.

"Yes," she answered, her mind snapping back to the present.

"All the customers are gone, and I think the final party has arrived. I heard someone come in. I'd be happy to take care of them and help lock up after if you'd like to go home."

"Thank you, but as much as I appreciate your offer, I think it would be rude of me not to welcome our last guests and thank them personally for the flowers if they sent them." Three more days, she told herself as she left the humidity and followed the waiter inside.

She lifted her apron from the hook and let it drop over her head. As she fastened the ties behind her back, she looked up. Her hostess was standing inside the door from the hallway that led to the dining room, staring at her, her face colored with confusion. "You didn't tell me you'd be dining with our last guest."

"Who said I was?"

"He did. He came in alone. I checked his reservation to make sure I had remembered it right and that it was for two. I did, so I led him to a table and asked him if anyone would be joining him. He said *yes, Ms. Beauvais will be joining me. Could you kindly let her know I've arrived?*"

Dominique released a low sigh, concealing her annoyance, and tugged the strings on her apron loose. "I suppose I should see who this gentleman is." Whatever he wanted besides dinner, he wasn't going to get. She wasn't interested, and she wasn't impressed. Despite how magnificent they were, did he really think a dozen bouquets of roses would lure her into being intrigued enough to have dinner with a stranger?

The irritation pricked at her insides. She didn't care to be manipulated into the company of a man. She whisked off her apron and tossed it onto the hook. She would set him straight. Pleasantly and politely, of course, but firmly.

She marched toward the door, and the hostess stepping

aside, pushed it open. Entering the small hallway, she headed toward the dining room.

She pasted a gracious smile on her lips as she stepped from the hallway and lifted her gaze toward the stranger's table. Her heart skipped a beat, and she stopped when she saw him standing there. She searched her mind for words, but none would come. The irritation she had felt dissolved under Ethan's gaze, replaced by a river of joy. She walked toward him again, not sure if it was of her own volition but under a force much more powerful than her own will.

"Good evening, Dominique." His voice washed over her like warm summer rain.

"Hello, Ethan." His eyes showed no trace of anger, no trace of hurt. "Thank you for the flowers."

"You're welcome." He took her arm, and it felt like a thousand pounds had been lifted off of her. "I wanted to surprise you." His hand slid down her arm, and he took her hand in his. He lifted it to his lips and brushed his lips over it. She thought she might float to the ceiling. "I'm in love with you, Dominique."

For a moment, she thought she was dreaming again.

"For you to think anything other than that shows what a fool I've been."

"You're not a fool, Ethan. I'm in love with you. I fell in love with you before you even left Monteaux. I couldn't—"

"Shh," he whispered. "I know about Gianna's threat. I understand the position she put you in, but I wish you had told me. I would have handled her." He drew her close and touched his lips to hers. "I can't live without you, Dominique. I want you in my life. We belong together. Come home with me. We've wasted too much time already."

"Yes. I want to be with you. I'm so happy you came here." Tears glistened in her eyes as she stepped back. "Let me tell my staff I'm leaving."

"No need. I already did."

When she stepped outside, she saw the limousine waiting. The driver opened the door, and she slid inside. Ethan slid in beside her, and the door closed behind him. The inside light dimmed, and his hand circled her neck. He pulled her to him, and when she parted her lips, he nearly sucked the life from her. The current of lust surged through her. She returned the kiss with equal aggression. It had been too long, and the desire was too great.

His hands groped her breasts, and the heat roared inside her. She fell back onto the seat and pulled him down on her. She felt every inch of him against her. She moved under him, desperate to feel him inside her. She slipped her hand inside his pants and wrapped her hand around him. When he reached up her skirt and pulled off her panties, she thought she would melt.

They rolled onto the floor, and she tore his belt loose. He unzipped his trousers and pushed them down. She took him again and skimmed her hand down the length of him. His heart felt like a time bomb clicking against her chest. Hers echoed in her ears like the beat of a drum.

When he entered her, she almost lost her breath. She felt his hitch. Each stroke tugged at her insides, and the heat in her belly flowed like lava. She was sure her insides would rupture, but he managed to keep her just on the verge. The delirious verge.

She felt his hands on her hips, and the rhythm of their movements climb. Every thrust delivered pulses of pleasure that rolled through her like a thunderous wave. And every pull drove her hunger for more. Together, they pushed her closer and closer.

When he said her name, she felt the heat between them combust. All control was lost. Passion exploded. Muscles convulsed. Nerves screamed.

ABOUT THE AUTHOR

Josephine Valent has lived and worked for most of her life in Southern California at the beach, in the city, in the country, and most recently, in the desert, which she now calls home. She enjoys taking cross-country road trips and has traveled coast to coast several times.

An avid reader growing up, she considers it liberating to open a book, leave life behind, and step into someone else's world.

When she's not immersed in the lives of the heroines she's conjuring up for her next romance novels, she's watching true crime shows.

She loves romance, dares to dream, and writes as if anything is possible and she is limited only by her imagination.